Willia

William Wall was born in C
of two previous novels, *Alice Falling* and *Minding Children*, both published by Sceptre to critical acclaim.
He has also written short stories, for which he has
won the American Ireland Funds/Writers' Week prize,
and poetry, winning three major awards including the
Patrick Kavanagh Award. His collection *Mathematics
& Other Poems* appeared in 1997.

Also by William Wall

Alice Falling
Minding Children

William Wall

The Map of Tenderness

SCEPTRE

Copyright © 2002 by William Wall

First published in Great Britain in 2002 by Hodder and Stoughton
A division of Hodder Headline

The right of William Wall to be identified as the Author
of the Work has been asserted by him in accordance with the
Copyright, Designs and Patents Act 1988.

A Sceptre Paperback

2 4 6 8 10 9 7 5 3 1

A CIP catalogue record for this title is available
from the British Library

ISBN 0 340 82214 7

Typeset in Sabon by Palimpsest Book Production Limited,
Polmont, Stirlingshire

Printed and bound in Great Britain by
Clays Ltd, St Ives plc

Hodder and Stoughton
A division of Hodder Headline
338 Euston Road
London NW1 3BH

For Ghosts

Madame de Scudéry, the most influential novelist of the day, devised the *Carte de Tendre*, or map of [the land of] Tenderness, which charted the journey true lovers must take across a symbolic landscape of seas of enmity, lakes of indifference, wastelands of betrayal in order to discover tenderness, in its varied forms, loving friendship as well as ardent passion.

Marina Warner
From the Beast to the Blonde

Part 1

I

A bright cloud hangs high in the stratosphere, catching the last light of evening long after darkness has fallen over the hemisphere. And down in the unpromising gloom of a Sunday second-hand market who knows what charm is at work, long after the objects found here have lost their original light, what powers of attraction and repulsion; the secret authority of order in the haphazard, the witchcraft of lines and lives crossed, love and friendship lying in ambush, fate passed from hand to hand like soiled coinage, as so often, among the usual people casually assembled. A space too cluttered with discards and mischance, blunders and wrong turnings and errors of calculation, the bygones of other lives – so many distractions and false trails I might almost have missed her.

An Irish Cabin. Emerald Series Printed in Ireland. I turned the postcard over and studied the strangely tinted image. A cottage leaned into the side of a hill. Beyond the gable was a golden-headed field of corn and a hedge of escallonia. There was a speck high above – a bird? Perhaps a hawk hanging upon its prey, a little too far away for the camera but caught in the act nonetheless. Two women and two children posed around the doorway, the woman's petticoat an unnatural green. Where was the man of the house? Away in the fields? Or labouring in London? The photographer is the familiar outsider composing them, getting the angle right, the balance, controlling the exposure. *Dear Mrs Delanty, we came to London on Friday and I am pleased to be among the bustling crowd again. I hope to see you shortly. Kind regards, Gregory.* The corners were dog-eared, the date stamp indistinct. 1907? I slotted it back in the rack. The cards were wrapped in cling film. I picked another at random, a full-breasted beauty in a lace-necked dress. *Miss Stella Gastelle.* An invented name? An actress, a society belle or a whore? I turned it over and saw that the message was in code. *Wvzi Qlv.* I bought it, wondering why someone would want to encrypt a postcard. Another showed a cunning-looking grey-haired woman in a cloak, driving a donkey and cart. A basket behind her clearly held eggs. *Going to Market.* It was the kind of thing my mother liked. I moved on. The next stall sold second-hand kitchen utensils. I studied an ancient steel mincer, turned the handle and watched the rusting worm-gear wind its blades without moving, the illusion of progress in a spiral galaxy.

'Not much call for kitchen mincers now,' I joked. 'Mad Cow disease et cetera.'

The stallholder nodded and smiled but I could see she hated me. 'It's a bargain,' she told me. 'Stainless steel.'

It was then that I looked up and saw Suzie.

In the jetsam of the afternoon she was marvellous as a seabird, glide-necked, shadow-light; a colour not in that day's gloomy palette. Her stall was selling Indian-style cotton prints, long dresses, caftans, blouses with elaborate designs, silk scarves in earth colours, Aran sweaters, tiny beaten bronze jewellery. I watched her from an aisle away where a man sold spare parts for motorboats. Five minutes

4

to examine a white compass with a black dial on it, watch the sluggish card spin and never settle on the meridian. Then I watched her from a place where a man tried to sell me an adjustable wrench, a set of spanners and a feeler-gauge in one lot at a knockdown price because he thought I needed them. She wore a jacket patchworked in autumn – beach-leaf, ochre, pale sky-blue, heather-purple. She had brown eyes. I drifted towards her for almost an hour, uncertain of my course, unsure of my ground, borne on a tide of bargain hunters, stalling here and there where the channel shoaled between magazine racks and second-hand plastic flowers.

I browsed the bookstall longer than usual because it was next to hers. Forty-year-old romantic novels in red cardboard covers. Old Readers' Digest Condensed Books, *National Geographics* bound in packs of twelve and tied with brown string, Westerns with handsome heroes whose date was out. I touched the side of a stack and it haemorrhaged pink paperbacks. Mills & Boons, their cover pictures dominated by a single family of wistful heroines and strong blond heroes. I bought a *Daily Mirror Yearbook* for 1927.

I followed her to the soup stall, the smell of sweet fat and musty clothes and incense, a fat woman and a thin man talking to her. The thin man had a stall that sold televisions, video recorders and radios, all guaranteed to be in perfect mechanical order. When they left I stepped up to the counter and got soup too, ladled into a styrofoam cup. My hand trembled and I saw the excitement transformed to tiny concentric tidal waves, shrinking towards the centre, cancelling each other. I drank the soup to still the waves.

'That it now, dear? Anything else?' the soup-woman asked.

I shook my head. 'It's good,' I said to Suzie. Suzie looked at the soup-woman and the two of them smiled.

'The taste buds are gone so,' the soup-woman said. 'It's straight out of a can. Hot water and castor oil. You better live near a toilet. If it's real soup you want you should come up and see me sometime.'

The three of us laughed together.

'You run the stall with the clothes,' I said.

Suzie nodded. 'Do I know you?'

'Beautiful colours.'

'Thanks.'

The soup-woman turned and leaned on the open pages of a *Mail on Sunday*. 'Well, would you look at your one,' she said, without indicating anything. She shook her head sadly. 'There's more there than meets the eye.' Below her T-shirt a pale layer of fat.

'See you, Olive,' Suzie said, about to move off. Olive waved without looking up.

I was suddenly aware that the contingent forces were about to shift once again, the ground moving slightly, secret cogs and wheels turning; in the instant the universe would move from one accidental arrangement to the next. In the sleight of hand my future would appear and vanish like a conjurer's cheat.

'I was thinking,' I said without looking at her, trying to sound careless. 'I was thinking, would you like to come out to dinner?'

She swung full towards me. 'What?'

'I was wondering would you like a bite of dinner sometime?'

She gasped. 'Who the hell are you?' The soup-woman swivelled her head to gape at us.

'No strings,' I said. 'Just dinner.' It was crass, but I could think of no other way of saying it. Fear? Lack of practice?

She dropped the half-empty cup into a bin and brushed past me. I stood where I was, a wash of nausea spreading upwards from somewhere below my heart. The soup-woman held my eye like a fascinated animal. But then she came back. I felt her tug my sleeve and I turned.

'I don't own it, you know. The stall.'

I grinned. 'I'm not after your stall.'

'It's my friend's. I'm just helping her out today. I'm a teacher. A music teacher.'

'So much the better,' I said. 'We were made for each other. I'm a writer.'

Held breath sizzled in escape. She moved to pass me. I shifted my balance to my left leg and the gap was too narrow for her to pass. She stopped, embarrassed.

'I often come here,' I said, 'but I never saw you here before.'

'So what?'

'You're so beautiful . . .'

'Jesus!' the soup-woman said, straightening from her *Mail*. She was grinning now.

'Look, I'm supposed to be looking after the stall . . . Allie is in hospital . . .'

'I'm not a weirdo. I'm an ordinary guy. It's just a date.'

She studied me and the soup-woman studied the two of us. 'OK,' Suzie said. 'Why not?'

The soup-woman said, 'Excuse me, dear. You're blocking the road.' She giggled. 'Would you ever do your coorting someplace else.'

We stood apart and she leaned across the counter between us. 'Mind him, dear,' she told Suzie. 'He's forty if he's a day. Old men are feelers.' The folds of her throat bubbled with laughter. Suzie grinned at her like an excited child. It seemed that a dozen transactions were suspended, as many stallholders staring at us.

'Chinese,' I said, desperately, trying to avoid the eyes, the winking, the smirks. 'Do you like Chinese?'

'Chinese is cool,' she said and I took her phone number.

I found a stiff-backed envelope in the bottom drawer under a stack of back-up disks and slipped the card and its translation inside. I wrote a note to my father and hoped that they both were well. I said the card was for my mother and sent my love to her. Something for her collection, I said. I could not say more, thwarted by my old obstinate hurt. The silent television flooded my apartment with watery blue light. The code on the back of the card had been a simple one – the alphabet reversed with occasional spelling errors: *Hope you have recovrd from the effecs of the wedding. Home on satuardy*. Most cards begin with the word 'Dear'. That was the key. *Wvzi Qlv – Dear Joe*.

Dear Joe.

My name dropping out of time, the coincidence of place and person across almost a hundred years, the card perhaps for the first time reaching the person to whom it is addressed. Why should *I* pick that card up, rather than someone else? What was the code for? The clandestine ordinary, the spectacular simplicity of the commonplace. The truth is in what is not said.

My first job had been as personnel manager in a box

factory – three years in a small country town where people kept secrets like tactical devices: revelling in the air-burst of a casual revelation, the collateral ruin of an exposed love-life, a shady deal, a wayward child. The factory kept the town afloat. It had been the brainchild of a local boy made good, now long gone with a golden hand-shake and a Mercedes from the grateful shareholders. We supplied packing cases to the fish industry, cartons to the co-operative creameries, flat packs for a company that transported duty-free goods. There is considerable variety in the personnel problems of box factories, although it is not infinite. Chief among them was the effort to retool in time for the great cardboard carton revolution and the subsequent redundancy of those whose place was best supplied by machinery. Suddenly everything from milk to washing-machine liquid was coming in paper pack-aging and we were there at the start, lining the shelves and firing personnel – I was not supposed to think of them as people – at the cardboard spearhead of the great economic recovery.

But the germ of my first novel came from the story of a young woman with three children and an invalid husband whose life imploded quietly when SimPak con-sidered her unnecessary. My job was to convince her that the redundancy package grudgingly negotiated by my boss was really a glowing tribute to her eleven years with the company. The man who took my place is now more appropriately described as Head of Human Resources because in a successful company people are stock, more or less troublesome to handle.

The town had a small writing group, where I found myself by accident one evening and became one of the few who stayed the course. There were old women writing their memoirs, girls with romances they hadn't lived through yet; the only other man was an elderly farmer who wrote poetry and sang the results in an ominous *basso profundo*. We were not effective: we took each other's work over-seriously, and we understood very little of what we were doing. But for a year or two we shaped our myths, named books and authors, absolved each other's pasts.

Joan was my first lover, a newcomer to the group like me, a dreamy desperate outsider to the small-town world, the only girl in her class who read books. She was working on a novel about her ancestors, full of Civil War battles and dull domestic lives. She illustrated the better scenes with beautiful, naive line drawings. More than once I told her that her gift was with lines not words. We used to walk home arguing about things, and sometimes we found ourselves in pubs talking about what we were reading. She believed passionately in her power to make a book what she wanted it to be, that once a story came into her hands it was hers, the story of *her* life and not anyone else's. She let me take her clothes off in a room on the first floor of the Ivernia Hotel. I was crazy for her body, in love with the sight and smell and taste of it. When she lost her secretary's job (another company with someone like me to sweeten the poison) she told me she was going to Australia where her sister lived and I suddenly understood the seriousness of what we were doing to each other. She wrote to me twice, then there was a postcard – *Dear Joe* – and signed *With Love*. No more. And no more than I deserved.

Sometimes I catch the odour of stale carpets and unemptied ashtrays and I recall her small breasts and the way she sat at the dressing-table mirror in the mornings, lining her eyes, and I am back again in that pathetic room, or climbing the backstairs holding her hand and hoping.

I wrote a desolate novel in that grey-faced town, picking out the words during quiet times on the office computer, taking it home on a disk and transferring it to my tiny Macintosh. I worked with the materials to hand, trawling memories indiscriminately, crowding it with friends and family: a young woman, made suddenly redundant, struggling with a sick husband and parents who never wanted her marriage. Melancholy made me reckless: The Ivernia Hotel was there, and my mother, and that first pointless love. The book would rip through my life like an ungoverned engine fuelled by loneliness and hurt. I never considered that they would read it, never really believed it would be published, never for a moment dreamt they would recognise themselves. There is no undoing that initial brutal plagiary: nobody is absolved for stealing suffering. I should have held my peace and found another theme.

2

There was a tiny second-hand bookshop on my way that I knew sold sheet music. In the window, on a brass lectern, a volume of Theobald's Shakespeare was open at the title page of *A Midsummer Night's Dream*. Nearby a book in French. From its cover and title – *Le Barbe Bleu* – I took it to be a fairy story. A scattering of modern texts. I saw Virginia Woolf's *A Room of One's Own*. Inside I bought a second edition of *O'Neill's Music of Ireland* for Suzie. The ancients knew that no one with pity can trifle with the bringer of gifts. I had seen the book on a previous visit, and had noticed that someone had annotated the tunes – arcane insect shapes in a sepia ink that seemed to be fading even as I watched.

I gave it to her on the street, too giddy to hold it back, and she took it and thanked me, a little too restrained. I wondered if I had overstepped, too much too soon. I was aware of something unsteady in me, a forward tilt that I could not account for.

We had to ring a bell to gain entry to the Lotus Restaurant, and when the door opened I was momentarily afraid that we would not be admitted because of the book, which Suzie was still leafing through in silent consternation. 'Wrong culture,' I imagined the owner telling us. 'Very sorry.'

*   *   *

The tinkling background was someone's idea of Chinese music; her smile was the foreground. She glistened with tiny flecks of glitter, varnished lips, weird jewellery. When I touched her huge earrings they tinkled like oriental instruments, like part of the backing track. 'My next thing is a tongue ring,' she laughed. 'My friend Allie has one. The girl who owns the stall, remember?' I didn't remember. 'I had my ear pierced five different times. I only have three left. They all closed up. I have incredible healing skin. Allie got a tattoo when she was in Ibiza last year. Her boyfriend didn't want her to do it but she did. It's incredibly small and delicate. You should see it.' Three silver rings flickered at me when she turned her head. Only one pierced ear.

'I should?' I said, grinning lewdly at her. 'Where is it?'

She chuckled and put her head down. 'It's only on her ankle. It says Long Life and Happiness. In Spanish.'

'Is she sure that's what it says? It doesn't say, I was screwed in Ibiza?'

She laughed again. 'There's a guy I know who got one put on his shoulder.' She looked around warily and then leaned forward. 'It's these incredibly beautiful Chinese letters, you know the ones. He thought it said – I forget what. Same thing as Long Life and Happiness except in Chinese. What it really says is, Chicken Curry Fried Rice.' Her laughter attracted the attention of the elderly man and woman at the next table. 'Chicken curry, fried rice,' she said to them, and they nodded. I noticed that they each had a lamb chop and chips. One of them said, 'You never know what's in them Chinese things.' And we all laughed together but at different things.

'It's on his arm,' she told me. 'Here.' Pointing at a place just below the sleeve of her T-shirt. I saw the tiny dead circle of her polio vaccine. 'He'll never go to Hong Kong anyway. At least not without a proper shirt.'

She told me about her brothers whose outstanding characteristic, according to her, was that they all played indoor soccer. They had scattered after school, each to a different small town, each to a different job. There was an auctioneer, a diesel mechanic, an insurance salesman, a hotel clerk, a plasterer; but no matter where they went they discovered a group of like-minded people whose lives revolved around the local gym. They were forever turning ankles, smashing knees, putting their backs out. 'They should start a professional five-a-side team and call it The Cripples,' she said. 'If they all lived in one place they'd keep the local hospital open.'

Behind the counter a bored waitress watched a miniature television. In the lulls of conversation and wallpaper music that occasionally coincided like rests in a melody I could hear the rumbling sound of a talk show.

Suzie was idly swilling wine around her glass, a tiny translucent tide. 'So, enough about me,' she said. 'What kind of things do you write? Am I going to be in one of your books?'

'I learned my lesson,' I said. 'I only write about strangers.' She didn't smile.

She was suddenly quiet. Her eyes were a kind of amber brown, a strange liquid mix, opaque and obscure at once. I could not tell from them what she was thinking. 'What kind of a lesson?'

I had never tried to put it in words before – simply because there had never been anyone to say it to. I wasn't sure I could do it now. 'It's too complicated,' I said. 'My first book . . . I was careless. You know when you read about writers, in biographies and so on, it never tells you how people really felt about being used. The people they wrote into their books. I suppose some people don't care, and some writers don't care whether they do or not.'

'You do?'

'I didn't once. I suppose I should be able to drum up an argument about great art needing to be free of considerations like that.' I stopped, hearing the pomposity of the words, not for the first time. There was a danger in dishonesty now, one that was not there before.

'Things are never simple.'

'Exactly.'

'What about your family?' The question startled me but she added: 'Any brothers or sisters?'

'One sister,' I said. 'And one niece. Mary, my sister, and her child. They're in Seattle now. I had a letter from her only last week.' Suzie waited quietly for me to continue. 'I'm convinced she's not the full shilling. Daft.'

'Brothers always think their sisters aren't right. It's a typical male delusion.'

'She's fanatical. Opus Dei, I'd say. Christian to the power of X.'

'A lot of people believe in God.'

'*And* go round shoving it down people's throats.'

'They do. And they're not mad.'

'This is different. Mary is obsessional.'

'Still . . .'

'Every letter is full of stuff about the latest cause. Anti-abortion. Dr Kevorkian – whom she always calls Dr Death, by the way. Gene manipulation. *In vitro* fertilisation. She has these subscriptions to weird magazines, born-again Christian – *The Way* or *The Truth* – they all sound the same. The last one she sent was way over the top. All about a Down's syndrome child not being able to get a heart transplant. It wasn't that part, though – it was the vitriol. The sheer spite directed at the doctors who made the decision. The article called them atheists and Satanists. And then the letter finishes with what Claire is up to now, or what they had for their dinner or something. From one extreme to the other.'

For some reason reading that article, I remembered the day before they went to America. In all the bustle of last minute bag-stuffing, checking of lists, phone calls, I was given charge of little Claire. I sat in the kitchen with a bundle of blankets and gazed into the placid face. Now I remembered putting my index finger into her palm and expecting her fingers to close over it. But the palm did not respond. Claire looked up at me with those unvarying eyes and her nerve endings ignored my gesture. That unclosing hand should have forewarned me: the primitive handshake by which the infant greets his humanity, that first acceptance of mortality – denied.

The right-hand edge of the cutting about the Down's Syndrome child was irregular, hand-torn, the corrugations of fingers still showing. The next article appeared to be a map or chart – a serrated coastline, a fragment of lines that might have been height contours or depth soundings or isobars. It could have been the weather map of a storm, a chart of some oceanographic discovery, a site map for a new housing development, the foundations of a new city. Or perhaps it was a treasure map, X marking the place where little girls could awaken and say Mammy and Daddy clearly and unambiguously, the true and undiscovered map of the land of tenderness.

I told Suzie about how Mary found the child through the agency she worked in, how they went to America in haste.

'Jesus,' she said. 'There's something funny there!'

'It's illegal, I think.'

'I think it's fucking criminal!' Her anger seemed disproportionate. 'What did you do?'

I shrugged. 'She's my sister.'

'What about the baby?'

The waiter came and took away our plates. She was a smiling Chinese girl, very small and neat, and unresponsive. She brought us tiny cups and put a cafetière on the table between us. The cups were delicate, almost transparent, but the milk jug was solid white stoneware, incongruously bulky and obtrusive.

'Mary went to work in this agency when she qualified. One of those places that offers counselling to pregnant girls. Apparently, to judge by Mary's boasting, their speciality was persuading girls not to go for abortions. I don't think they cared very much what happened to them after that. The big thing was to get them before they made the choice, hold onto them until it was too late and then move on to the next in line.'

'You're obviously on the side of the angels.' She was smirking at me over the rim of her coffee cup.

'Does it show?'

'I'd say you're a bit anti-Church.'

'The famous liberal agenda?'

'It's printed on your forehead.'

'Have to be honest with you.'

'I'll take that as a compliment. Carry on anyway.'

The music seemed suddenly quieter. I looked at the girl behind the counter and she was wrapped up in her television programme. Behind her, in an illuminated water tank, unlikely fish came and went without acknowledging each other. I wondered how they would react if I dropped a worm in there, and what my father would make of them, he for whom the humble dogfish was an exotic enemy.

'Well, I don't know if she got a conscience or if the whole thing came to her as a bright idea, but this girl came in determined to have an abortion. Apparently they got quite a few girls like that. Sometimes they came in to hear what the other side thought. For the sake of their consciences or something. I don't know. They must have been pretty mixed up to wander into that den of vipers, or lost. I can see Mary preying on lost souls. There's a thought. Anyway, Mary got to work on her. She was a zealot even then. In the end she made a bargain with her.'

'What kind of a bargain?'

I drank the remains of the wine, a grit at the bottom that trailed on the side of the glass, purple tea-leaves foretelling nothing. 'She seems to have decided one Friday, at work, that she would take the child. If the girl would go the full term Mary would take the child.'

'Jesus!'

'What happened when she went home and told her husband nobody knows, but by the following Monday the two of them were in it together. Matthew had been offered a job in Seattle and they decided to take it.'

'It's not as easy as that.'

'So I'm told.'

'So?'

I shrugged. 'I haven't a clue. All I know is she's over there now. I think he's working for Boeing or something. Claire is nine.'

She stared at me. 'It was a crime.'

I shrugged again.

'Blood is thicker than water?'

'I wouldn't put it that way.' But it was true. I could never have stopped Mary because the only way to stop her was to report the whole thing.

'But you couldn't go to the police?'

'No. And it would have killed my parents.'

'My father was born on an island,' she said after a pause. 'He went to sea when he was fourteen.' The coffee was weak. There was a biscuit in a plastic wrapper. 'I go back there often. To the island. I love it. I often think that's where I really belong. A calling in the blood.'

'I wish I had that.'

'An island?' She laughed.

'No. A family. A real one like yours. Blood thicker than water.'

'But you have. That's why you never did anything about your sister.'

I shook my head. I could feel the wine swirling in it. 'It was too big. That's why I didn't do anything. My life was small and the baby was too big for it. I was frightened. I don't think I cared really. I was never all that close to Mary.'

An elderly man at another table was asking for chopsticks. I wondered if his arthritic hands could even hold them, but when they came he took them in his fingers and began to eat. The bone-white sticks, like the attenuated fingers of a very old hand, carried the food without a slip, the casual practice of belonging.

'But what happened to the girl, the mother?' Suzie said. 'Who was the father?'

'Who?'

'Of the baby? What's her name? Claire.'

'Who knows? I think, from things I've pieced together, that the girl wouldn't say who the father was.'

'It could have been anybody.'

'That's a risk you take when you do things like that.'

'It could have been incest.'

The shock was intense. I felt it like a blow in the stomach, low down, below the belt. I stared at her but she was distracted by a drunk swaying at the door and demanding chips. The waitress was patiently explaining that this was not a takeaway, that he would have to sit down and order from the menu. I thought of little Claire, the blank face staring at me from my sister's happy-family photos, the contrast she made with the wild, weird, screaming, happy American children at someone's birthday party.

Suzie was leafing through the tunes in *O'Neill's*. 'He was a New York cop, you know,' she said. 'He took down all these tunes.' She stared at the annotations. 'It's a beautiful gift. A beautiful thought. I'm amazed that you remembered.'

And so it was all right after all, and I was not wrong about her.

We walked out into the night. The air was heavy with woodsmoke, coal smog, the tang of car exhausts – one of those times when the world's skin sits heavily. It was the smell of the city and I loved it. Neither of us wanted to go home. Somewhere, on the slope of a hill leading down towards the river, she volunteered her shoulder, edging into me and inviting the enclosure of my arm. She felt small to me, frail and beautiful. I held her tightly and in time we kissed. 'How long have we been wandering around?'

She shook her head.

'An hour maybe?'

'I don't know,' she said. 'I'm happy, that's all.'

'I love this stupid city. Even the stinking river.'

'That's what you are,' she said. 'A lover.'

'It's not a fault, is it? You make it sound like a fault.'

We watched the lengthened lights shivering in the river, the ships lying slack against their moorings, and we talked. The sky lowered slowly and became drizzle.

3

There were dates and other dinners, an awkward German film at the Kino, a concert: waypoints on a passage, the destination still uncertain. One day I waited in the rain outside the door of my building. She flapped flat-footed through puddles that were like small invasions in the no-man's-land of the car park. She was laughing. We clattered up the concrete stairs, stopping occasionally. The timed light timed out before we reached my door.

Her reaction to my apartment was, 'But where is everything? You're the one who was rooting around the market. I thought this place would be a museum!'

I told her I had a horror of junk, that I never bought anything except books and cards. 'Will I show you?' I was aware of a boyish eagerness, feeling suddenly much less mature than her. I took down the appliqué box where I kept my postcard collection and she marvelled at the incredible range and variety of such everyday things, things that had passed from hand to hand unremarked, and the simplicity of what people had felt compelled to commit to paper. I told her why I was fascinated by them: the openness of the message, to be read by everyone who took the trouble, the sorter, the postmaster, the postman, and the consequent necessity of being guarded; how each message seemed to me to say more by trusting less.

I showed her my books and she immediately borrowed

two. 'This wall,' she said, looking at the shelves, 'should have a secret door into another room. Like in the old horror movies.'

I held up my hands and apologised. 'Sorry, no secret entrances.'

Standing by my desk she brushed the space bar and my Mac jumped into life at a blank page. She seemed suddenly distracted, pensive. I followed her around the room, full of unaccountable foreboding. What if I failed the test? What if I said something wrong? What if I had misread her signals?

'And the bedroom?'

The bed was neat, for once, although I noticed a sock protruding from under the valance like a desiccated fish.

She paused for a time, examining the framed postcards that hung inside the door. Then she trailed along the wall of books and wondered if I ever had nightmares about a bookcase falling on me when I was asleep. 'I can see it,' she said. She held up her hands to indicate the spread of a banner headline: 'Writer drowns in books?'

My eyes were drawn to a verge of black lace below her skirt, a vexing fretwork that moved out of synchrony with her thighs. 'Suzie,' I said, 'I'm trying to control myself . . .'

'What gave you that idea?' she said – mock horror.

She had phoned an hour before. 'So you *do* live at this number? I was wondering. I thought you might have been a chancer, you know.' She didn't say what she was wondering about. 'I'm coming over. Where exactly is it?'

In due course I heard the enormous rumbling of her van in the street. The rain came just before she did, a downpour, blinding the city, softening the edges of things, blurring foregrounds and hiding distances. People went by cocooned in plastic. Everything is furtive in rain.

'It's Allie's van really,' she had told me. 'I have it on loan. More or less a permanent loan. Allie lost her licence.'

We had kissed in the hall, at the top of the stairs. We had to clockwork round each other once or twice, a dainty charade – I knew that – subtle urgencies transmitted in code. This was her first time in my rooms. Somehow the air realigned itself, furniture reclassified itself about her, and I knew that it would be different always now. Suzie was here. Already the print of her legs was in my bed, an augury of stray hairs on my pillow, a tacky ellipse on the rim of a cup was her lip. If we did not fall for each other these marks would mock me as long as I owned the place.

'So, I've been thinking,' she said. 'A lot.'

'I can't stop thinking about *you*.'

She laughed. 'Do you ever tell a lie?'

I did not say that fiction was my stock-in-trade.

Carefully we lay down side by side on the bed and began our first real day together. Mostly we talked but in between we touched and murmured. In the afternoon sometime we climbed inside the blankets and allowed the room to cool slowly around us. Later I brought her tea and jam sandwiches. That was the first time I heard her sing. When she saw the tray she said, 'Is this a proposal of marriage?' She threw back her head and closed her eyes and, in her clear pure voice she sang for me: *I'll buy you a paper of pins, 'cos that's the way that love begins, if you'll marry, marry, marry, marry, if you'll marry me.* It was simple, beguiling, touching. It seemed to loosen a sail of memories that carried us abroad into childhood. I told her about my parents, the farm, my mother's collecting, a little about why I never went home now.

And in return for the gift she said, '*My* father sent me to fiddle lessons. Fiddle lessons!' She was indignant or mock-indignant. 'When all my friends were learning the piano or the violin or even the guitar. It was the fashion. Girls should have *something*. Well, I learned the fiddle from a man who believed in the existence of aliens and spent all his weekends playing dance tunes in pubs for people who only wanted to watch soccer. I was the butt of everyone's joke. The funny thing is, I still play the fiddle and not one of *them* could even hum a tune. He had the gift and he gave it to me.'

She had a way of lying absolutely still so that only her eyes moved. Every now and then she would swallow, her mouth still slightly open, and I would hear the metallic clicking of saliva in her throat.

'I can see you with a fiddle.'

'I believe in it,' she said.

'The music?'

'Everything. Every word the singer sings is true.'

'Doesn't it bore you?' I was thinking of the repetitive dance tunes radio stations used – supposedly proof of their commitment to tradition.

'But the music is incredible!' she said. 'Some kind of poetry, that's what it is. First there's the tunes. That's only the start. Then there's the graces – *cranns* and *rolls* and things. Then the repertoire. The best guys have thousands of tunes. They don't even remember half them. Some guy will say, Do you know "The First of May"? Everybody'll say, No, no, we don't know that one. Then he'll play a few bars and they'll all say, Oh yeah, that's "The Red-Haired

Boy". We know that. And they'll be off. Everybody at it together.'

'Sounds like an orgy.'

'It is. It is. A bit, anyway.'

The door in the flat next door closed with a bang and the sound of a television was suddenly too loud. I heard my neighbour moving about in boots of iron, damaging everything, and the six o'clock news talked about Chechnya. She was listening too, her head turned towards the sound so that her hair fell straight to her right shoulder. Down from there golden skin drew almost to a point at the bud of her right breast, sagging a little so that a shadow fell under it. There was a faint shimmer of sweat where the curve rose. Her arms were thin, slightly out of proportion to the rest of her body. Skin rippled at her neck and another wave like a seismic echo rippled at her waist along the faint suggestion of a sun line; and below that the quilt was a mound between her legs.

'I like your flat,' she said. She told me that the first time she ever lived in a flat was after she got her job at the college – one dingy room in a four-storey building. There was a toilet just below on the half-landing, with a cracked bowl that seeped water onto the lino, the cistern hissing constantly. A tiny yard held a criss-cross of clotheslines that would contain whatever the people in the eight or nine flats had to wash. In midwinter it would be buntinged with soggy underclothing and socks. Rats flickered among the bins in the corner. One night in late November she would see a young man from the next floor standing naked in the middle of the yard, pissing into the tiny shore in the centre, talking loudly to himself. The next day he would be gone and his flat would be let again within a week. The stairs smelled constantly of urine, battered fish and wet clothes. 'The one I'm in now isn't much better, but at least there's no rats, no naked men – that I've seen anyway – and no lino. The landlords in this town really rip you off. Your place is heaven by comparison.'

I looked around and wondered what she could see in it – a lot of books, a few prints, framed posters, a single mahogany balloon-back chair. It wasn't a kip, and I had made something of a home here over the last few years.

'The neighbours are noisy but decent,' I said. 'It's a good neighbourhood. Up and coming.'

We both laughed at that. From the outside the building was indistinguishable from the warehouses and slightly down-at-heel offices that surrounded it, despite the fact that it was purpose-built as an apartment block. 'Well, we have no yuppies,' I said. 'There's not a mobile in the house.'

Nobody sings in this country any more, Suzie said. People have to be drunk. Or they have to have backing. Karaoke trad. We were in a pub somewhere, another day of the weeks or months since her first visit. Still there is a television at the corner of my eye, and young men in an arc around it, watching a soccer match on a luminous green sea over which stick-men propel an invisible balloon. Suzie believes in music and soccer is only something that has crippled her brothers. The young men hang motionless in the unreal light of another world.

'If you want to know what has changed most about this country, forget all that crap your sister says in her letters, the evils of TV, the end of the traditional family, all that stuff. There's no more singers. That's all there is to it. This is a country that doesn't sing.'

My mother sitting in the front room, polishing the silver with a soft chamois cloth, singing: *It's not for the envy of my sister Kate, It's not for the grief of my mother* . . . Or my father twirling Mary above his head and singing, *Vote, vote, vote for De Valera.*

Dee Valera, he always said. Mary was wearing a white dress. Perhaps it was her communion day.

Sometimes, Suzie said, listening in the soundproof booth in the Music Archive, she gets so wrapped up in it that she thinks the staticy spitting of the old recordings she studies is part of the music – the crackling of an excited crowd, bar-room noise, the singer's own tarry lungs: Joe Heaney with his inside-the-barrel voice, '*Bean an Fhir Rua*', 'The Rocks of Bawn', Nioclás Tóibín singing 'The Connerys'. The big songs. When she sings, she said, she can feel the weird tumbling, turning, stopping and starting of the song, the *sean-nós*, the old way.

'Do you know the way the song suddenly stops and then goes on again?' I didn't but I nodded anyway. 'That's the way it is with the *sean-nós*. Long lines and short lines, the tune catching up on itself, and then, for no good reason, it all stops for a second. That silence. Sometimes I think it says more than the words or the tune. That stop is for all the people who never sing any more.'

'But what about your teacher?' I asked. 'The one who believed in aliens? Do you ever see him now? Did they ever show up?'

She put her head down and her hair fell like a blind to hide her face. 'He poisoned himself two years ago.

Paraquat. A weedkiller. By all accounts it's a hard way to go. I couldn't go to the funeral. I couldn't face it.'

I knew what paraquat did. A hazard on every farm in my childhood. I had seen cattle poisoned by it, an accidental spillage into beet pulp, my father called to plunge his long blade into their bellies, the escaping gas, the green piss bubbling from the wound. The dead eyes and stretched throat. There was no hope for them.

And now high bottle-glass windows filled the lounge with submarine light and let uncertainty in. What was real was the darkness that underhung the tables, the shadow on her face. I wished the aliens had come, for the sake of her teacher, for her sake. To spare that death.

I squeezed her hand – the universal vocabulary of pain – and held her tears back by main force.

'We're alike so,' I said. 'You were taught by a teacher who believed in aliens and I was taught by people from another planet.'

She shook her head as though to clear it and laughed.

'Is that what you think of priests?'

'No. But you should have seen the ones I had.'

'What did they do that was so terrible? They educated you. Now you're a writer so it can't have been all wrong.'

'Where will I start?'

'Oh God,' she said, 'not another story about priests abusing children.'

It was a neat balance – her teacher and his aliens, my alien teachers – but the connection was merely formal. Now that I was required to explain I saw that there was no connection. Her friend had died. My pitiful little brush with love was no counterweight, a fibrous root dangling through the roof of my childhood that (failing to find sustenance) failed. I couldn't tell her. I changed the subject.

'You know, I worry about my sister Mary.' In any case Mary was never far away from my thoughts in any talk of God or Church. 'And little Claire is not right. Mary never says so, but she's not right.' The beer was affecting me too. I could feel its insidious persuasion, the urge to simplify, to sorrow and to brood. 'You know I'm fond of her although we're always fighting. She *is* my sister. And Matthew, her husband, is a fool. A crackbrain religious fanatic. I know she is too, but she gets depressed.'

'Joe, that's the first important thing you've said about your family in the whole time we've been together.' She turned right round to face me and gave me a beer-wet kiss, full on the open mouth.

'You don't know what you're taking on,' I said.

'So tell me,' she said, grinning at me, happy that she was penetrating whatever frail armour I owned.

I tried to concentrate, conscious of a passing moment in which to fix a mark, a chance to lay down lines by which we might safely transit, bring our keels home over the shoals. Or just to close the circle of uncertainty.

'The things you remember from childhood, you can never be sure of them, Suzie. Like old movies, you run bits and pieces together. Something from this one, something from that. You end up with a composite but you think it's the real thing. I'm afraid of it.'

It was true. People think the writer is God, with the power to hammer up a tabula rasa, and then install the axioms and necessities, wind the people up and determine their lives. Instead he takes what's given and reduces it to something purposeful: the billion eccentricities of real life are discarded, only the useful matter makes it into the machine, with the proportion probably ten million to one.

'I'm afraid of the way I'm piecing it all together into something smooth and continuous and meaningful. Once you start to explain things you begin to lie. Things don't really have a meaning, you know. They just happen. My mother almost died when I was a kid. I can see the hospital, I think. But I don't remember fear or worry. Do kids know about death? But I remember wondering about how different things would be if she died. I remember just mentally cancelling her. Lifting her out of the things she did. Cooking. Doing the books. Tucking me in. Washing my hair. All those things went on but she wasn't in them. That's the way I saw it. It didn't seem so terrible.'

'Oh Joe,' she said. 'You were only a little boy.'

'That's my nightmare. Remember you asked me if I had nightmares the day you came to my flat? Well, that's the frightening one. Me. Cancelling her out.'

She stared at me and I stared back. Someone failed to score on the luminous sea behind us and hoots of derision punctuated our silence. Then the barman came and took our glasses and there was nothing else to do but ask for more.

My father liked her. He liked her directness, her obvious affection for me. I suspected he was already thinking of the wedding. There was a smell of roasting meat and the table was set with glasses and china mugs. He must have recognised the domesticity, the smell of home. I could not bring myself to explain that we were only getting to know each other, that it had only been a few months, that it was *her* wish to meet him.

'If he comes up every month, why don't I cook him a proper dinner?' Families were important to Suzie.

'He's just as happy with pizza,' I said and she laughed scornfully.

'A man your father's age is never happy with pizza!'

It was a sharp day and for a long time I noticed how his big hands scrubbed and warmed each other, how the skin looked translucent, and the veins clear as rivers on a frozen landscape. He had come straight from the hospital, he said.

'You had the check-up?'

'Are you not well, Mr Lyons?'

'A thing of nothing,' he said. 'I have these blood tests once a month. That's what brings me here.'

'I give him his dinner,' I explained. 'The old cheapskate.' That made him chuckle.

'I'd be better off in McDonald's,' he told her. 'Joe doesn't know the difference between cooked and burned. And,' he winked broadly at her, 'what about the traditional Irish takeaway pizza? God between us and all harm.'

Suzie had taken charge – there would be no burnt offering today, no takeaway.

'Anyhow, I got the all clear. It comes down to balancing the tablets. One goes up and one goes down. They adjusted the rat poison today.'

Warfarin. To thin the blood. To prevent strokes. Also the rat poison of choice.

'Give your mother a call, Joe,' he said unexpectedly. 'She's not inclined to talk these days. She's a bit down. You might draw her out a bit. It'd do the two of you good.' I saw Suzie nodding approvingly. I nodded too, and looked away.

As always he respected my silence. Neither of us wanted to revisit the past.

He jerked his thumb towards the blank grey screen of the computer. 'How's the work?'

'Nothing doing,' I said. 'A dry patch.'

He looked sympathetic. 'I'm inclined to think you should go in for something else. I read that Maeve Binchy book the other day. One your mother got a couple of years ago. The penny candle one.'

'Not my style, Dad.'

'You might change. Earn a few bob for once in your life. I'm told she does well enough out of it.'

I said something stupid about leopards not being able to change their style of writing any more than Christians could become lions. He wagged a finger at me mockingly. 'Now, now,' he said. 'Leave your sister out of it!'

'I had a letter from her recently,' I told him. 'The same old Mary. I'm surprised they didn't martyr her over there.'

'Ah, she's not as bad as that.'

'She's a lunatic.'

He chuckled. 'She takes things a bit too far all right. Will I tell you what? Your sister is the kind of person that might be waiting at the gate of heaven on the day you died. She'd see you struggling up the ladder full of expectation like a child going on a holiday. She'd wait till you were level with the gate, holding onto the last step as hard as you could. And then she'd give you one good kick in the face.'

His laughter was breathy and hollow but wholesome, forgiving. We laughed together like children.

'She's one of those Christians,' he said, 'that takes a lot of interest in other people's prospects of going to hell.'

The roast came from the oven sizzling and spitting crackers of fat, and my father stood to carve it, as he had done every Sunday of my childhood. For the first time in years I recognised my mother's absence at the table, perhaps because Suzie was there.

Suzie charmed him, that was certain. 'Have a piece with a bit of marbling in it,' she said, passing him a slice of beef shot through with swirls of fat. 'A small bit won't do any harm.'

'God bless you, girl,' he said. 'You're a comfort to my old age.' They laughed together and I could see that she was used to old men – something surprising.

They fell into an easy complicity, the old man and the doting daughter, a natural relationship that has kept houses for thousands of years. After dinner he moved over near the radiator again and warmed his hands over it, rubbing them together and flexing and straightening the fingers, talking about the weather and gently extracting the story of Suzie's life. 'Would you be any relation of . . .' 'Let me think now, I knew a man down there one time, a fellow by the name of . . .' In twenty minutes they were talking about common acquaintances like friends who had been parted by unfortunate circumstances. My father was the kind of countryman for whom a knowledge of a person's ancestry was equivalent to a long-standing friendship. Once he had established that he knew a cousin of hers on her mother's side from his days dealing cattle, that in fact he had sold him a pair of heifers for a particularly good price, they settled down. The afternoon moved in a kind of enchanted quiet, the ordinary conversation passing from one to the other as though each word were a well-intentioned gift.

'She's a nice girl,' he said to me afterwards, when we were standing on the street. 'Mind you behave yourself.'

'What's that supposed to mean, Dad?'

'You know very well what it means. She's well-brought up. Don't you do any harm to her.'

'Do I look like I'm going to take a kitchen knife to her?'

'Is she living with you? I suppose she is.'

I nodded. 'Not all the time though. She has her own flat. She's very independent.'

'I can see you're sweet on her.'

I did not deny it.

'What's this she does for a living? Teaching?'

'Music. Her speciality is Irish Traditional.'

'Are you going to marry her?'

'We haven't thought about it.'

'Well, you'd best get started. You could do a lot worse than that girl.'

'I'm fond of her.'

'She's fond of you, I can see that. You'd be lucky to get her. I'd say she deserves better than you.'

'What do you mean by that?' I was beginning to lose patience, never appreciating him in his hectoring mood. We mustn't upset Daddy, we used to say. 'None of your business. Any of it.'

He laughed. 'Don't get your dander up. All I'm saying is, she's a nice girl. I could be fond of her. Your mother would like her. If you're thinking about asking the question, don't waste time.'

I should have listened: *Don't waste time*. Words are supposed to be my profession.

4

In the café they said that the usual island ferry was being overhauled. Engine trouble, they said. The relief boat would take us out instead. They grinned at my shocked face and said that she had weathered worse days than this; the gale-force forecast was for the west coast, not here; we'd find it easy enough once we got into the lee of the island, and other mocking consolations. Suzie was elated. 'It's going to be great *craic*,' she said. She held a piece of wafer-thin pizza to my face and said, 'Eat. Something in your belly will make it easier.' I stared glumly at the white water in the harbour.

'I'll tell you this one to take your mind off your dangerous voyage. This Irish couple have twenty children so the pope decides to present them with a special medal in honour of their contribution to the spread of the one true faith. The bishop himself delivers the medal. Makes a speech on the doorstep. But there must be some mistake, the couple say. We're Protestants. Sweet sufferin' Jesus, the bishop says, we minted a medal for a couple of sex-mad Protestants!

'It's the end of October,' I said. 'This is crazy.'

'Drink your coffee. The ferry is coming.'

I saw an ancient wooden boat chugging across the harbour. 'That?' I could see she was enjoying my naked fear. Every now and then she clucked in mock sympathy and stroked my wrist.

'That's it. She's the old ferry. She's been here since the 1950s.'

'That,' I said, 'does not inspire me with confidence.'

Only yesterday we had been sitting in a cinema, holding hands companionably. *The Golden Bowl*, Merchant and Ivory. Something about the Italian setting turned my head. I said, 'Suzie, let's go away for a bit. Let's go to your island.'

She thought I was mad. 'It's practically winter already,' she said.

'You have a week,' I argued. 'The half-term and so on. Why not go? A week by the seaside?' Earlier, outside the cinema, queuing with plastic cups of coffee burning our hands, the evening had been balmy. There were boys in front of us in shirtsleeves. The city was drowsy with people enjoying the Indian summer.

I was sorry now.

The two men who managed the ferry greeted Suzie familiarly. The younger of the two, a crop-headed young man of about twenty-five, reached her a hand as she stepped off the pier. There were three other passengers, two English girls and an elderly man who made for a spot in the stern. There he could lean against the structure of a kind of hut in the shelter of an open door. Suzie lifted the tarpaulin on the deck cargo and I saw cardboard boxes on a pallet. One hundred quarter-pounders. McVities Digestives. She stowed our backpacks under the tarpaulin. When the time came for the ferry to pull away she took one of the ropes. The older of the two men cast off at the bow and for a time the little ship rested lightly against the pier, as if lingering out of affection. Then he stepped into the cuddy and I saw him twirling the wheel. The engines changed their note and the boat began to reverse slowly and slightly sideways.

When we cleared the harbour we slowed to half-speed and pointed our bow into the long blunt swells that were coming in from the south-west. I saw a distant headland engulfed by a squall, white water at the base, black cloud on top. Beyond that again an obscure range of mountains was brightened by a gap in the clouds. Water came over the bow and the boat seemed to rush into it so that the whole length of the deck was gleaming wet. I was exhilarated by it. I turned to Suzie and she kissed me, our cold faces touching numbly. I held onto her and leaned out into the icy spray. It seemed to score my face, a great flail swirling up from the deep. Suzie laughed and tightened her grip.

The humpback of the island was ahead of us, a giant whale breaching in a welter of white water. Scattered around it were dozens of small islets and rocks, none big enough to support even a colony of gulls, but all suggestive of the dangers of the passage and the uncertainty of our journey. I watched Suzie chatting to the skipper, jammed in the doorless opening of the cuddy, one heel propped against a piece of machinery, one hand jammed forward against the framework to brace herself. Her hair thrown back from her face was the colour of the bleached teak she was holding. She was at home here, the city girl, the musicologist, the college tutor, but also very much the island child connected in some profound way to all of this; whereas I, who grew up on Durrus Strand, was the outsider, completely lost on this sea.

They landed us at the island pier, a deep cleft in the rocks filled with mirror-calm water and a few boats. We passed a line of parked cars, each more rust-eaten than the next. A boat with its back broken was dragged up on the stones near the base of the pier. A small Portakabin said *Leabharlann*/Library. Through the salt-darkened windows I could see orderly rows of books, all new-looking and impressive. A wayside shrine had a statue of the virgin and a rounded standing-stone with three irregular crosses incised in it.

A car passed with the two English girls sitting in the back. The driver rolled down the window and shouted, 'Do you want a lift, Suzie?'

'Thanks, Con. We're all right.'

At the base of a steep hill I heard him slam the car into first gear. Suddenly it was enveloped in a vivid blue cloud. The engine raced. The car shot up the first thirty feet of the hill, then settled into a steady grind. The smoke died out about halfway up.

'They pay no tax or insurance,' Suzie said. 'There's no guards here. If anyone ever asks them who owns the car they say they haven't a clue.' We passed a BMW estate. Someone had covered the bonnet in handprints in white paint. Where the number plate should have been were the letters RIP 2. 'They bring cars onto the island,' she said, 'but they never take them off. With all the hills they never get out of second gear. Wherever you go you'll find car graveyards.'

The steepening hill was already defeating me but Suzie was jaunty, pacing ahead and then slowing to allow me to catch up. I loved the way she moved, her body swinging on angular hips, the small adjustments that caused her head and breasts to move together, the way her legs separated like a dancer's with a defined and deliberate movement, the suggestion of a full-formed body, of warmth and ripeness beneath the ordinary clothes.

Surprisingly, when we breasted the hill there was a bay ahead of us, as if we had, in five minutes, traversed the entire island. Later I would notice that the hill we climbed was on the narrowest neck of land, a deep fjord encroaching on each side. The swell that had made the ferry roar and plunge was thundering into this inlet, huge rollers coasting along the smooth bastion of a pier on the far side, breaking white. Every now and then the continuous roar was punctuated by the *crump* of air compressing in a sea-cave somewhere along the cliff.

There was a boat rotting near the house, its ribs emerging from the grass like the legs of an upturned spider. The stempost was solid but the transom had fallen outwards. Four or five planks with rusted nails bent at right angles and a single spongy seat. Scutch-grass was drowning it.

But the house itself was modern, spartan but dry and warmed by electric heating. There was a comfortable couch, two chairs, a well-equipped kitchen. Upstairs there were three bedrooms – ours a double bed and an en-suite. 'Con built it himself,' she tells me. 'It's hard to get anything built because you have to ship all the materials from the mainland. It can take years to build a house. Builders won't come out, so the islanders learn to do it themselves. He rents it in the summertime.'

'And now? What is this costing us?'

She had a way of looking sideways, her eyes gleaming like scorched leather, a mischievous curl to her lip, the tip of her nose pulled down by it. 'Con is a cousin. We only have to pay for the electricity. He says we're keeping the damp out.'

How did they warm themselves, these anchorite island-ers, before there were generators and windmills? There never was a tree here, no species that could stand up to the screaming Atlantic gales. We stroll along roads sunk between dry-stone walls crazed by lichen. Bracken inhabits limestone folds and takes possession of the mind, a persistent memory. *Raithneach rua.* Long-forgotten Gaelic begins to trouble me, words and phrases welling up, fed by the unkindness of the landscape. The smell of it now is sufficient to conjure an exact locality, the boundaries of rock, the patchy grass and the low-growing, yellow-speckled furze. There was no turf cutting, no tell-tale strips of cutaway bog that can be found anywhere in the West. Driftwood and salvage would have been welcome. Planks from some faraway beaten ship hauled up and dried, used for building or burning. In such a place even existing was hardship.

Now there is electricity, a submarine cable from the mainland, two powerful generators for the time of storms. A single white windmill twirls its skeleton arms on top of the highest hill. They have too much electricity here, too few houses. They export power to the mainland grid – to Ireland, they say sometimes. A wry smile on their faces. *Are you going out to Ireland? Out of the island?*

We turned on the heaters in every room and boiled water for bottles for the bed. We found coal at the back of Con's house and lit a fire in the tiny hearth. We pulled the couch in close and ate bread and drank hot tea. We wrapped our arms around each other and listened to the island at sea in a gale. Suzie said she loved me and I kissed her.

Her father sent her to cousins here during the summers of her school years to learn Irish, and she had grown up with many of the men and women we met in our walks. She had the exile's love of detail and was forever pointing things out to me – a stone with worn ogham markings, a well where certain illnesses could be cured, the building where the Magnetic Company had set up its telegraph in opposition to Reuters, the house where a man had composed a lament for his two sons drowned while fishing in sight of their own windows. She could even sing a few verses of the song.

'We'll go up to the *Fir Bréige*,' she said that first morning on the island. '*Fir Bréige*? False men? It was during the wars against the French someone got the idea of setting up these boys on the cliffs looking out to sea and dressing them up in red coats, stone men. I think it was the bailiff, or the commander of the sea-fencibles above at the watchtower. He had plenty of stones for the job anyway. It looked like the place was alive with soldiers. They're called the false men.'

We climbed the long steep slope to the southern headland, along a track between stone walls. The walls were the incredible thing. Miles and miles of them, set at every conceivable angle to each other. Some six feet thick at the top and more at the base. Each field a citadel. Gates were sally-ports. So much stone on the island that the fields could only be made by piling them high, taking advantage of some that could never be moved to base a gate, the foundations of a hut or shed, a house – island pyramids, monuments not to hubris but to the futility of fighting the land. The houses themselves were solid stone. No mud huts here, no flimsy timber. The merest cabin was a citadel, strong enough to withstand cannon-fire, narrow windows looking out through two or three feet of stone, rifle slits, embrasures.

I was fascinated by them. I climbed up on a particularly wide wall and measured my length across it. I peered through the window of a disused shed and saw only night.

'Why hasn't someone painted these?' I said. 'There should be a school of painting here. Like on Tory Island. The scale is incredible.' I kissed her and her face was dry and cool and there was a salt taste on her lips.

There were fewer houses high in the upward scoop of the hill. We came out on top to see the bright Atlantic, a heaving glittering desert speckled with white water and the shadows of charging clouds.

She explained the topography of the mainland coast to left and right. Distant mountain ranges were named, distant bays, the lie of the land westwards.

When my curiosity was satisfied she said, 'You're writing again? You were up early this morning.'

'I like to work in the mornings.' Once the day comes in, it brings distraction, but there is a simplicity in the early morning that frees the mind. 'The morning is the easy part.'

'What's the book about so?'

I shrugged. I was uncomfortable talking about it. The truth was there for her to read, written for her. But I could not give her the raw fact, not until the net of words had been woven and the trawl laid out. I needed the enclosing form and metaphor to win her. To reveal it half made would be too dangerous, too risky. She might slip out and away and I would be lost. I needed time. I thought by recreating the past I could impel a future into being; art is no less spurious than any other form of augury. At that moment I believed I had all the time in the world.

'A love story?'

I nodded. 'A loss story too.'

'Not about us so.' She was watching me in the corner of a brown eye.

'Love lost as soon as won,' I said, smiling.

'I like happy endings.'

'What about your songs? The one about the dark-haired woman.' *Sé bean dubh an ghleanna, do bhreoig mé – It is the dark-haired woman of the glen who has made me sick.* Most of her love songs were sad.

'They're the truth, Joe. But people want to live fairy tales.' I told her there was nothing to worry about, that tragedies were only for books, and even in books they were structural tics and squints, quirks in the great formula of happiness that was literature.

'Count the happy endings, Suzie. They outnumber the catastrophes. The factor is incredible. All the romantic novels, the fantasies, the romances, the comedies . . .' And, I wanted to say, there were so many happy families that there had to be more than chance in the equation. The memory came to me of my parents at some Farmers' Association dinner-dance, the two of them swinging off around the floor in an old-time waltz, my mother's pale small hand resting – not clasped – in my father's big rough paw: the happy dancers. When I thought of them together they were always in movement, walking or dancing – a coalition of grace and happiness, a physical alloy as durable in memory as love itself.

'You're puffed,' she said, standing back, hands on her hips. She was grinning at me. 'You're breathless after the hill.'

It was true. I tried to control my breathing but my efforts ended in spluttering laughter. When I had recovered I confessed to a more sedate lifestyle. 'I'm too old for you, Suzie.'

'Ten years,' she said. 'I know. You look it too.' She grabbed me and dragged me against her. 'But all cats are grey in the dark.'

We laughed. Below us a dark shadow that might have been a cloud or a whale moved on the water. A gull glittered against it.

'Are you going to tell me?'

'About what?'

She turned her back on me, facing inwards to the island. 'I brought you here. Now tell me what you're writing.'

I tried to shrug it off. 'I don't know yet.'

But she was adamant. 'I want to know. I'm entitled to know.'

'Suzie, please. I can't do it yet. You don't understand.'

'That's not much good to me.'

'I'm sorry.'

'Bastard.'

'No. I'm serious. If I talk about it, it'll vanish.'

She shrugged and waited.

'You come from a normal family . . .' I said. But I did not go on.

Eventually she said, 'Is that what it is?' She turned towards me again and I saw that her eyes were moist.

46

'It's just that you know how to relate to things, people. I don't seem to be able to do it. Not easily. I don't know why.'

'It's called selfishness,' she said.

'No. It's the way I work.' But I knew she was right. It was the mark of all my loves and friendships.

'You're frightened. That's all. You won't share your work with me. It's a kind of cowardice. Or lack of trust.'

'I'll tell you everything,' I said. I saw my mother sitting at the mahogany table, her notes in front of her, her face grey with fury: *Do you remember this place? You ate me up and spat me out.* I knew I would never risk it again. 'I don't want to make the same mistakes, Suzie.'

'I don't want to read your old book anyway. I'll see it when it comes out.'

I laughed. 'You're not allowed to change your mind. You're compelled to listen. That's the deal. It's like a magic spell, or one of those bargains you make with witches or leprechauns.'

She did not laugh.

'You were in love before, Joe. You told me that,' she said, as if I had been schooled, should know the rules. 'You have to give.'

There was only one false man. The ruins of others were nearby. He was a mound of stones without a head, his trunk canted a little towards the sea. We sat with our backs to him and ate Mars Bars and drank milk. She came around in time, warmed by the winter sun.

The weather forecast reported the approach of another storm; the isobars, circling tightly, looked like a deep well. The islandmen shook their heads and hunched deeper over their pints. Con said there would be no boat tomorrow, or the next day most likely, and everyone agreed. 'You'll have to phone in,' I said gleefully. 'Tell them you're trapped on a remote island and you'll be here for the winter. Tell them you've been kidnapped by a madman.' I was beginning to imagine us isolated from civilisation by the three miles of boiling water that was the Sound. 'Jesus, look at that storm!'

The summary chart said winds of seventy miles per hour with severe gusts. A dangerous weather alert was in force with damage to buildings and trees expected. No unnecessary journeys.

We went down to the water's edge, in the calm of the evening, and watched the enormous glassy swell that came into the bay and rose and tumbled on the shingle and stones. A hundred yards out a seal floated and dipped, his big blank eyes watching us. It was easy enough to believe that this was the natural condition of the ocean, that it would be the same the next day and the next, our one week's escape accompanied by the thunderclap of collapsing waves, the still air, the extraordinary light. We imagined walking by the beach, watching the gannets diving for winter strays, the oystercatchers gathering in conclave on the wet sand of the northern side, the smell of bladderwrack and kelp. For a time a mother and daughter played at the water's edge. The child wore a Hallowe'en mask and black cape, but she took off her shoes and socks to paddle. There was to be a party in the island hall that night – everyone invited – ghosts and ghouls included.

'Mandy Kelly,' Suzie told me. We watched the little girl trying to pull her socks on over still-wet feet. 'English originally. A new age traveller, Con says. Liverpool Irish, I think. Her partner took off when the child was born. They say he couldn't sleep at night with the crying.'

'What brought her here?'

'She's also a trained nurse.'

'She's rearing the child on her own now?'

'There's worse things.'

Out in the deep evening the seal was calculating our chances of survival. He must have thought the four of us an unlikely species, the odds stacked against us, considering the unnecessary complexity of our mating rituals.

5

The wind came during the night, pouring out from the well of the storm. I woke at one o'clock to what sounded like something hammering on the roof. I listened for a time, awed by the raw force of it, then drifted into an uneasy sleep, dreaming about animals and burglars.

When dawn came I stood at the window and saw gobbets of foam rising over the distant cliffs on the other side of the island and carried two hundred feet up to fall like snow on our side. A man went by leaning at forty-five degrees to the ground. In the gap between two headlands I could see a mass of white water. A dog at the door of a house that did B&B was barking at the wind. We snipped the plastic band that bound the one bale of turf briquettes that we had been able to find, and piled them into the damp grate. Suzie took a burning taper from the gas cooker and shoved it where the firelighters were concealed. Then she sat back on her heels and watched the flames.

'When I was a child,' she said, 'I was always delighted when there was a storm. I used to wrap myself up in the blankets and listen to it. I felt cosy and safe. But my father hated storms. Think of the sailor, he used to say to me. Pity the man that's at sea tonight.'

'We used to go down to Durrus beach to see the mounds of kelp washed up. Bits of lobster pots and ropes. Once they used to haul the kelp up to the fields as fertiliser.'

'We're safe now, anyway,' she said. 'Unless there's a tidal wave.'

Wind thrust down the chimney and forced the smoke-and-petrol smell under the rim of the fireplace and into the room, sweet and unpleasant and mixed with the brown smell of the turf and damp coal. Outside we could see it prowling over the scrub and furze, and shaking the low-growing heather that hugged the hill. Its voice was hostile. We listened to it in each room and nowhere was it lessened.

At midday we struggled down to the tiny shop to buy something to cook. Our heads full of noise, we watched a dozen crows blow away in the wind, black jets keeping low for safety. A sheet of iron groaned and banged, only partly attached to the rafters of a shed.

There was no meat. We could have cooked Heinz beans, bananas, Bounty Bars or butter. A bearded young man who spoke with a Dublin accent waved apologetically at his shrunken stock and told us that the ferry had not been in that morning and so there was nothing new. His smile said: This is island life, it's hard, but I chose it just the same. I envied him his composure. 'We're expecting her any minute,' he said, and another gesture indicated what we hadn't bothered to see, that the pier was full of cars, each occupied by one or two anxious islanders staring out to sea. And as we watched they left their cars and crowded to the spot on the quay where the boat came in – *Leaba Bháid an Phoist*, as the notice said: The Berth of the Post Boat. We hurried out to watch with them.

We were in time to see the boat emerge from a rampart of white water that ran from a tiny sea-swept reef to the main island. The people seemed to relax a little.

We heard one man say, 'He hadn't much room for a mistake there.'

Then the boat came sideways on to the seas, rolling so far to one side that it looked as if she would roll over. 'I can't watch,' Suzie said, dragging me by one arm. 'This is terrible.' But I was fascinated.

Twice I saw the boat turn directly into oncoming seas, white water coursing at her above the height of the cabin windows, spray flying. Then she was in the entrance, travelling fast to counter the effect of the cross-swell. Men scurried for hawsers coiled on the quay. Thinner heaving-lines with weights on the end were hefted. The boat came on, a white smoke at her forefoot. Suddenly the captain was out of his bridge and shouting to young men on the deck. The side was festooned with orange balls and bruised car tyres. A man on the quay made a strange gesture, as if he were giving something up, giving up hope or resigning himself to something, and the heaving line was flying out of his hand, coils uncoiling, the weighted end flying across the afterdeck. It was caught deftly and the heavier hawser pulled out with it. A second line was flying at the bow. The islanders around us were relaxing and beginning to talk with animation. The boatmen made graceful gestures, swinging ropes and winding them onto cleats. A passenger came out to waves from the crowd. His face was pale. He waved back and leaned against the cabin with one hand in his pocket to show that he wasn't nervous. The boat was in.

On the little beach inside the breakwater an old man was trying to drag an open boat onto the shingle. The waves were sweeping the stern to left and right. Even from the pier I could hear his foul-mouthed ranting, Gaelic and

English mixed. I went down the steps and jumped onto
the beach, landing short, up to my ankles in freezing water,
Suzie calling to me, too late, to mind my shoes. I waded
out to the stern and held it steady, ice-cold waves coursing
between my legs, and between us we lugged the boat up
above the high-water line. The old man made the painter
fast to an iron ring in the quay and turned to gaze at me.

'Well,' he said. 'You got your trousers wet.'

There was something demented about him – an ardent
unvarying eye, a suggestion of menace in his bearing, even
the skin of his face seemed to be distressed. Without a
word of thanks he strode up the hill, still swearing fluently
sotto voce.

Suzie stood above me on the pier, giggling. 'Well, Joe,'
she shouted, 'you got your trousers wet!'

'That's Nioclás,' she told me later. 'The poor man.'

'He could have said thanks.'

'Fools rush in where angels fear to tread.'

'I thought he couldn't manage it.'

'Only every day of his life.'

News came with the ferry. Reports of damage up the
west coast – a satellite mast destroyed, power lines down,
trees blocking roads. In Galway a falling chimney had
peeled away half the gable wall of a house. For once
there were no injuries. I looked around me at the bare
back of the island and knew that if ever it had excess
baggage it had long ago been torn away by the violent
air. I imagined the southerly seas, a fetch of two or
three thousand miles, sweeping up the North Atlantic;
the winds driving them born in a ripple of the jetstream
around Pico in the Azores, perhaps, or in the icy valleys
of Newfoundland. By the time they reached this place they

were irresistible, ferocious animals wrestling everything in their way.

The entire force of nature bent itself to send disaster here, to paint white water between the island and the main, to turn the flood and drown the boat; the islanders, with skill and grace and instinct, evaded its thrust. The ferry boat came in. There was never another time, never a second chance. One false turn and the sea was in, the engine choked, the helmsman helpless.

There was more than skill to this, some kind of belonging that drew the boat safely in, that pulled the islander home.

And there is always home. If I had known the sea-marks I might have found the way in. If it was not already too late.

The power went out at five o'clock and we were left with the flickering of the fire, an icy uncertainty invading the room. One by one we pulled on sweaters, overcoats, woolly hats. Soon we were hunched over the fire, hands outstretched like workmen huddled around a tar-barrel in a roadway. 'Don't worry,' she said. 'They'll get the generators going. We'll have power again in an hour.' But there were lights in the other houses perched in the hillside niches, and the sign for Con's Bar blinked and brightened in the usual way.

'I'll go down and tell Con. Will you have a pint?'

'I'll follow you down.'

She opened the door and the outside screamed at us. She slipped through and was gone.

I went upstairs and lay down on the bed fully clothed. The sky outside was alive with clouds, the three-quarter moon flickering on and off behind them. A pair of her panties was thrown on a chair; the blue checked shirt she wore yesterday was lying on top of the half-empty knapsack; the room was full of noise and the sweet smell of her body.

When the storm blew out, the island came to life again. Con came and reattached the wire that brought us power. He was cheerful. 'Plenty of work to keep you going around here,' he said. He was hanging from a pole, a huge canvas belt dangling tools so that he looked himself like a gadget inside out. A mechanical digger appeared suddenly below us, on the road to the beach, and began to hammer at the rock. 'Road widening,' Con said. 'Would you believe that? The County Council thinks we need wider roads.' The sun came out, watery but warm.

This was our last day. Across the way the mainland seemed unbearably indifferent, commonplace, tractable, unchanging. Tomorrow we would make the crossing again. We had decided to walk the length of the island and she took me up onto the hill that formed the spine. 'We'll take the short cut,' she said, 'the old road.' We climbed a steep cliff, following the ghost of a track in the heather, weaving right and left but going upwards all the time. We came out on a relatively flat area on top of the hill. The view was astonishing. In the clear wintry air we could see the mainland stretching northwards indefinitely, the sea filling the south as far as the parabola of the horizon. There were tiny trawlers trying to look busy at a snail's pace, and a small coaster ploughing westwards in the remains of the storm-swell.

'This is one of the old ways, the old roads,' she said.

'From before the time they put tar on them.' Underfoot was grass, but where it was worn away I could see a bed of limestone, sheets of rock occasionally. 'This is Coinlín,' she told me. 'Look. That's the old village down there.' Slightly below us was a collection of ruins nestled against the rock. 'Let's go down.' She was different this morning, more detached if anything.

There were six houses, in what must once have been a tiny hamlet, high up above the sea but protected from all sides. Some of them had been partially dismantled over the years, their stones used to build walls or patch fences. She led me to one that was intact except for the roof. Four walls, high gables, ridges where the roofing timbers had rested. She led me through the door. I saw her brush the stones with her hand as she entered, as though pacifying the household gods.

It was a single long room, a huge chimney at one end. Windows on one side looked down the hill towards the glittering sea; on the other they looked inwards to a sheltered yard, the dry bones of a fuchsia bush filling one corner. She showed me the hearthstone, the trace of the fire in it still, although fifty years of weather had bleached it grey. In the chimney there was a crossbar of oak, blackened where the crane for the pot had worn it. There were two small shelves let into the stone on either side. I imagined some ancient island man standing his pipe there, some island woman taking a teabox from that shelf, or replacing a teapot where it would be hot. I saw the house full of warmth, the voices of children.

Roughcast mortar formed irregular shapes on the walls, moss and lichen growing over everything. A few skeletal weeds clung to the beaten earth and heaped rubble.

Something was growing on top of the gable beside the chimney.

'They lit the fire in November,' she said. 'They called it a six-month fire. *Tine leathbhliain.* They all watched to see who would be the first to start a flame. When they saw the smoke going up the chimney they brought a sod of turf to take the fire away with them. There was a special blessing for that first fire.' The air was full of the babble of people coming for the gift, coming to the island Prometheus. 'My father remembered that,' she said.

There was a blessing for me too, if I could take it. I could come for the fire and take it away, husband it through the winter, blowing on the embers and watching it crackle into life when it was needed.

'He never came back, Joe. He sent me here to learn Irish, but he never came back himself. He couldn't face the memories.'

'Was he right? Maybe he loved the place too much.'

'How long is it since you went home, Joe?'

'That has nothing to do with this.'

'You're not a whole man, Joe. That's what I think.' She was shaking her head very slightly, from side to side, small repudiations that shook me in turn.

'What are you telling me, Suzie?'

'I don't know. It's as simple as that. I just don't know. But . . .' She looked at me gravely. 'I'm scared. I'm sorry, Joe.'

'Of what? Scared of what?'

'What you can't say. What you won't face up to. It's too much.'

'I let them down, Suzie.' I felt suddenly undone by the simplicity of it. There were pieties to be observed, truths

to be upheld, lies to be bolstered. That is the structure of
the family, the skein of half-truth and received mythology
that binds the occasional days of love and happiness. 'I let
the side down, I gave away the secrets. A tell-tale.'

'You wrote a book, Joe. A good one too. It wasn't your
fault that the cover looked like your mother. That was a
freak. And it wasn't your fault that she thought it was
about her. You drew on your memories. Your experience.
Every artist does that one way or the other.'

'It's there in black and white in the book. I should have
asked their permission. To use them.'

'You had a right. An artist's right.'

'But not a child's.'

'You can't be a child for ever. First you're a child and
then you're the next generation. They have to live with
what you are. They gave it to you along with all the other
things.' Her eyes were grave, she barely moved. 'This is
the house where my grandfather was born,' she said.

She was leaning against the wall, one hiking boot
propped on a stone. Behind her head a patch of lichen
had colonised the mortar, an empire in little, marching
over the stony landscape. There was something desolate
about her, desolated like the house itself, as though time
had robbed her, emptied her. Her head was tilted back
and sunlight brightened her forehead, but the shadow of
the missing roof was there, the wasted hearth, the sightless
windows.

She caught and held me and we made love in her grandfather's house. Afterwards, going out, she touched the lintel
again, and I wondered if the gods had been propitiated or
angered by that one act: an appropriate ritual or a ritual
desecration. The answer, I knew, depended on me.

6

We screamed through the dreams of sleeping children and the silences between moments of excitement in 'The Sunday Game'. Dogs woke in kitchens and lifted their ears. An old man stared at us from an open door, his arms folded defensively across his chest. Street lights flashed by at irregular intervals, punctuating long stretches of darkness. There were occasional houses, occasional oncoming cars, and Suzie's speed scarcely changed as the bearings of her Hiace van died in agony along the winding road out of the West.

She was telling jokes to keep herself awake. 'A man on a business trip phones home and his son answers. Son, get Mammy to come to the phone, the man says. I can't, Dad, she's upstairs in bed with the milkman. Son, the man says, get my shotgun, load it and shoot the two of them for me. The boy goes away and he hears two shots. The boy comes back after about five minutes. They're wasted, Dad, he says. I blew them out the window. They're floating in the swimming pool and the whole pool is full of blood. What are you talking about? the man says. There's no swimming pool in our house.'

I said, 'Where are we anyway?'

'Halfway through my latest batch of bad jokes, halfway home,' she said. 'At our speed anyway.' She coughed, giggled and shifted out of second gear. The screaming sound went down an octave. 'That'll be another shagging bearing.'

'The bearings are all right,' I said. 'It's the van that's a wreck.'

'Do you want to walk!'

'Suzie,' I said. 'I'm lost. I was asleep. Half asleep anyway.'

She stared at me for two full seconds while the van veered towards the hard shoulder. 'I am Lazarus come back from the dead,' she quoted. She turned back to the road. 'I will tell you all.' Then she was chuckling again, repeating the punchline: 'Son, there's no pool in our house. I like it.'

I turned the radio on and heard the reader on the ten o'clock news say there had been an earthquake in Turkey. Then the jingle and a voice saying that RTÉ was turning the spotlight on Ireland of the welcomes, Ireland's gay community living in fear and loathing. Too easy, I thought – a cliché in itself – the reality more painful, more dangerous, hurt and lonely. I remembered Troy in boarding school, clasping the cords of his pyjamas, his tear-streaked face, and later, kicking through the leaves, hands in his pockets, hunched against the desperation of another year in the trap. And Joan, waving and walking away – 'I can get this anywhere.' I didn't want to be lonely. But most of all I didn't want to lose Suzie.

The heater was permanently stuck at ON so that we had to drive with the windows cracked open, but the air in the van was all our own. We dropped down into the city from the western ridge, the lights linking from street to street like chains, late-night houses going out even as we watched. My hand rested on her thigh under a traffic signal and when she released the clutch I felt her sinews changing place under my fingers.

'Not tonight, love,' she said, in answer to my unspoken question. 'I have to get home. I have to get my things done. I'm back at work tomorrow. Do you realise we didn't wash anything while we were out there?' On the street I kissed her through the window, our faces angled because the glass never dropped below halfway, permanently neither up nor down, and she said, 'I'll see you?'

'I'll have a look at that wheel tomorrow,' I said. 'See what that noise is. I'm handy with engines.'

Something useful from the past, my father and me standing on the front wheels of the tractor, leaning into the grease and diesel: pass the spanner Joe, we'll have to take the cylinder-head off to get at that scraper, you keep your eye on the torque while I tighten, do you see that belt?

The van jerked into motion, almost decapitating me. 'That's not all you're handy with,' she shouted, and as she drove away I could hear her singing over the noise.

My flat was cold, full of the settled damp of rooms abandoned in autumn. I saw the blinking red light on the answerphone and almost pressed the play button. But I stopped, conscious of the frailty of this interregnum; there would be time enough in the morning to talk to my agent or my publisher or my bank manager or whoever it was that had left word of tomorrow's imperatives.

I slept fitfully, dreaming of the air and sea-smell of the island, the place in the hills where the village had been, where I first believed she needed me. Then I woke to the November darkness and made coffee, watching TV with the mute button on – silent chat shows and cartoons, the mischief of other people's lives, other people's calamities, while all the time the tiny light on the answerphone winked like a lighthouse at the edge of memory, saying, if I could only place it: *here* is the shipwreck, the outer danger, prepare while there is still time.

But I was fascinated by *their* unhappiness, the *otherness* of pain; the faces that opened and closed, the host bustling along the seats with his microphone, other wrecks, false lights. A caption at the bottom of the screen said, 'My partner fooled around with a member of my family.' Softball out back in the yard? Goofing off? Or was this a family witch-hunt, the witch tried in his or her absence? Raw sex, thoughtless and uncomplicated, twisted them in their seats. Here was a young woman with a cartoon nose, thin for half its length but bulbous and upturning at the end. Her eyes were solemn. A fat man wept. A boy of perhaps ten told a long story. In the cold light of the studio he looked anaemic. He had a powerful facial tic, a kind of seismic blink that involved both sides of his face.

Applause.

Applause for courage, dignity, sorrow, generosity, but most of all for revelation.

Applause. Applause.

Thank you. Thank you.

And thank you Michael/Travis/James/Hank for being so honest and up-front with us. Thank you for sharing that with us. Thank you for your pain.

I changed stations and watched nightmare figures fly weirdly realistic spaceships through empty galaxies. Flick again and a rat was talking to a bear. I saw that the rat's face was intelligent, his eyes focused, his mouth set thin and firm. The big bear was dumb, though. His head made slow rhythmic movements as he spoke, a kind of music-less bopping. I ate my toast and thought of the ferry's bow plunging through an Atlantic swell, green water running along the side-decks, Suzie's face gleaming in the afternoon light, her eyes shining because I was coming to her place, her island, her past.

The voice on the answerphone said not to be alarmed. To phone home. I pressed rewind and played it again. And again.

My sister Mary.

For a time I could not reconcile the thought of Mary and home. I saw her standing in some kind of television apartment in Seattle – open-plan kitchen/living room, leather couch, picture window. Was it a joke? For an instant my version of her life fused with the chat show and I saw her holding Claire in her arms and glaring across an overlit studio at her husband, daring him to reveal the intimate details of some family spat.

Then I thought that she must have flown home while I was away and that my father was dead, the balance finally out, the rat poison gaining the upper hand or losing the battle. I sat down and tried to force the thing out of my mind. For some odd reason the unbidden memory was of him squatting over a basin of worms on a wet strand years before, our unbaited hooks winking from the sand.

I picked up the phone and dialled home.

Mary answered. 'I've been here for four days,' she said. 'I couldn't get home any quicker. We were trying to get you. Where were you?'

I wanted to say: None of your business.

'I was away on a holiday.'

65

'At this time of the year?' The implication was that I was simply not answering the phone.

'For God's sake just tell me what's wrong. Is it Dad?'

'No. It's a bit of bad news. About Mam. Not as bad as you might think. Not too bad.'

'Tell me!'

'Look, you know she hasn't been well. We all knew there was something wrong.'

A cough? I knew about that. Dad kept me informed. What was a cough? Bronchitis? Or a nervous thing, a habit even. She always had these nervous tics, an odd hand movement, a grimace, a tendency to tap her foot. Then I thought of cancer of the throat. I once met a man who spoke through a voice synthesiser. He had been a major in the British Army, ramrod-straight back, unwavering eye and a voice that whispered through a faulty amplifier. He had written a book about General Montgomery and the Africa campaign.

'What's wrong with her? What is it?'

She gave me a name that meant nothing, that sounded like a place in Asia. She had to spell it out for me.

It was a slow thing, something she'd had for years, Mary said. She said nothing of my absence from home: why weren't you there? her tone insisted, you live here in Ireland, couldn't you let bygones be bygones, forgive and forget? You should have known about this.

'How long?'

'Since we were kids. Teenagers anyway.'

I couldn't believe that.

'It's true. Now that I think about it I can remember things. This is a very slow thing – in the beginning anyway. Dad and herself found out about it around the time I went to America. But she's going downhill fast now. They can't hide it.'

You might have seen it if you visited, was the implication.

'He talks and talks. All the stories, you know the way he loved a good story. She started forgetting things, big things – how to cook, shopping lists, people's names. She hated getting into crowds. She was losing track of things at mass and standing up in the wrong places. Buying things she didn't need. She put bacon on to boil once and forgot to turn it down. The handles melted off the saucepan. Dad was doing more and more for her, organising her. And there were these movements.'

'What kind of movements?'

'You might have seen it if you were around.' It was out now.

'I could say the same for you.'

'I was in America.'

'Couldn't you get farther away?'

'You let that stupid squabble keep you apart. How could you do it? Your own mother.'

I sighed. 'Look, Mary, I said it before. I'll say it once more. The people who designed the cover had no idea that it was like her. I didn't see it. I suppose I was too caught up in the whole publishing thing. It was a mistake.'

'But not what you wrote about.'

'I used some of the things that happened in our family. But the people in the book weren't us. It's fiction, for Christ's sake.'

'The collecting?'

'It was an image.'

'She thought it was about her.'

'How bad is she?'

'She thought you were punishing her.'

'How bad is she, Mary? What does Dad say? Is he coping?'

'The least you could have done was come down and apologise. You could have made your peace with her while there was still time. A little bit of Christianity wouldn't go astray on you, Joe.'

'Mary, I was blue in the face from apologising. She was obsessed. She wouldn't even talk to me. I tried.'

'Well, she's past all that now.'

And that would be the truth. In a few minutes of conversation I had come to feel the finality of certain actions: a man closes a door on a friend and never sees him again; a child goes out to school and never comes back; a lover kisses her beloved goodnight and wakes to find him dead. Such things had happened, even to people I knew. I had held the hand of a young woman who found that death had overtaken her husband between the time they came home from the cinema and the ringing of the morning alarm. I remembered her catalogue of might-have-beens – words, gestures, acts. Now the finality was mine. I had quarrelled with my mother and my last words had been a closure. What were they? I tried to remember exactly how we had parted. Too long ago. Too many hard words. Too many closing doors. I could hear the bleak laughter of minutiae. The small things are what count in the end, the discarded things: they were what made the coherent whole. Whatever my words were as I opened or closed that door, made a gesture, set my foot on the threshold or the flagstone at the front step – whatever I said or did, that was my farewell. There would be no reconciliation. I could never call it back.

'Dad is in the kitchen,' Mary said. 'He wants to have a word with you. I'll get him.'

'Last Christmas she had a bit of trouble,' he told me when he came to the phone. 'A bit of a problem swallowing. She was inclined to cough up her food. And she's not talking much. She's down to one or two words at a time now. She's very bad the past month.' I could hear his characteristic tendency to understate. I knew she would have been much worse; probably she would have been vomiting everything, implacably silent.

She was irritable, he said. And she was getting things into her head. She wouldn't leave well enough alone. 'You know what the poet said, Joe, about things like that. You know: thin partitions do their bounds divide? I was worried for a long time. You know what I mean? You should see her, Joe. She doesn't weigh as much as a bag of feathers. She's like a rasher of wind.' I could hear the catch in his throat.

'Why didn't you tell me, Dad?'

'Ah, Joe, the way it was between the two of you . . .' Silence for a time, then in a quieter voice: 'Will I tell you the truth? What would I be lying for now? She made me swear. She didn't want any burdens on you or Mary. That was the way she always was. Independent. And then, I was afraid if she saw you it would only make things worse. I was always thinking that she'd come round. Get used to the idea – the book, you know what I mean? That she might get over it.' He may have heard my half-suppressed cry – exasperation or anger, I don't know which. He changed the subject after a short pause. 'Seemingly it's been going on for years in a small way. Maybe twenty years. Small things. Like the twitching. I always thought she was one of those impatient women. Inclined to want things done yesterday. And then she was getting forgetful, and sure I was that way myself. You see? Old age? I put it down to the two of us getting old. If there wasn't the fight and all that, you'd probably have noticed it yourself.'

'I could have helped.' It was not a statement. I was pleading for a reprieve.

He told me that she had said things that even he was hurt by. That she had developed a cruel temper. That if I had come down he was afraid what she might have said. 'She made me promise to tell no one. From the time she found out. They diagnosed it a good while ago. Let me think. It'll be seven or eight years ago now.' I could hear the weariness of the waiting years. 'They told us all the symptoms, and I could see straight away that she had a share of them. The temper was one. And the confusion. Forgetting. And the future wasn't too good. They laid the whole thing out for her. That's the way she wanted it. She didn't want to be hoodwinked. She's a very strong character, your mother is. The doctor was very good about it, in fairness. He was kindness itself. I couldn't fault him. And your mother faced it all head on. She spelled it all out, exactly the way she wanted things. She didn't want you and Mary troubled. She said so. They have their own lives to lead, she said. I'm sorry, Joe. I tried to tell you once or twice. Without saying it in so many words. Hinting.'

'It got worse quickly?'

'Seemingly, she has a quicker kind. Slow to begin, but then faster. That's rare. The doctor was surprised. The whole thing is rare enough anyhow. I think he said less than ten in a hundred thousand people. What are the odds,

Joe? Ten people in one hundred thousand and it has to be my Eily?'

He had been able to manage on his own until lately. 'The shaking got very bad. That's the way it goes seemingly. The doctor says it's part of it anyway. Her legs. She keeps moving and twisting. Even when she's just sitting looking at the telly her legs are going. Half walking. Kicking. But slow enough. Anyway she can't sit up now with a while. She starts out to do something and she stops and sometimes she doesn't even know she did it. And I have to watch her all the time.'

I could hear the fear in his voice. He would be standing in the hall, holding the phone in the tentative way he had, the earpiece not quite touching his head. What was left of his hair had been almost completely grey for the past five years, and he was balding gradually. The overhead light would be gleaming on his pate. How often had I seen him stand there discussing the price of cattle, the weight of a fish, the details of some committee meeting or other? The winter chill of the hall, a draught filtering through the ill-fitting front door and the blast of heat from the kitchen at his back. 'Close that door,' my mother would say. 'If it was a gate you wouldn't leave it open.' And without a word he would reach out his left hand and push it gently.

Who warmed the house now? Who struck fire into the grate? Who closed the door?

'She left the gas on a while ago. Back before the summer. She forgot to light it and left the oven turned on. Only that I smelled the gas myself we were all gone.'

He paused.

'I needn't tell you,' he said carefully, 'that it was a mistake. Your mother wouldn't do that on purpose.'

71

'I know that, Dad.'

A long pause.

'She's inclined to see things,' he said. The words fell into my silence like a stone crashing down the sides of a well. The depth was so great that the splash was inaudible. It was some time before I realised that I was holding my breath.

'It's terrible,' Suzie said. 'What could I do to help? Anything. I'll come over straight away.'

But I could not cope with her sympathy now. I felt a strong urge to hang up, to cut her short. Feeling my own unpreparedness, her strength. Self-pity surging in. And the accompanying contempt. 'Suzie, I'm hardly able to think,' I said. 'I couldn't cope with you. I can't afford sympathy. I have to keep my head straight.'

'It isn't sympathy.' I heard the sudden crackle of ice, a passage closing in a frozen sea.

'I'm not the one in trouble. I can't afford to let self-pity get in the way.'

'It's love.'

Another thing I should have known.

Like the rush of the spring tide pulling boats straight on their moorings: I heard the sound of water crackling through bladderwrack, between stones, lifting the strands of sea-grass; helpless tears streaked down my face. I struggled to control my mouth, my voice.

'Joe?'

'I'm here.'

'You go down. Talk to them. There must be something you can do. When you come back, I'll be still here.'

'I love you, Suzie.'

'You don't deserve me.'

I laughed. The sound surprised me. 'You're right. You're not the first one to say it either.'

'What's going to happen to her? Do you know?'

I had checked it on the Internet. More than a thousand hits. No time to check them all. I had written down the definition from one site: *Inherited as an autosomal dominant disease that gives rise to progressive, selective (localised) neural cell death associated with choreic movements and dementia. The disease is associated with increases in the length of a CAG triplet repeat present in a gene called 'huntingtin' located on chromosome 4p16.3.* Cold. Definitive. The disease was progressive. Neural cell death. A death sentence.

'I'll be here when you get back.'

Too many things to be done. I had the strange feeling that I was putting my affairs to right, as if it were me that was dying. I paid two bills that had been overdue. I sorted my mail and answered a letter of enquiry from the British Library, emailed a review that had been sitting on my hard disk for a month. I closed the blinds, unplugged all the electrical appliances, poured disinfectant into the toilet and opened the doors of the built-in wardrobe. Then I threw some clothes into a bag and walked out.

The roads were wet, speckled with mud, pocked with holes. I drove down the distance, watching the miles reel in, listening to the drive-time programmes, the mindless banter and infill, the lyric-less songs. People on cellphones drove by with their heads tilted into their shoulders. Evening came down quickly. Night enlarged the space between villages. Lights polished the roads, warmed houses. I wondered how long the disease would take, what resources my father had for her, what kind of care the state would provide. And I tried to come to terms with the fact that my mother was dying. That we had never been reconciled. That my father, who had always been cared for, must become the care-giver. That Mary and I would have to play our part. And I wondered what the disease would do to her. What would she look like? How would she react when I arrived?

Mary.

The splinter of resentment still there, a shape under the skin to worry at. I wondered how would she defend her God now, who handed down a death sentence buried in genetic code, one that struck the innocent and guilty alike. All her puritan certainties, her easy platitudes, her pieties.

I crested the last hill and saw the stretch of darkness where the coast of my childhood should have been, a fainter grey marking the sea. On my left the cluster of the village, and beyond that again the gently sloping hill speckled with farmhouses. One of those lights was home. My father would be waiting there, standing at the window, perhaps, as I had so often seen him do. 'That's for rain,' he would say, indicating the night, as though we could see that the wind had changed. 'There'll be nothing done this week.' And it would be harvest time and the harvester would have to be postponed again. Or it would be springtime and the fields would be wet and there would be no question of the harrow until everything had dried off a bit. And a bad day for the farmer was a good one for the fisherman, he used to say. 'On a dark day they have to go by smell. They can't see the trace. It's an ill wind that doesn't blow some good.'

Part 2

7

When my sister Mary was born part of my mother died. It was not just her womb – a catastrophic loss in its own right – but some piece of the contrivance failed, some cardinal property, the absence of which changed her for ever. In dark times now, knowing that it could not be so, I think that mortality nested where my sister burrowed out.

I see the grey face of a hospital, four or possibly five floors high, the tallest building I had ever seen. In the canon of death and disease it was laid down that little children could not touch their mothers, so the closest I came to her failing body was this vision of the monstrous through the misting windows of a Morris Minor. Idly I wondered if my mother would ever come out – at that age nothing much matters – and fiddled with the handle that raised the glass, the creaking cables of a theatre backdrop: *hospital car park, foggy day/The same, fog has cleared, a suggestion of cold.*

She had haemorrhaged, a ruinous insult to her thin frame, and the only guarantee that she would not endure the same damburst again was hysterectomy. That was the day my aunt and my father confronted the surgeon. They had discussed the condition as though it belonged to someone else, calmly going over the options. And at first it seemed as if they were rich in futures, all the things that modern medicine circa 1967 could do. But one by one they found that none of them would end her bloody flux, and though they circled and sallied forth through hopeful developments, important work, new drugs, the latest research, the nexus of all their talk was death. The surgeon was sorry to have to tell them, but (here he shrugged very slightly, in my father's telling, bowed his head a little, looked at something on his desk) all they could do was hope and pray that God would not call her away. With weary patience he explained that these things happen, an occasional consequence of parturition. My father must reconcile himself to God's will.

My aunt, a nurse trained in England and on her way back there in a matter of days, said the word *hysterectomy*. The surgeon, ignoring her, turned slowly towards my father, hands held out palm upwards.

'Do you see these hands, Mr Lyons?' he said. 'These hands were blessed by the pope.'

'Does that mean that you won't do a hysterectomy?' my aunt asked.

He shook his head – at my father.

'You are aware, Mr Lyons, that hysterectomy is a form of contraception?'

It was probably at this point that my aunt, my mother's elder sister, began to shout. They argued for a time and eventually she said she would fly my mother to England to a doctor she knew in Guy's Hospital, London. She would mortgage her house to pay for it; then she would sue the surgeon to redeem the mortgage.

The hysterectomy saved my mother's life and the surgeon went on to commit other offences against his conscience, one or two of which involved the removal of other wombs. Nevertheless, in his sixty-third year, he was awarded a papal knighthood for his services to the Church. That was a time when such honours counted.

When my mother recovered she became a collector and the things she accumulated hid the thing that was lost.

And then there was reassurance in them, each item in each collection a small thing, a mere term in a series, an element in a great unforeseeable substance, each new item adding a promise of the next, an earnest of futures. Each collection was infinite in its capacity and each contained sets of further infinities: she never made collections that could be completed, the possibilities stretching forwards and backwards in time out of mind. She did not, for example, collect Irish coins. She simply collected coins. She collected china. There was never a suggestion that she might have collected a sample of every kind of china, or that her coin collection was nearing completion. There was always the next lucky find, or the sought-after rarity. The house filled up with old glass, postcards, stamps, shining sixpences and brassy threepences. The hatpins were extraordinary. There were silver butterflies, exotic feathers, copper snoods, arrangements of wire, glass beads, imitation rubies, straight pins, geometric shapes. They winked and gleamed in different lights, displayed in specially procured pincushions. And each room had its antiques, all unique for some reason: the looming forms of two-door wardrobes with bevelled mirrors and odd figures in the silvering; the brass bedsteads; stiff-backed chairs. Many were named for the original owner – Mrs Chale was a delicate lady's dressing table, Mrs Weir a Victorian potholder – Protestant ladies whose lack of children resulted in auctions of household effects, sundry antique furniture, bric-a-brac, books in lots of ten tied with white fibrous string and numbered with a brown-paper tag, and gardening implements.

When old Mrs Weir died, my mother said, 'When the woman dies the heart goes out of the house.'

Mr Weir called, unsteady on his legs since a shell had exploded behind his back in 1917. 'Come down, Mrs Lyons, and have a keepsake,' he said. And my mother took the potholder. She held his hand at the door and said, 'Don't want for anything, we're only down the road.' His rheumy eyes gazed unsteadily at something behind us, and he gave me a shilling.

Mrs Chale's sister, also a widow, came from England to organise the auction of house and effects. My mother bid over the top for the dressing table. 'You can't be looking for a bargain from a neighbour,' she said. My father, who bought and sold cattle with his neighbours all the time, did not understand.

She took me with her to the auctions as if she were training me to a trade: the auction-goer. She had an elaborate technique designed to lure other less canny buyers away from her favoured purchases. She would walk up and down the lines of the display watching everyone else. When someone paused at a piece she didn't like she would drift in that direction and begin to examine it. She would make brief comments to me. Opening a drawer she would point at a crude joint. 'See that,' she'd say. Then in a stage-whisper: 'Typical. Georgian.' And a shake of the head. 'It's amazing how rough those old Georgians were. Still it's old enough. Worth a bit. That'll be a bargain.'

Or dismissing an ugly table as 'early Victorian', she would add, 'The old bitch. She gave five pounds to the famine relief.' Meaning Queen Victoria, whom my mother despised.

When a true Georgian piece came up, a plain, bluff, beautifully finished chest, for example, or a rich mahogany table, she would ignore it completely. These pieces glowed in my mind like imagined objects. 'Don't go near that,' she would say, and the table or chair or teabox or mirror would become the centre of gravity in the room. Every step I took would be in relation to it. When the auction came she would be disgusted to find that the people who really understood furniture were all bidding for the same pieces anyway, as often as not well beyond what she could pay, and her Georgian table went for twice what she had hoped to get it for. 'The dealers are here,' she would say by way of explanation, pleased, in a way, that at least her judgement had not been wrong. Afterwards, when the pieces were all bought and paid for and there was no danger of revealing the true worth to the uninitiated, there would be a small soft-spoken tutorial on Cuban mahogany, mortise and tenon joints, marquetry and veneer, the Victorian walnut-frame sewing chair or the Georgian commode. All of these things, it seemed to me, were supposed to be valuable in themselves, a value that was completely unrelated to function. We did not need a commode of any age, but the wood was so fine, the grain so elegant, the patina so lustrous, the brass hinges original and so very finely made, that it would be impossible to pass up at the right price.

Our house would have exploded with antiquity but for the fact that the price was almost always wrong.

When my sister Mary was old enough, and I was already away at school, she became my mother's foil; and strangely, from an early age, she seemed to have the required single-mindedness and a capacity for small deceptions. By eight or nine she was drawing my mother's attention to bevelled mirrors with only a little of the silvering missing, to dressing tables with wells in them, tables with ball-and-claw feet. There may have been something whimsical in the way she was attracted to the stranger features, but the truth was I never saw any of them. Mary would step into an auction room and her face would take on the intensity of a child in a secret game. She would prowl the aisles and return, whispering that there was a brass oil lamp near the top that still had a globe and shade. My mother would suppress a cry of delight and together they would contrive to pass it twice without seeming to look at it. They were a comical pair at the bidding, my mother desperately trying to restrain Mary's enthusiasm.

'Keep your hand down or he'll think you're bidding.'

'But we won't get it!'

'We can't afford it, child.'

'It's only five pounds more.'

'No. Sit on your hands.'

Somehow their love was forged among the bric-a-brac, something more elemental than I was capable of, or so I thought. It made me, bit by bit, a spectator – my father too.

I can see our kitchen, the Aga cold because it was summertime, tea-things cleared away and standing by the big oak draining board. It was Saturday night and there was the ritual of a bath, hair washed in the kitchen sink, the comforting smell of wet towels and Lux soap. Cleanliness is next to godliness. My sister looked glum, her arms straight by her side, her mouth crimped closed, the square-faced bottle of clear liquid and the spoon hovering before her face. The turgid movement of the liquid on the spoon.

'Open your mouth,' my mother said.

'Go on, Mary,' I said, 'it's good for you.' The television flickered quietly in the corner, Lucille Ball's implausible face surprised by yet another risible coincidence. The picture above it showed Pope John, Pope Paul and John F. Kennedy, a triptych of past, present and a deceptively simple future. Beside it a new purchase: a historical map of Ireland, oak poles at top and bottom to keep it spread, picked up in a job-lot at an auction in a teacher's house. Only an hour earlier they had been hammering nails into the powdery mortar between the stones of the kitchen wall.

'You know you'll get constipated,' my mother said. 'You always get constipated.' Still my sister would not open her mouth. 'You'll get a headache and you'll be complaining about it.' A small shake of the head.

'Right so,' my mother said. She turned and put the bottle back on the sink. Carefully she ladled the spoonful back into it. She stood the spoon in the empty milk jug. We watched her, mesmerised by her stony silence.

'Come on now, love,' she said, melting suddenly. 'Don't let me down. It's for your own good.' And Mary was in tears, sobbing against the blue housecoat, saying sorry, Mammy, sorry, over and over again. My mother saying, 'There, there, child, it's nothing. Look at the big map we bought. What'll Daddy say to that? Look how small Ireland looks.'

And then the sound of heavy boots in the yard – my father come whistling to the back door. When he saw Mary and my mother he began to sing: *My sister Mary heard the express, she ran downstairs in her morning dress, a hundred guineas I will lay down, to see my brother safe in Wexford town.* He saw the map and his eyes opened wide for a moment – in shock or surprise? Then he winked at me and said, 'Well, Joe, we can't go around hugging like the ladies.' He was in a laughing mood. 'Leave it there, boy.' He held out the flat of his hand as the cattle-dealers did. I slapped my palm into his and we grinned foolishly at each other. And then he saw that Mary was crying.

In school Mary had the same unerring acquisitive instinct. All through primary she hit ten out of ten in everything. She was held up to the class as an example of perfection, and she carried her reputation with her into the convent school. She collected ideas and facts with equal relish. The chemistry of a reaction was as valuable to her as Macbeth's cry of anguish for his dead wife. She outpaced everything I had done, and I had been a marvel to my parents and teachers. It was effortless for her. *Out, out, brief candle, life's but a walking shadow*, she would chant. Over and back on the creaking old floorboards, the book folded over her thumb, held behind her back. And later she would show an even greater aptitude for science, juggling the letters and numbers that stood for substance, the symbols that meant relationship, interaction, reaction. Her notebooks were full of terse statements about catalysts, compounds, reactions; beautiful drawings of glass jars, bell jars, burettes, pipettes, their transparency hiding everything.

There was once an elegant Trafalgar chair, with a rattan seat still intact, brass bands at the feet, beautiful rope-work carving in some fine timber at the top rail.

It stood in the dusty corner of some antique shop, towards the back and behind a modern wardrobe and a cheap laminated table. It was the only one. As usual Mary saw it first. She was carrying a pair of new denim jeans in a bag. My mother had a glossy fold of dry-cleaning, the thin plastic cover magnetised to her. They never passed an antique shop without looking in, always hoping for a bargain, something the shop-owner had missed – the collector's/gambler's/alcoholic's dream: the lucky strike. A glance at the chair was enough to tell them what it was. They called the owner down and enquired about the laminated table. They tut-tutted over the price and then, casually, enquired about the old chair. They walked out. The usual drill.

Later they brought my father in.

'It's a thing of beauty,' my mother hissed. 'Cheap at the price.'

My father shook his head. 'We don't need another chair.'

There was a sliver of anger in my mother's eyes that was a crack in a wall, lighting the way inwards to something alive and burning, the brain turning against the coming indignity, a tiny nebula that fizzed and dissipated. I should have sensed the shock waves lifting and dropping us, shifting us apart by infinitesimals, but how was I to know? Even children can't see into the future, despite not being overburdened by the past.

'I have a bit put aside,' she said. She was the one who reconciled the books, balanced the cattle or beet sold, the lambs brought to the block, against the seed bought and sown, the ram, the weanlings, the diesel oil and the thousand outgoings of a busy farm and house. And who managed to set something aside each week with which to purchase perfect forms – a butler's tray last week, a pound note from the Civil War, a collection of smooth brown half-pennies, a hand-tinted postcard date-stamped 1908: *So sorry we missed each other at Passage. Hope this finds you well, as it leaves me. Till Sunday then, Your fond friend Tom.*

'It isn't that.'

'What is it so?'

'It's not the money.'

'Well, what is it so?'

I saw my father hunting in his memory for the reason and I saw that he was lost, confounded in pointless opposition. I saw his mouth set in stubborn lines, his shoulders hunch a little as though preparing for an attack. This once, I could see, he had determined to make a stand. Mostly he pursed his lips or shrugged his shoulders, confounded by the astonishing range of the things she found beautiful or necessary. Sometimes he indulged her, praising her taste, her eye for a bargain, or the elegant grain of the wood, or the perfection of a veneer. Just once he had used the word 'obsession' and her fury unsettled him for weeks.

'God almighty,' he said at last, 'as if we haven't enough shagging chairs!'

They argued in hissing shadows until my mother stalked away, wet-eyed, and my father thumped the laminated table with his fist. Mary and I ran out and waited in the street, caught between my mother's disappearing shape and the gravity of my father's anger. Mary was in tears, desperation written all over her.

In the car he said plaintively, 'The house is full of things. It's not natural, Eily.'

We drove home in silence. His driving was erratic at the best of times, a tendency to cross the road to see what so-and-so had planted this time, or to count heads, Short-horns, Friesians, Herefords, the new strange Simmental. Now he was weaving across the white line and swinging back in, almost putting the wheel in the drainage ditch, grass rustling underneath, briers scratching the side. He raced the engine, changing gears as if he were still driving the old Commer truck he used to have that needed to be double-declutched at each gearshift.

We came to an uncertain stop in the yard and when he switched the engine off the car rolled a few feet on the slope. My mother was getting out before he jerked the handbrake on. I remember that it was a crystal-clear night, frost in the air. A night for echoes, in which voices travelled long distances, the barking of dogs repeated over miles. He went from room to room turning the lights on, opening and closing doors.

Sometime around ten o'clock – the long talking over – there came a hiatus. He was standing in the kitchen, a mug of tea on the sink-top. The big black Aga range was cooling. In the silence of the moment I heard embers fall through the grating and drop dead into the tray of ash beneath.

My mother began to say something and then stopped. She looked down and our eyes followed hers. Her hand was moving from her lap towards the nearest corner of the range, a strange, awkward, rotating movement, unlike anything the sinews were programmed for, the fingers rippling slightly as though she were playing the piano very softly. It stopped halfway and the movement became a tremor. Then her hand returned to her lap. It took no more than two seconds. She stared at her hand for a moment afterwards, her face a mask.

'Something moved my hand,' she said flatly. 'Like magic.'

My father sat down suddenly, glad for once that there were too many chairs in the kitchen. 'Did you see that?' he said, as if she had not spoken. 'God almighty.'

Mary came in and said something that started the whole argument about the chair again, quieter this time, my father retreating carefully, eventually surrendering. 'Buy the chair,' he said, 'if that's the way you feel about it.'

But my mother said, 'I feel washed out, Daddy. I'm tired out.' The air was suddenly full of urgent flaws, pressures that neither Mary nor I could chart.

It is Mary's contention, somehow predicated on the college course she took in behavioural psychology and on the flimsy evidence of a period spent as a counsellor in the anti-abortion clinic, that everything is related, each small fault reaching out for others, acquiring structure by its relationship to other faults, a monstrous fabric growing out of the one atom of despair and the other atom of joy, the sinister and the innocent coagulating to a single complex membrane. If so, then we should be able to identify the first small piece in the patchwork, the first axiom in the geometry of the sinister.

So, there is no excuse for blundering. We were there at the time.

Object by object, word by word, we crowded out the air and light: no drawer, no inch of floor, no windowsill was barren – our house was filling up with the debris of other people's lives, the scatterings of other family disintegrations, other people's childless marriages, distant bankruptcies – the whole structure trembling on the verge of rupture, as if one day a wall would go and this ample womb would spew onto the street.

8

When I was twelve he took me fishing for the first time. 'The day after your birthday,' he said, and all day I waited for it. I waited through school – it was my last year in primary – daydreaming over the wallchart of pelagic species, following the sawtoothed coastline on the classroom map and wondering which bay or rock my father would perch me on. I admired the green and black elegance of the mackerel in the wall picture, a humble figure that yet managed to convey speed and purpose and intelligence. I had seen them herding sprat into the crooked arms of the bay and spurting through the silver shoals like torpedoes. When the big boys brought them to the door in August their bodies were curved and rigid as though they had died in the act of evasion. I knew my father scorned them. He said that mackerel fishing was murder, that the fish almost committed suicide, gave themselves up. There was no skill in it. Instead he would take me out tonight and initiate me in the pursuit of superior fish: the delicate plaice; the subtle dab; the sole; the codling; the bass; the brutal dogfish; the pollock; the conger eel whose jaws would seize upon a human hand in its death-throes and must be prised apart with a crowbar. We would stand together in the dark by the luminous edge of the ocean and place our lures where they might be found. An elaborate dance with an invisible partner. A game where the rules could only be guessed at.

The end of that schoolday was long in coming. When I was sent out to ring the bell, I rang it to bring the walls down because only a catastrophe could release me quickly enough.

We drove into the twilight in his ruined old Ford Escort estate, the boot smelling of brine and beet-pulp and cow-dung. He told me solemnly that he would teach me about the sea. I wore black wellington boots, two woollen scarves, an Aran jumper.

He was full of talk, old stories and stale jokes. He loved to show off his powerful memory by quoting weighty chunks of the poetry he had learned as a boy – Shakespeare, Keats, Goldsmith, James Clarence Mangan, and the great patriotic favourites: 'Who Fears to Speak of Ninety-Eight'; 'The Man from God Knows Where'; 'The West's Awake.' Sometimes he would sing an old ballad or something by Thomas Moore. This evening it was 'Oft in the Stilly Night', delivered in the soft, slightly nasal tone he favoured, a wandering labourer crossed with John McCormack. His memory was a capacious mansion in which were placed, in their perfect places, exact inflections, precise variations on words or spelling or pronunciation, the detail of a chance remark overheard fifty years before. He could remember, for example, the exact instructions for firing a rifle given by a drill-sergeant in the local defence force almost half a century back.

'Oft in the stilly night,' he sang, ''ere slumber's chain has bound me, fond memory brings the light of other days around me.'

And we seemed to be moving through the light of other days, the magic twilight travelling with us and fading into darkness.

Soon the headlamps were picking out whitethorns and arthritic fuchsias and occasional houses and people. Darkness falls early and sudden in winter; when we turned in to the gate at Durrus Strand the beams swung out to infinity, projected over the edge of the world and onwards into the galaxy. The rattle of the car died and was replaced by the sound of a gentle sea collapsing on sand.

We pulled on our boots, our army surplus jackets, our woolly hats. We joined the ends of the rods and snapped the traces on in the weak glow of the tail-lights. Then we tramped over the strand and down to the water's edge, the ebb-slaked sand solid underfoot. He lit a small lamp. Out of an army surplus knapsack he took a Heinz beans can and the flat square top of a biscuit tin. He tipped the worms from the can onto the biscuit tin and poked among them with his fingertips. 'Lugs,' he said. 'Most of them are lugs. But look, see that one? He's a ragworm. Rags are the best for flatties.'

He stared at them. Too long.

'Are you all right, Dad?' I whispered, as if the darkness were peopled with listeners.

'Why wouldn't I be?' he said brusquely. He flicked his hand at the distance as though pushing something away and bent his head again towards the dish of worms.

He showed me how to thread the hook through the worm's mouth and follow the body downwards without breaking the skin until the very last moment. The tiny spurt of worm-blood when the hook went in.

We walked out into the tiny waves, phosphorus sparking all round, and cast our lines into the deeper water. I heard the whirr of the line unwinding, the swish of the whirling lead and gut, the silence and then the distant plop. At first my line fell at my feet and several times I had to thread new worms on the hooks, but in the end I cast to my father's satisfaction and we walked together back to the sand.

He showed me how to hold the line with my finger pressed lightly against it. He explained the small tremors and the larger pluckings that were the current or the tide or the wave, and I realised that he was echo-sounding the bottom through the thin gut, as though the creatures of the sea were sending their fear to him, plucking at the heartstrings in the darkness like blind harpers. 'Do you know, Joe,' he said, 'when a man stands beside the ocean he's standing beside his own past and his own future?'

'How's that, Dad?'

'Look at it. Man crawled out of the sea millions of years ago. Crawled up and laid hold of a brain somehow and decided he was the heart and soul of the party. That's where we came from – the sea. Then when he dies he's put in the ground. Six feet deep. That's meant to be safe. Six feet down, people say, as if they were laying the foundations of a fine solid house. But the sea is eating up the land. Look up there.' He pointed to a place where the path had fallen away in a recent storm. The gable wall of an old cottage still stood, the rest of it turning gently into sand fifty feet below. 'I knew the family that lived in that house. They were decent people.

'And you know, Joe, we did *Hamlet* in school. I often told you that. There's a very good part about how a person dies and ends up food for a worm and that worm is eaten by a fish and a beggar eats the fish. Well, how do we know we're not eating the last remains of Alexander or

Caesar when we eat our flatfish? That'd be a turn-up for
the books! So you know what, Joe? I always feel humble
when I'm standing beside the sea.'

'Me too, Dad,' I said, and he smiled.

'Look up at the stars, boy,' he said, as though directing
his son's attention to a wall-map of the universe. 'See the
Pleiades, look. They're like a kite of stars.' And, jerking his
thumb over his shoulder, he said, 'You know the Plough.
You always know where you are with the stars. If I dropped
dead now and you had to find your way home you could
follow the Plough.'

He laughed. 'Follow the Plough.' He stopped for a
moment and tilted his head as though listening for something. Then he began to sing softly – *When I was a young
lad I followed the plough* . . .

I remember that our rods were propped in wrought-iron
stands and he had brought a tiny folding stool. He sat in
a pool of light, hands folded into his armpits, collar high
around his ears. I had taken to wandering up and down
the beach, in and out of the light, stamping my feet and
rubbing my ears and nose. There was a smell of snow in
the air, the invisible sky thick with cloud and moisture.
I remember he said that the temperature had risen in the
past hour, a sure sign of snow, but to me it felt colder
than ever.

I returned every now and then to read the Morse, finger
straining gently against the line. I felt the rolling of the
lead way out there on the bottom, below the low water
mark, out where people have never been. I felt the strange
knockings and twitchings that could have been fish or
waves or drifting kelp or wrack. Sometimes, not knowing

where the line went when it left the rod, with nothing to see even in the faint light of the lamp, I imagined I was wired to the universe and the outward drag of the ebb was the galaxy loosening its grip, stars and planets spinning away from the centre, the infinitesimal degeneration of everything.

I would say, 'Dad, feel this. Is it a fish?'

He would come over and test it for a moment and shake his head. 'When you have a fish you'll know it,' he would say, maddeningly sure of himself. He might wink and say: 'Fish not with this melancholy bait,' one of his favourite lines from Shakespeare. Or sometimes he would not get up at all. 'You'll know.'

And I did know. When the fish took the bait I felt his first speculative touch. I felt his testing mouth checking for humans on the line, the rap of his body against the trace as he flared off in fright, and the gentler stroke when he returned. Then a sudden snap. Then quiet. Then a steady tug and the tip of the rod began to bend. A little at first, just the very tip. I was winding the reel and calling for help. The weight was astounding, a wary fish turning the ocean to his good against a small boy. My father stood up and clapped his hands in glee. He shouted encouragement. I wound the reel and pulled and relaxed the rod trying to gain on him. Every once in a while the clutch slipped a little and a span of line screamed out, and I cursed myself for not tightening it properly as I had been told. In the end I knew the fish would win so I turned and ran, throwing the rod onto my shoulder and sprinting for the high tide mark, hoping there was enough distance in the beach for the line. Before I reached the rocks I heard my father shouting at me to stop. I turned and saw the silver thrashing in the last inch of water, my father splashing towards it. 'A bass!' he was shouting. 'A big one!' The lamp in his hand swung wildly. I dropped the rod and ran, my wellingtoned feet filling the night with gunfire.

He brought him home and laid him out on the draining board on several sheets of the *Cork Examiner*. The guts came out in a tangle of purple and red and black and were scraped into a bucket. The head stared up at this unexpected end, dead eyes and a false grin. 'There's the nerve, see, this line here,' and his knife indicated a fine parting of grey that ran along the side from head to tail. 'That's how a fish feels the water. And look at these scales. Beautiful when you look at them.' A ridge of silver wafers where the blade had scored the flesh. 'Now, Eily,' he said, turning as my mother came into the kitchen. 'The miracle of the loaves and fishes. We got the fish. Is there a loaf of bread in the house?'

Another night he stood staring at the grey whiplash body of a dogfish, the thin straight mouth, the sandpaper skin. 'You have to kill them,' he told me. 'Never throw one back.' He held the body with his foot, pressing it into the sand, and forced the hook out of its mouth with a pliers. Then he caught the fish by the tail in his gloved hand and threw it far up above the high water mark. I heard it thud among the rocks. Two days later it was still there, eyeless now, its unwholesome body troubled by gulls.

'It's terrible,' my sister Mary said. 'He must have choked to death.'

'He'd be drowning,' I said. 'We drown in water. He'd be drowning in air.'

I had watched other fish in his bag. For long periods they would be quiet, struggling to make sense of the thin fluid that passed through their gills, imagining water in it. They would hear the eerie noises of the world and wonder where the sea was gone, the familial certainties – the chatter of dolphins, the crash of the swell on rocks, the muffled scream of gulls from the other world. Then they would straighten or jump or twist, some violent spasm that should have hurled them backwards into the sea, but instead was frustrated by the yielding fabric of their grave.

'Cruelty,' Mary said.

'Fish don't have any feelings,' I said. 'They're cold-blooded.'

'That,' she told me imperiously, 'has nothing to do with it.'

But my father never varied in his hatred. All other fish were welcomed, even the extraordinary barbed gurnard, the coarse horse mackerel, the John Dory, although he would eat none of these and threw them back immediately. But the dogfish must die. Once I saw him catch the fish by its tail and whirl it onto a rock repeatedly, a kind of cold frenzy.

Was it that year or the next that Mary changed? Or had it been going on all the time like a tiny mould, a billion cells colonised before the first pinhead is visible? She wouldn't eat the fish he caught or the meat my mother bought. She wouldn't wear leather shoes or belts and insisted on plastic even though we pointed out that the production of plastics was probably harming more animals in the long run. 'Eat your meat,' my father would say. And she would cut the steak or chop and shuffle it around her plate, hoping,

98

by making it smaller and smaller, to reduce it beyond visibility.

She had strict rules about food, a kind of monastic rigour. She would never eat unless she had exercised first. She would walk a mile before tea in the beginning; later she jogged or ran the distance. She did press-ups in her room although she never seemed to develop any muscles. She ate her potatoes dry, when everyone else smothered them in butter or gravy. She did not eat eggs or drink milk. 'Have some compassion,' she would say when I talked about food. 'What about the animals you're killing for your own satisfaction?'

And I would say, 'Cabbages scream when they're pulled. I read it in the paper. Vegetables have some kind of communication. They talk to each other. They're probably saying, She's eating more of us than the rest of them. I'd say they hate you.'

'It makes me sick,' she said.

And it did. I had heard her vomiting in the toilet. In school I had been reading that the Roman patricians gorged themselves and then vomited. *Latin for Today*. Our teacher, a big priest with a face full of broken veins, spoke the words with disdain. 'They used to go into the *vomitorium* and make themselves puke.' He pronounced the V like a W. 'And then they'd go back in and start eating all over again. These days we'd say the sin of gluttony.' My classmates giggled at the thought of all those elegant patricians in their purple togas, puking their guts out. But I remembered men coming late from the pub and leaning their heads against a wall. The sounds they made. The roads streaked with vomit and rain. And my sister Mary, locked in the bathroom, rejecting everything.

9

Water hissed somewhere in the high cold morning air, the ghost of the distant sea sifting through pebbles, and a boy in another cubicle beat out a drum riff on his bare knees. The man who built the boarding school had churches in mind, vastness the only understood proportion, marble floors, stone walls, high windows that rattled in bad weather, that leached heat. Frost made cold sinks of them. Here in the toilets the remote ceilings were stitched with mould and the scars of leaking pipes; the tiled floors were icy underfoot. Alpha and Omega, a cold heaven and cold hell. St Keelin's Secondary School for Boys.

A toilet rushed water and a cubicle door opened and swung creaking back against the jamb. Footsteps going away. In the stillness another faint human sound, like a distant brawl but transmitted somehow through the fibre-board partitions. I listened awhile but could not make it out. Now there were other noises: the drip-drip of water falling into the cisterns overhead; a guttural hawking sound that I identified as a running tap; a man whistling on his way to work beyond the walls. Ten minutes to bell. Ten minutes of solitude. I pulled my dressing gown tighter on my knees and rucked the Aran jumper over it, doubling it almost. I was reading *Lady Chatterley's Lover*, contraband wrapped in the cover of *St Alphonsus Ligouri – A Monograph*. That was how they came to us – *A Clockwork Orange, Ulysses, Quiet Days in Clichy* – all clad in the overcoats of the pious or the innocuous. Sometimes the covers were more mysterious than the books, some of them so rare it was hard to imagine a source. *A Clockwork Orange* had the cardboard jacket and dust cover of a first edition of the poems of Joseph Mary Plunkett. I see His blood upon the rose and in the stars the glory of His eyes.

A shuffling sound distracted me. I sat upright, spilling warm air from the unfolding Aran. Sometimes the priests descended in dawn raids, scattering out among the dormitories. They pried and despised. They flexed thin canes. The crows. *Nix* was the word if you saw one. *Nix* passing along the ranks of iron beds. A seismic notice, sensed and understood.

It was *nix* now.

I could smell him out there, a black bird perched in the unconscious. A hint of hair oil, the smell of a soutane, the laundry where the nuns purged clerical underclothing. The crows got special treatment. The crows had the nuns all to themselves. The crows. *Nix* was the word.

I stuffed *St Alphonsus Ligouri* into the flannel pocket and stood up, humming noisily. I shifted the seat of the toilet so that it grated. I reached up to where a mahogany knob ended a brass chain and pulled hard once, twice, three times. Water churned in the bowl, carrying water away. I imagined the icy purity of the Blackwater river rushing downhill to the sea. I saw the sea dropping on Durrus, a cold green tube rolling pewter on top. The blistering cold of memory. A blink of pain. Then I opened the cubicle door and saw Father Drake holding his finger to his beak and pointing his cane at me.

'Stop there, Lyons,' he hissed. 'Don't move.'

He tiptoed across the moist tiles and stood before another door. He rapped with his cane on the top. 'Open up immediately,' he called and rapped again, tattoo tattoo like an open sesame, a door-opening code. Small sounds within, something like despair or dread. What is the difference? The door opened, sticking halfway against a body that twisted suddenly to allow it to pass bang against the wall. I saw two boys inside, one still fumbling with the shaggy strings of his pyjamas and crying. A boy called Troy. The other, a sixth year, wearing a polo-neck shirt and striped pyjama legs, staring defiantly.

'And what is this?'

'It's a devotional book, Father. *St Alphonsus Ligouri*.' I handed him *Lady Chatterley's Lover*. He looked down at the sombre cover, his lips moving silently as though spelling out the letters one by one. '*St Alphonsus Ligouri*?'

'I didn't start it yet. I'm only just down.'

The crow jiggled something in the pocket of his soutane. 'So you came down here to . . . ?'

'Meditate a bit.'

'Well, to think of it! On the one hand we have yourself coming down here to meditate on St Alphonsus Ligouri and on the other hand we have that that abomination taking place nearly next door. It's sacrilege. No more and no less.'

The crow surveyed the cold cubicles, the chipped basins, the yellow-seamed urinal. He shook his head. To indicate the sadness of human existence, the essential irony of things.

'Anyway, the president will want you. Just tell the truth and you'll be all right. You'll be fine.'

'Can I have St Alphonsus back?'

'God bless you, sonny.'

Lady Chatterley changed hands again. 'Thanks, Father.'

'Father Cale will want to see you. He'll want a full statement about all of this.'

'Yes, Father.'

'I read it myself years ago,' he said, pointing at the book. 'A wonderful work. God bless you, sonny.'

'Thanks, Father.'

The hollow sound of an institution. Echoing voices. Footsteps on marble tiles. Opening or closing doors. The smell of Mansion Guardshine polish and Jeyes Fluid in the long colonnaded hall.

The president's door was marked by a brass plaque:

THE PRESIDENT
P. I. Cale DD Ph.D.

The carpet was bog deep inside. I was disconcerted by the dead drop of my footsteps. I found himself standing before a dimly lit desk in a dark room. On my right a window, heavy with brocaded curtains, glowed coldly; on my left a long sideboard with three cut-glass decanters and six glasses. The president toyed with the pages of a ledger, a capstone of paper on the expanse of mahogany and green baize. Then he ticked twice – abrupt attenuated gestures – with a black fountain pen, leaned a sheet of blotting paper onto the ticks and looked up. A civil-service style partner's desk, impressive but cheap, because big furniture is hard to sell. No partner, just Dr Cale, celibate.

'Joseph Lyons, is it?'

'Yes, Father.'

'You were in the toilet, is that right?' Brusque, business-like.

'I was, Father.'

'What were you doing in the toilets at that hour?'

I said that I was going to the toilet.

'That's not what I heard!' The president was angry, numerous tiny red spots pimpling his cheeks. 'You were reading something. Reading in the toilets!'

'It's true, Father. I was going to the toilet. There's the other thing too, but I don't like to mention it, in case I'd be presumptuous.' *St Alphonsus/Lady Chatterley* was long gone, passed into eager hands. Too great a chance that he might ask for it.

'What? What other thing?'

'*St Alphonsus Ligouri*, Father.'

'That's what Father Drake said.' He seemed puzzled. He smoothed his hand over his chest and down as far as his belly where the flap of the soutane bulged outwards, exposing black buttons. His tone was suddenly softer, almost apologetic.

'Now about this other thing . . .'

'I was in the other toilet, Father.'

'Certainly.' A flash of anger. 'We didn't think you were in the same one.'

'No, Father. Sorry, Father.'

'You didn't know about this other thing? You didn't hear sounds?'

'There was another boy. He played the drums on his knees. You know, just slapping his knees with his palms. I think it was "Rock Around the Clock".'

'Rock around the clock?'

'A record, Father. Bill Haley and the Comets.'

'Who was he?'

'An American, Father.'

An angry grunt. 'The boy in the toilet! Who was the boy in the other toilet?'

'I don't know, Father. He was there when I arrived and he left before Father Drake arrived.'

'What happened next?'

'I flushed the toilet and came out and there was Father Drake. He told me to stay put. He made the other boys open the door of their toilet and there they were.'

'You saw them?'

'Not really, Father.'

'Could you name them?'

'I didn't look, Father.'

'You didn't look! That's what you want me to believe?'

'I was embarrassed, Father.'

The president flicked the pages of the ledger on his desk, a rapid flickering of insect shapes in ink and blank space. Two nights before, at study I had made a movie with stickmen dancing and waving on the edge of *The Geography of Europe*. What were Father Cale's men doing? Not just waving. He flicked them again. During the second flick he began to speak. 'You will name those boys and corroborate the testimony of Father Drake. We don't need it, mind, but this is a serious case. It's all very well to stand up for your schoolfellows, but – but there could be possible criminal proceedings . . . proceeding from this matter. Do you understand me? You will tell me now. On pain of expulsion.'

*   *   *

'I didn't rat on you,' I told Troy as the refectory queue clammed up for a moment.

'Thanks,' Troy said. 'Thanks for nothing. I was only going to the jakes,' he said and I said, 'You were and a half.'

Although I could not tell whether he was telling the truth or not, it seemed unlikely.

And after refectory that night – tea of potato cakes and bread and sausages – Troy vanished. It was a mystery at first, but word came down from the seniors that he was in the infirmary. The sixth year was not in the infirmary but confined to his room. A separation.

Keeping the lovers apart, someone joked.

Absence makes the heart grow fond.

I thought of the frail threads of the frayed ends of the pyjamas. People in the infirmary had mumps and measles and were ministered to by a nun with a nose shaped like the head of a hatchet. Some people claimed to have ways of shamming sickness so they could have a night or two in the warmth. One third year put blotting paper inside his sock and fainted in Latin. He arranged with his friends to take the blotting paper out when Winker Walsh was gone for Sister. Another swallowed toothpaste but his temperature did not increase as he had predicted.

The father of the sixth year was an accountant and Troy's father was a county selector. It was said that the president had played the accountant versus the selector and the selector had won. Perhaps the school did not need an accountant, whereas boys who played Senior for the school would have a good chance of being selected for the county and that would bring honour and a sense of purpose to St Keelin's.

I made an effort to recall the details for the others but failed to produce anything better than the story of how Father Drake had handed back the dirty book and said it was a wonderful work, that he had read it himself years ago. (Their laughter was malignant: the dirty bastard, reading dirty books, the dirty mind. People came up to me and winked or nudged me and said: 'The dirty bastard, hah?')

There was the icy cold of the toilets, the hissing, the stains. I tried to recall the expression on their faces. Troy was crying but he looked as if he had already been crying for some time. The older boy was brazen or angry. Troy was tying the strings of his pyjamas and the ends were frayed. I could not detect, in the thin detail of the morning, the substance of whatever it was that had brought this catastrophe on them.

There were three more interviews with the president. By the third he had sent for my parents and I was no longer afraid. It seemed I was to be punished for my silence. The accountant was threatening legal action, so the rumour ran, and they would need someone to stand up in court.

Why could my father not have come? I had imagined him facing the president and gradually subduing him with his quiet strength, as if it would be a physical contest and not a test of wills. But it was my mother who arrived in Tim Quinn's car. Daddy wasn't well, she told me. Some gastric thing. What was all this nonsense about toilets? I tried to explain what had happened but faltered over the detail. She walked through the halls with me, not asking questions. 'Don't say another word, Joe,' she said eventually. 'I know what you're trying to tell me.'

The bishop was coming on Saturday for some meeting

or other and the crows had decided on High Mass to mark the occasion. As we passed the chapel I could hear the choir rehearsing the *Kyrie Eleison*.

'Mary sends her best,' she told me, blessing herself automatically as we passed.

The president was unctuous at first, asking after her health, my father's health, some relations of ours that he knew. He offered her tea and me biscuits. We sat, perched in the odour of book leather, floor polish and stale clothes, sipping and chatting. Eventually he came to the point.

'You know, of course, why I asked you to call on me?' He made it sound like a casual visit. 'Joseph here is being very obstinate.'

'How so, Father Cale?'

'Well, Mrs Lyons, it's a matter of a very important thing, a thing I can't really go into with you because of the private nature of the . . . thing, the matter in hand.' It was unlike the president to repeat himself so much. I sensed his nervousness and something of my mother's effect on other people. 'Joseph is not directly involved, but as a witness. A witness, now. It involves an older boy, three years older. Not even in his class.' He picked up a pair of black-rimmed glasses from the desk and put them on, then he looked over them at me.

'He is not being honest.'

'Are you saying he's lying about something?' I knew from the unsubtle coding, and they both knew, that my mother knew exactly what had happened, and that neither of them was going to mention it.

'No. No, it's more a question of not delivering the whole truth. You could say he is withholding the truth.'

'But he's not in trouble himself . . . ?'

'Not at all, not at all. Not directly. Except that he won't tell us what happened.'

I foresaw the end of the contest. My mother was becoming pale, a sure sign of anger. Her foot was tapping its light tattoo. She would explode and I would be expelled. It did not seem altogether a bad ending – there were other schools.

'Are you trying to tell me that all this is because my Joe won't tell on some other boys? Do you mean to tell me you'd expect him to turn informer?'

'Well, that's not the way we see it . . .'

'Well, I'm going to tell you something instead, Father, about the way I see it. You dragged me all the way up here and my husband sick in bed, and all because you want my son to do the thing that you can't do yourself.'

She took me out to tea, a thing that only ever happened to other boys whose parents could afford to take time off to visit them. There was a small teashop that was part of a bakery. We passed it on our way to the playing fields, which were right on the other side of town – every Saturday morning thirty hungry boys walking through the smell of fresh bread. We never had anything fresh in ref. In the cold of the morning the smell of bread was home on the wind.

'Don't tell me anything,' she said. 'Tim Quinn had the whole story coming up in the car. Butchers know everything. Still he was good enough to drive me up. Just tell me one thing, Joe. You weren't with those boys, were you?'

Why did my answer feel like a betrayal?

'That's my boy.' She brought me to the counter where a

series of plates, stacked one above the other like the layers of a fairy-tale fountain, the fulfilment of every boy's wishes, contained every cake I had ever imagined. 'Take two, Joe. We can afford to splash out today.'

Sunlight slanted through a window, dazed with smoke and dust-motes, and caught her like a glory. I knew now why she came, and that my father would have been the wrong one. She was an embassy from love, charged with the authority of family and fireside.

'Mam, thanks.' I held the cake up like a toast, but she knew what I meant.

'You're doing the right thing, Joe,' she said to me. 'It's not your business to give them away. Let the priests do their own dirty work. Stick to your guns, that's my boy. Anyway,' she confided in me, 'I wouldn't give it to anyone to say that one of mine would turn informer.'

But after tea and cakes she was flustered. She searched for her purse and, when she found it, could not count the change. I took it from her and placed the bright shillings and brown pennies on the plate, counted them twice.

Sunshine had enriched the shabby town. We stopped at a curiosity shop and she bargained for ten minutes for a silver pencil that slid back into itself. It had a tiny piece of amber in a head that twisted open to reveal a chamber where the spare leads were kept. 'It was for you,' she said. 'Pity he didn't come down a bit more. What he was asking was highway robbery. I wouldn't give it to him to say.'

I spoke to Troy only once more, two years later. An evening in early winter I caught up with him, walking among the roses and blackened dandruffy cherry trees that bordered the path to the ball alley. A priest in dungarees was burning rose cuttings, the faint smell of petrol wafting along with the smoke. He leaned on his rake and watched us, winking and nodding his head because it was his habit. That was why he was called Winker. Father Walshe. The roses were his joy. He bought manure from a man who kept horses. In springtime his shoes smelled of shit.

'I never told on you,' I said. 'I never said a word.'

I was remembering my final interview with the president. 'You have disappointed me, Lyons,' he said. 'I thought you were the kind of boy who would stand up for his Faith. Anyhow, I'm telling you now that you're under starter's orders; starter's orders, do you hear? You give me one ounce of trouble and you're out the door.' It was bluster, the usual thing, far less frightening than his ominous goodwill.

'Thanks,' Troy said. 'You stuck your neck out.'

'It's your own business as far as I'm concerned.'

He bridled. 'What is?'

'Whatever you were doing. That time.'

He was watching a wren bobbing from branch to branch, assiduously leading us away from its nest. He pointed him out to me. 'He's a cute bastard, that wren.'

Then he said: 'Did you ever, you know, try it?'

'Not me,' I said quickly. 'It's none of my business but I'm not up for that myself. Sorry.'

The set of his shoulders indicated pain. He had gambled something and had lost it. Privacy perhaps. His question had been speculative, open, capable of repudiation. My apology had told him everything.

'Me neither,' he said. 'I just do it for the laugh.'

But it wasn't funny.

'I'm going to be leaving next year,' Troy said. His eyes

watered. 'His name was Gahan. I suppose you didn't know him. The other fellow. They were suspicious of Gahan before. That bastard Drake might have followed him. He might have been watching him. How else did he know to come down at the right time? Anyhow, they didn't need your word for it. Only if you had ratted they'd have got me as well. Sometimes I think I'd have been better off if they'd thrown me out too.'

'You'd get a name. You'd never get in anywhere.'

'Bollocks!'

'What happened to Gahan?'

He shook his head twice. Even I could see misery in it. 'I got one Christmas card. He didn't sign it, just XXX. My father tore it up and burned the bits.'

'Look, you'll be out of it in six months. You'll be free.'

'It's nearly teatime,' the priest called over the rose bushes and the leaves, a suggestion of panic in his voice. Two boys being alone in the darkness at the very end of the rose garden was a danger too great to be countenanced. 'Get along now! Get out of it! Go on up for ref!'

Troy glared in his direction and for a moment it looked as if he would strike out, charge through the thorns and strike him full in the face. But then he subsided and misery took possession of him again. 'Who cares now anyway?' he said.

'I hate this dump.'

'Me too.'

'I have the feeling everything is changing outside and I don't even know about it. It's like a prison.'

'Like when you come out nobody knows you?'

'I'm wasting years.'

'A waste is right.'

113

Winker Walshe crunched along behind us through the frosting grass, a shepherd minding his flock. Darkness was gaining ground among the trees. The flames were gone, leaving behind a faint glow in the rubbish. A pair of blackbirds scuttled together, disturbing papery leaves.

In Gehenna children were sacrificed by fire and later the refuse was burned. But where is the place that children were sacrificed by cold? In the high rooms of St Keelin's the flesh was shriven by accident. There was no purpose in the pain. The windows looked out on a heedless town that stretched along the bank of a black river, which ran recklessly to the remote Atlantic. Cold salmon squirmed in the pools. Trout ghosted in shadows. The cold of the mountains came down in a mass that swept everything clean and debouched into the sea. Alongside this great cleanser the school stood. Children came one September at twelve or so and left at seventeen or eighteen in the month of June. In between they became men according to a certain definition. They clustered in the polished hall on the first day, arrivals at the terminus of childhood and heard the president's lecture about the usefulness of cold showers and the school's motto, which was very close to that other German one about work and freedom.

One hundred and thirty boys. The noise at table was unbearable. The farting. The spitting. Pass the fucking bread. My job as table prefect to slice one loaf into sixteen pieces, each exactly even and no one wanting the heels. Come on, Lyons, someone says. We're all waiting. Here. The breadknife passes along, handle foremost. I stand and manhandle the loaf. *Et tu Brute*, I say and one or two chuckle. Then the blade crunches down, sawing backwards and forwards, grinding out dust and flakes. Someone makes a kissing noise and everyone laughs. Winker Walshe comes in, his soutane swishing. Someone hisses, 'Crow. *Nix.*' And everyone goes quiet. He glares at our table. Then they are eating. I hear the sound of the crust disintegrating in their mouths.

10

My father had an arrangement with Tim Quinn, the butcher in the village whose son was a year older than me: that he drove the two of us to school at the start of term, and the butcher collected us and brought us home at term's end. He used to joke that I was the sacrificial lamb, delivered by the farmer to come home in the butcher's van.

For days before the holiday began the school would be winding down the heating, saving a few pounds where possible, the classrooms becoming cellars, the dormitories ice caverns. For the winter holidays frost formed on the insides of the windows. Boys would hang around, hands in pockets, jackets buttoned up to the neck, waiting for the crunch of wheels on the gravel, eyes turning to the window to register the arrival of a classmate's parents. When Tim Quinn's car came through the gates there was always a slight turn of disappointment in me.

On the road home he and his son would discuss hurling, working outwards from the parish team to the county and the province, the big names, the prospects, the chances of beating this or that traditional enemy. In the back seat I would huddle in the fug of the heater, my coat around my ears, and dream of home. Mary and my mother would greet me at the door, my father still working somewhere, the noise of a tractor in a distant field, cattle moving sleepily along a headland, or it would be mart-day and he would not be expected home until late.

Tea then, real meat in a steak-and-kidney pie, apple crumble – a hero's portion after the burnt offerings of school. 'I made your favourite,' my mother would say.

'Tell us all about it,' Mary always asked. 'What is it like living with all the boys?'

Afterwards I would not be allowed to help with the washing-up – 'Time enough for that when you're settled back,' as though surviving the journey home was heroic in itself.

I watched them with envy – mother and daughter – the actual air charged with their intimacy. Unspoken messages lingered at the edge of perception – *Did you say something? I thought you said . . . I know what you're going to say.* Uncompleted sentences, gentle forgettings.

I was becoming a summer visitor, supplemented by occasional weekends and festival days, abducted by school to another world where affection was twisted, transformed to cruelty, banter or deception. Even then I knew the dangers, and that I would have to use all my cunning to survive.

They used to hold hands walking. I see them stepping between weeds and puddles on some springtime lane, the bramble reaching blindly towards them. I see them coming from Sunday evening devotions, incense travelling with them. They took each other's part always.

'Eat your vegetables, Mary,' my father would say.

'Leave her alone, Daddy, she's minding her figure. Aren't you, Mary?' And Mary would nod and that secret signalling would flash between them – the code for love, I thought.

* * *

Christmas of that year, I saw my parents dancing, alone in the kitchen. Where was Mary? At evening devotions or a sodality meeting. It was one of those unseasonably warm nights that give the lie to all the Christmas cards. There would be no snow, as there never was. Instead a frontal system brooded over the country, stalled by some hopelessly powerful cold force that dominated Europe. Perhaps there was rain coming – I can't remember – but my mother had lit the Aga that morning and the kitchen was an oven. She threw the windows open, opened the door into the hall. I was in the yard kicking a football against the darkness when I heard some tune on the radio. It swirled out into the fluid air and I heard my father say, 'Come on, Eily. Give us a dance.' I saw him stretch his right hand towards her, palm up. She put away what she was doing, dropped her fingers into his and stepped into him and, without any sign of a transformation, my parents became a couple.

And they could dance.

My mother was feather-light. Although they swirled around the kitchen table, the scattered chairs, none of her was in motion, or perhaps all of her was in motion but each part was constant, unchanging, a simple flowing grace.

My father's dancing was elegant but purposeful. He moved only below the knee, his feet changing places like shadows.

When the music stopped they stepped apart, laughing, perhaps a little embarrassed. I heard my mother say, 'You're a holy show in that shirt. I never danced with anyone in a dirty working shirt before!' My father grinned and pulled the shirt off over his head. Underneath he wore a long-sleeved vest. Her laughter clattered out to me and splashed into the liquid evening. 'I thought you were bad in the shirt,' she told him. 'You should see that vest!'

First the child is a participant, part of an organism that is parent and child. Then it becomes the outsider looking in. A time comes when it sees its parents, first as individuals, then as a couple. Why would two such people marry? For years the question never occurs. Then, if he is lucky or attentive, staring through an open window, watching them turn and turn, the harmony and the ease, the child understands. The world begins with his birth. From that time, and perhaps before, they have always been a pair.

Sometime around her third year at secondary school Mary became fascinated with Egypt and Egyptology. Even then I could see that it was an extension of my mother's collecting habit, except now the collection was vicarious and on a vast scale – I think it was the idea that someone could take possession of an entire past that drew her in – and I became aware that the wellsprings of her collecting habit were different to my mother's. She bought a wall-map of Ancient Egypt and put it over her bed. Her windowsill was stacked with books about Champollion, the Rosetta Stone, Tutankamun, the Nile valley. Once, when I was home on one of my mid-term holidays, she took me up to her room and showed me its treasures; all wide-eyed with the discovery, she told me that there are passages in the Great Pyramid of Cheops aligned with the belt of Orion, two extraordinary corridors that lead out of the King's and Queen's chambers towards the stars. One, however, comes to a dead end, walled from the outside world. Why was it there? she asked. And how did they make the calculations?

What instruments could they have used? And how did they make the alignment? She had a long cardboard frieze above her head on which the stick-men and women of Ancient Egypt played out their symbolic lives. I imagined a stone mountain in the whistling desert night, a hollow place that was its longing for the stars, an empty finger stretched from the King's Chamber towards the silence of space. But the Queen's Chamber was blind. A sterile womb.

Once I saw her standing in front of the full-length dress-maker's mirror in my mother's room – a bargain from an auction of the contents of one of those ancient ladies' clothes shops that sold silk blouses and woolly under-clothes in equal quantities.

'What are *you* admiring yourself for?'

'Joe, do you think I'm fat?'

'No. Why?'

'Look,' she said. She pinched a roll of skin on her forearm. 'That's disgusting.'

I remember that the mirror had a black malacca rim that gleamed in the evening light. The glass was very slightly smoked. A flattering glass, my mother called it. Mary wore the shapeless clothes of the day, a big jumper in earth colours, a print dress. Still she looked angular, more like a gadget than a living thing, a bundle of rods and joints surmounted by a pale gaunt frightened face. 'Mary,' I said, 'you'll make yourself sick.' She was the possibility of death for me then, not the remote and poetic Death of the texts I was studying – *King Lear*, *Wuthering Heights* – a piece of fine language, a dramatic full stop; she was a bag of bones and I feared for her.

'I don't know what you're talking about.'

'I see what you're doing.'

'What am I doing?'

But I had no name for it.

She had taken to wearing loose clothes, baggy jumpers, wide flares and bell-bottoms. She bought a kaftan on a shopping expedition to town, a strange hybrid of Indian patterns and hippie styling. 'Look at you,' my mother would say then. 'You're the picture of health. You have your good looks from my side of the family, wherever you got your brains. You're as slim as a model.'

There is no chart or pilotage here. The complexity is unimaginable. No one can follow another through the looping and branching of their mind. When we pass close enough to touch, slowing between the shoals, in the narrows, we must greet each other and share the news. Such meetings are necessarily brief.

And rare. The pilot sees the branching channel and swings to left or right. The choice is random, the probability of success, or of finding another vessel in the road, is low.

I had already made my turn.

'They're going to bring in the contraception,' Mary said at dinner time one mid-term. I can't remember which government was in power. Jack Lynch had remarked that we couldn't put contraception on the long finger, a pun he may not have noticed at the time, and all the talk was of how to avoid touching it at all. French letters would be available from slot machines, people were warning; children going to the toilet in pubs would be exposed to filth. There was talk of making the contraceptive pill available on prescription 'for bona fide family planning purposes' – as though no one had noticed that it was all about *not* planning to have a family. People were beginning to think of sex as something you could have a little or a lot of without facing catastrophe. The Church was infuriated by the very terms of the discussion.

Mary was angry. She had her catalogue of certainties, a little set of universal truths kept oiled and ready for action. This was a skill she had learned in auction rooms and shops: that the strength of a single term depended on its relationship to the others in the collection. No truth stood alone but on a foundation of other truths. In argument her tactic was to wear the opposition down by presenting to every objection always the next absolute in the line. Her thoughts were strange forms supported by contiguous shapes so that the whole improbable edifice looked massive rather than solid; yet no wrecker could find a gap into which to put even a tiny piece of dynamite; every window and door was plugged with doctrine.

It was a sin, she said, not only to buy and use contraceptives, but to pass laws that would allow others to buy and use them. It was tempting people, leading them astray. A person who led another into sin was himself committing a sin.

Mary's school friends were dating and going to discos. They were smoking in the school toilets and smuggling vodka into alcohol-free school dances while Mary was going to mass and evening devotions. They talked about boys and hit records and the Top Ten. She retold comical stories that priests related in sermons, horror stories about immoral people, miracle stories from the great Church miracle sites; she was a loner, pointed out and giggled at, holy Mary. At the time, because we were siblings, it seemed the proper reaction was contempt. Pity might have been better. Love would have been best of all.

And my mother made that cutting gesture with the flat of her hand that we had become used to. It meant: change the subject, don't mention contraceptives, don't provoke Daddy. We had developed the habit of eating in silence. We would listen to the news on the radio and if a safe subject came up (the troubles in the North were out, so were contraception, the EEC and Margaret Thatcher) we might chat for a minute or two, my mother watching him surreptitiously for any sign of anger. We mustn't upset Daddy, she would say. Sometime between childhood and leaving school we had come to accept that he was not well, although there had never been a diagnosis, a clear statement of fact. My mother worried about the colour of his face, the amount of fat he liked on his meat, the butter on his bread. Sometimes she said, 'Calm down. You'll burst a blood vessel.'

'Once you let in the pill you'll have abortion next. Then it'll be euthanasia. You can't draw a line. If you have one you have it all. Anybody can see what's going on.' That last point was directed at me.

'Look,' I said, 'you're trying to force your religion on people. This is the 1970s not the 1790s. There's other people in this country besides Catholics!'

'Atheists!' she said scornfully. 'How many atheists are there in Ireland?'

'Protestants,' I said.

'Protestants don't want abortion either.'

'You're so stupid! You believe everything they tell you!'

Mary was white with fury. 'I am not stupid. I'm top of the class and I'm going to college!'

'You should join the nuns. You're half a nun already.'

'You want to murder unborn babies.'

'They're foetuses. By definition you can't have an unborn baby.'

My father stopped cutting and placed his knife and fork side by side on his plate, fork down.

'I'm eating my dinner,' he said.

'But Dad, he's against the Church. I hear him talking to his friends.' Her voice was plaintive.

'He's entitled to his beliefs,' my father said.

'You're an atheist,' she shouted at me. 'You're all for free love! This is a Catholic country, why don't you leave!'

'This is a republic. It's not a theocracy yet!' That was one I had heard on the radio.

'It's only a republic where sex is concerned!' she hissed. I gaped at her. What did she mean?

'For God's sake,' my father said. We all stopped and looked at him. His face was deep red, blood pressure climbing. The knuckles of the fingers on his knife were white.

'What, Daddy?' my mother said.

'There was an old saying about all that kind of thing when I was small,' he said. We held our breath until he looked up and smiled. 'That and pig-rooting will never be stopped.'

Our laughter had the power of healing broken paths. But we laughed a little too long in the end, conscious of the fleeting moment, trying to prolong the ordinary, while the nation danced its crazy dance outside our door, each leg rattling like a piston, the body politic wearing itself out; bystanders remarked how a nation could dance itself to death and still smile.

I I

Mary's boyfriend. She had almost finished college before it happened, and I was away at work, but even the idea of it sounded strange. He wore corduroy trousers and a knitted jumper. He shook hands with each of us in turn. 'Come in, come in,' my mother said, excited and puzzled. 'Mary only rang us on Wednesday. We never knew.' The classic case: daughter brings her intended home for tea – implying some kind of intention; conclusion – this is the man she will marry. Mary was about to take her degree. Matthew had just qualified and was working with Siemens. I toyed with the idea of punning on the name.

'This is my atheist brother,' Mary said.

He shook my hand with great delicacy, letting it go quickly. No lingering here. No contamination. Shake hands with the devil. 'Pleased to meet you,' he said.

'Ditto,' I said. 'Never mind the atheist bit. I'm only a lapsed agnostic really.'

'The dinner'll be spoiled,' my mother said. 'A nice bit of roast lamb.'

Matthew rubbed his hands together and made comical 'yum-yum' noises. My father narrowed his eyes and stared at a distant ditch, as if he had just spotted a gap in the fencing of which a lively bullock might take advantage.

We tramped into the hall and on into the kitchen. The house was alive with the sound of crackling fat, heavy with the rich smell of lamb, potatoes roasting in the juices, cauliflower. My mother had cooked a cake the night before. Summoned to meet 'the new boyfriend' I had driven miles on the strength of the words, 'I have a fruit cake in the oven.' Glorious memory pulling me home. But, unaccountably, she had forgotten. My father rescued it before he went to bed, but the outside was a carapace of charcoal. Only fragments of the tantalising smell remained.

'There's more to this than meets the eye,' my mother had told me earlier. 'Who brings a boyfriend home just like that? She's bringing him to meet the in-laws, that's what it is. Mark my words, there's a wedding in this.' Her hands tugged irritably at the buttons of her cardigan. One broke free and played a small tune in air, a nervous habit of hers.

'Good for her,' I said. 'I hope they're happy.' I was thinking of a room in the Ivernia Hotel, a girl I would be seeing there soon. I had my own secret.

My relationship with Joan had become something – what I wasn't sure. I knew I wanted her body but I was often impatient with what she said and thought. She had never left the town, moving from school to secretarial job as custom and family needs ordained in the time-honoured way – the boys to college, the girls to work first and then marriage. Was I that end? After each writing workshop we lingered in the bar until it was empty and then, with a nod and wink to the desk clerk, booked whatever room was available in the almost always empty Ivernia Hotel. In the beginning she seemed transparent enough; now I was beginning to think I had no key to her life, no way of really understanding her. I could not say I was happy. She certainly was not.

'But so sudden, Joe? She's only what? Nineteen or twenty? Is she twenty-one? I think Mary'll only be twenty-one this year. And she'll have to finish college.'

'Plenty of time for that.'

'I don't know. You better come down anyway. Lend us a bit of moral support.' I let the irony pass.

When Matthew closed his eyes and joined his hands in front of the enormous plate of roast lamb, I knew she was right.

'Do you mind if I ask Matthew to say grace?' Mary said.

'We thank thee, Lord, for these thy gifts which of thy bounty we are about to receive, through Christ Our Lord, amen.'

He kept his eyes closed for a few seconds as if adding some personal aspiration that we could not be privy to and I saw my father frown across the table at my mother. When he opened them again my father said, 'God helps those who help themselves,' and began to cut the meat on his plate.

'You never said a truer word, Mr Lyons,' Matthew said. 'He does indeed.'

My father looked shocked. 'It's only a saying, Matthew. I say it every time I sit down to a dinner.'

'Still. It's true.'

'Matthew is an electrical engineer,' Mary said.

'Where did you meet my daughter?'

Matthew smiled at her. 'A very good question,' he said. 'I was passing out leaflets outside St Dominic's. She took one. She didn't know it then but I recognised her. We had a friend in common. A guy from Engineering. But when she took the leaflet I somehow knew that we would meet again.'

It had happened at the end of Mary's second year at college. I was twenty-four and bogged down in my own problems, already hating my work, writing by night and firing people by day, clinging to furtive Thursday nights with Joan. Mary's college days meant nothing. It had never even occurred to me that she would have known boys, much less been pursued by one. What did she know of me? I had dated one of her classmates for a time. She would have heard of that. Otherwise our visits home rarely coincided, apart from Christmas. Neither of us would claim to miss each other.

'So you met her again?'

Mary smiled at him. It was one of those half-sad, half-secretive smiles. I felt sick.

'He made a point of meeting me,' she said. 'When we talked, we had so much in common.'

They were here to announce their engagement, Matthew said later. He was standing with his back to the range, a curiously nineteenth-century pose. Apparently, he wanted nothing better than to make Mary happy.

They shook hands and my father wished them both long life and happiness. They were delighted, my mother said a little breathlessly, as though she had been running to keep up all afternoon. It was very sudden but she was delighted. She was sure Matthew would make a very good husband for her daughter. Even though she had only known him a few hours she already felt that he was a good man.

But when the others were congratulating each other I noticed that her eyes were full of nervous questioning. 'Don't worry, Mam,' I whispered once. 'She's a grown woman. She can take care of herself.'

When my father produced a bottle of whiskey Matthew

and Mary toasted each other stiffly. Clearly unused to spirits, they coughed and spluttered as the whiskey burned down. My father chuckled and winked at me and my mother fussed, and Matthew and Mary looked pleased and embarrassed, standing together at their end of the room with their backs to the Aga. Two lone swimmers, I thought, both half dead from the cold and the isolation, struggling onto the same beach. They rescued each other. They were alone on a desert island unmarked on any globe, a Pitcairn of the heart; what else could they do but fall in love?

There was no delay. The date was set, the trousseau bought and paid for, the hotel booked. They had cards printed edged in silver. Mr and Mrs M. Lyons are pleased to announce the wedding of their only daughter Mary, etc. RSVP.

In the cheap open clothes-press of the Ivernia Hotel it was just visible like a tongue between lips in the side pocket of my jacket. I should have left it at home.

The other hotel guests, if real guests there were, had a secretive way about them that never ceased to amaze me. Sometimes there were footsteps falling dead on the carpeted corridor outside, rarely voices. Joan and I often found ourselves tiptoeing to the room. There were nights when we made love in whispers, pulling the bed away from the wall because the rapping of the frame seemed to echo back. Once we heard a shower running in a room above, but it ran and ran, and was still running when we turned away from each other to sleep.

'What's the card?'

The sheets of a new story were rolled in the other pocket but her eye had caught the silver edging.

'My sister Mary,' I said.

She was sitting on the edge of the bed with her back towards me and I was fiddling with the hook of her bra. Her skin was pale, almost white, and there was a dark red mole just above the strap. She smelled of 4711 Eau de Cologne and cigarette smoke.

'An invite?'

'She's getting married.' The clasp separated and her breasts relaxed. I slid the straps off her shoulders. My right hand brushed her nipple.

'I love weddings.'

I rested my chin on her shoulder and cupped both breasts, my thumbs stroking the aureoles, feeling the nipples tighten and stand alert.

'I told you about Mary,' I said.

She nodded. She let me play with her skin for a moment.

'I got an invite too.' She stood up and turned to face me. 'My sister out in Brisbane.'

I stared at her. 'Are you going, Joan?'

'What's here?' She gestured at the room, the faded carpet, the chipped Formica bedside table, the cheap lamp with the burn hole in the shade, the imitation watercolour of the Lakes of Killarney. 'This isn't much.'

I felt suddenly exposed.

'There's never much going to happen to me in this dump.'

'I could change your mind about that in five minutes.'

Her look was withering. 'I'm being let go.'

I had suspected as much. I heard things through the network, through the company. I had known they were reducing staff. I had not known where the axe would fall. Why hadn't I warned her?

'I hate the place anyway!'

'You always hated it. There's plenty of work out there. I'll make enquiries.'

'No thanks, Joe.'

'A better job with better pay.'

'I said no thanks. I'm moving. I can't stick this shitty town.'

'What about me?' I was nervous now.

She glanced at my jacket and then looked away. She did not reply.

'I love you,' I said, in desperation. Even at that moment I knew it was because she was standing there with her scooped breasts and the mound of her pubic hair pressing against her plain white panties, desirable and immediate. Even then I knew it was a shabby lie, but there would be time for guilt later.

'What do your parents think of the wedding?'

'They're a bit confused. He's a very strange kid, Matthew. A bit weird. Outside their experience.'

'Mary is lucky so,' she said.

'Why's that?'

'She found her match.' She went to the open press and pulled the sheaf of typescript from my pocket. The captive metal hangers clanged like damaged bells. 'What's this? A new story?'

'An old one reworked. Maybe we might look at it later. It's about us. I didn't want to read it to the group.'

'I haven't written a word in months.'

'I told you before. You're an artist. You should be drawing not writing.'

'Do you think I'm beautiful?'

'You know you are.'

'The fine days are coming now.'

'Yes,' I said, wondering what she was getting at.

'Summer won't be long.'

'A month or two.'

'It'll be autumn in Brisbane. The upside-down world.'

I got up and walked to the press. I swirled the jacket against the noisy bells and pulled the invitation out. 'Here,' I said, passing it to her on my way back to the bed. She opened the card and looked inside.

'Nice,' she said. 'Expensive.'

'I want you to come.'

'To your sister's wedding?'

'To my sister's wedding.'

'Do they know about me?

I shook my head.

'Well, I can't. I'm going to Australia.'

'What about us, Joan? This?'

She looked around the room and then at me.

'You can get this anywhere.'

12

The wedding was a small affair, turkey and ham, a rich cake baked by a neighbour who specialised in weddings and christenings. Matthew's parents were worried that Mary was so thin. They each mentioned it at different times, leaving room for me to elaborate. I gave them nothing; she was still my sister. I could see them estimating her chances of surviving pregnancy.

Fifty miles away Joan was packing. A few days to go before she flew out, first to London to an uncle, then onwards, crossing lines of latitude that separated worlds, date lines that marked the changes in civilisations, eras. She was excited. We had met again, most recently a week before, in a café first, then the bar of the Ivernia, then the room. She was suddenly careless – or free. 'I needed this,' she said afterwards. 'I'm bottled up. I can't wait to escape.' I was learning hard lessons as she abandoned me. I told her I was leaving too. I would give the job three months, look around for a flat in the city, and throw caution to the winds. I would finish the book. There had to be another way to live. She nodded agreement but her eyes said otherwise; already she had me down for a talker. A failure. This time I was the one who went home before breakfast and she stayed on to eat bacon and eggs among the travelling salesmen.

Matthew's brother got quietly drunk, sneaking out to

the hotel's second bar and knocking back double vodkas before returning to dance with anyone who would accept him. He told me that Mary was a lovely girl and his brother was very lucky. He told me that his brother was very religious but he was normal himself. He told me that his father worked for the county council, a surveyor, and that he himself was a linesman with the ESB. Then he went out into the garden and vomited into the hydrangeas.

Mary was crying before they left. 'Goodbye, Joe,' she said. 'Take care.'

'I'm not going anywhere, Mary. Remember? You're the one going on the honeymoon.' But the figure I imagined flying away, full of happiness, the bride of new things, nothing borrowed, nothing blue, was not Mary, and she was not coming back. Loneliness – or envy – was corroding me.

She had changed into her going-away clothes, a sober cardigan and slacks. We were walking in the hotel garden and I was trying to steer her away from the shrubbery.

'We often fight, Joe,' she said. 'But I'm fond of you. I don't mean it.'

'I *am* consoled,' I said, making a florid bow, an Elizabethan supplication. I was a little drunk. When I bent forward I felt my centre of gravity change. I had to straighten quickly to save myself. 'Pray tell, what don't you mean?'

'I don't think you're going to hell.'

That startled me. I knew where my centre of gravity was then.

'I just think you took a wrong turning, that's all. That's what I told Matthew.'

'You told Matthew? What?'

'He said you'd rejected God. I said you were still search-ing for him but you were looking in the wrong place.'

'So he thinks I'm going to hell?'

'He doesn't know you.'

'Fuck the bastard!'

'Don't say that, Joe. He's a good man. I want you to like him.' I could sense the urgency in her. I knew she was driven to this, that it was of great importance to her. But I could not give her the blessing she needed, the very last man who could bring any kind of benediction.

'Tell him from me, he can go fuck himself.'

She had caught my arm earlier, steadying me a little. Now she let it go and stood back. 'Don't,' she said.

'What right has he to pass judgement on me? What does he know about me? A stupid ignorant bastard like that? You tell him from me, Mary, if I ever see his stupid face again I'll smash it for him. Tell him that.'

A door opened behind us and the babble of the wedding party drifted out. I saw that it was Matthew's brother again, veering towards the same patch of hydrangeas. 'And tell him his fucking brother is an alcoholic.'

Matthew had a good job and a company car and Mary started work for a counselling agency as soon as her finals were over. They were lucky, given the economic climate of the time. They rented a suburban semi-d and went in for shopping together and taking long walks. From my remote eminence they appeared to be ten years older and wiser, one of those slightly embittered couples who would eventually get involved in petty politics. I knew what their politics would be. The pro-life movements were beginning to organise. Soon there would be a political party, although like all fundamentalist groups they would be fragmented. Real political parties, being amoral, have the ability to compromise on apparently essential doctrines, but the pro-lifers lived by absolutes, unbending in their hatred, ungenerous in their charity.

My parents would never understand exactly what Mary stood for, so when the news of the adoption came they took it with pursed lips and the slightest shaking of the head. Adoption would not have been for them, they said, but Mary had her own life to lead. That they should not interfere was an absolute. They had seen friends and neighbours meddling in their children's marriages and had seen the trouble that bubbled over into public fighting, separations, affairs. They blamed the parents for getting involved. For their part they asked no questions, accepted the little mite for what she was – a mistake in someone else's life not quite corrected in Mary's.

It would never have occurred to them that anyone would bring a child into their lives for purely political reasons.

They drove to town and bought a new pink Babygro, a white lace hat with a floppy brim, two blankets and an imitation patchwork quilt. What did they say to each other? I could imagine the tight little silences. We're good at coping, they would be thinking. Our generation, we're used to disaster, we have learned to take life as it comes. Least said soonest mended. We just have to grin and bear it. And they would be telling themselves that a child is a child, that it must be loved, and after all there were worse things in life. It was not the adoption, they would say, but the way it was done – the haste, and so soon after the wedding; who would have believed that an adoption could happen so quickly? And then, adoption was really a kind of last hope, they would be saying, when there was no chance of a real baby. Surely Mary and Matthew couldn't know that yet? Had they been to a doctor? Tests? It was all very sudden. They would hope that Mary was not becoming unstable, that she was not falling apart.

The pink Babygro and the blankets were conventional gifts, but the floppy hat was a tilt at joy, a wish for sunny days. They could picture the little mite balancing on its broad bottom in a field of daisies, the sun shaping hard darkness around the rim, the eyes protected.

Mary took these as tenders of approval, tokens of their willingness to love the interloper. Next time I saw baby Claire she was wearing the funny hat. There was something strangely old-mannish about her, like an Englishman who had just come in from the garden, the brim falling down at one side, slightly raffish. Her eyes were tired and dry. I was reminded of a fish that had been a little too long in the air, the way the watery glaze of the pupil evaporated and the eye looked like a cheap imitation. My parents noticed it too. I saw the way they handled the little bundle, hefting it, holding it awkwardly, studying its face. Once they asked Mary a question about the mother, probing a little too deep: who she was, or where she lived, I forget exactly what. But Mary reacted by picking the baby up and walking out. I could see in those few weeks before they left for America that the cooing and coddling was as much a cover as anything else.

And Mary and Matthew went in for it in a big way. They bought all the right clothes, pink for the most part. They talked about being awake at night with the rueful pleasure that young parents always have ('Look what she's doing to me, the little beauty'). Mary complained her greatest sorrow was that she couldn't breastfeed. 'Don't you think the bond is so much stronger?' she asked my mother, who shrugged and tried to pretend that the subject had not been raised. 'I can imagine the little mite snuggled up to my breasts,' she said. 'Her little mouth slipping off the nipple as she fell asleep.' She sighed. My mother coughed. She found it difficult to reconcile the images of the Child of the Legion of Mary and the earthy mother. *She* certainly never mentioned her breasts, why should her daughter?

'Matthew takes his turn at the four o'clock feed,' Mary said. 'I just roll over and listen to the two of them. He talks to her all the time. What we do now is, we keep two bottles wrapped in blankets. It doesn't take long to heat them up.'

It was as though she had been granted a kind of absolution, as though some burden had been lifted from her shoulders. She had a penitent's joy in the smallest safe thing, the slightest pleasure that could be indulged in with impunity. Sex was a sordid singularity by comparison with this intense and seamless love. Passion for a child was not idolatry.

But what was her sin? What error was excused by Claire?

'We can't talk about the parents,' my mother said. 'She's very touchy about that.'

'I don't know,' my father said. 'It's a strange turn-up.'

'She liked the funny hat.'

'I don't think Seattle is like Florida. I think it's nearly as wet up there as it here.'

'Highest rainfall in the United States,' I said.

'There now,' my father said. 'Joe agrees with me. What use'll they get out of that hat?'

'It's the thought that counts.' I winked at my father who ignored the signal.

'The mother could have been anyone.'

My father sighed. 'This is the age of equality, Eily. Couldn't you say the father could have been anyone just as easy?'

'Adoptions take months, don't they? Or even years.'

'She's as bright as a button, that child,' my father said, proving that the distance from wish to belief is never greater than the span of a single infant step.

'I wish she wasn't going away. I know they're all doing it now, but Matthew has a good job. Why would you be emigrating if you had a job?' She was agitated. I noticed her left leg jigging up and down, a tiny, crazy dance.

'Look on the bright side, Mam. You'll be able to collect postcards from the States now.'

Her look withered me. I saw the darkness in it, the trivial blinking of coins and the dull gleam of polished mahogany, the brusque notes that spoke of rainy holidays a century ago. I saw the cluttered past, the Pandora's box of senseless things closing out the daylight. She let me see, that one time, the baleful bride hiding among second-hand treasures, other people's intimacies.

'Look,' my father said, 'turn on the news there. Let's see what's going on in the world.'

'You don't approve, I know,' Mary said to me. I could hear her own contempt crackling down the line. She had been packing, she told me earlier, trying to fit everything in – who would expect a baby to need so many clothes? 'But you wouldn't understand an unselfish act if you saw one.'

'It's none of my business. Approval doesn't come into it.'

'Why don't you ever say what you really think?'

'I'm glad for you,' I said. 'You have a baby. That's a joyful occasion. We shouldn't be talking about how I feel.'

I heard a sound that might have been a sniff or a short laugh.

'At least I'm married.' A reference to my irregular lifestyle. I thought of Joan's parting shot – *you can get this anywhere*. 'You should see her this minute, Joe. She's a dote.' Outside my window rain was falling through space, nothing tangible between the window and infinity. It had rained for three days and nights and cars swished through puddles fifty feet below my flat; lorries brought their own mist-filled atmosphere with them.

'You know what they say, Mary, a pet is for life not for Christmas.'

'How dare you!' I thought she would hang up, but the covenant of childhood and kinship required us to run through the ritual; the *Dominus vobiscum* was still to come.

'Mary, I'm just thinking. It *is* Christmas. It's an emotional time of the year. You're what? A year and a half married? Maybe you should have given it time. You know what I mean.'

Her voice was cold. 'Whether Matthew and I have children of our own or not won't change my love for Claire.'

'It's none of my business, you're right, Mary. None of my business at all. But, you know, these things should be given time.' I thought Matthew's parents were right: her skinny frame hardly had the physical capacity to bear a child.

What kind of a being would issue from that austere and inflexible womb? 'Don't be offended now, but Matthew and yourself – you shouldn't give up hope after only a year.' A bundle of bones like her, a bundle of fanatical beliefs, Catholic guilt and anger and neurosis all wrapped up in a half-transparent fabric of skin; someone like Mary would find it very hard to let herself go in bed.

'I'm not offended,' she said.

'Isn't there a waiting period anyway? For adoptions? An assessment procedure? How could it all happen in this short time?'

'We did all that. It's all finalised. We have the papers.' Snap. The sound of a door closing. The sound of a polite enquiry being cut off.

'Well, of course,' I said. 'But I thought adoption took a long time. We all did. Mam and Dad.'

'I thought you'd be glad for me,' Mary said.

'I am glad for you. I told you that. A new baby is a joy. I hope you and Matthew are very happy in America.'

'It's three of us now. Matthew and me and Claire.'

'Wonderful.' But I was thinking that there was not a bleaker prospect for a little girl to face.

'We're going to give her a happy home. Matthew organised a nice apartment in Seattle. She'll have a good life. I'm not saying we're perfect, but we are capable of a lot of love. That's something she wouldn't have had before.' I thought, because then I didn't know the circumstances, that this was several kinds of presumption, not least that the birth mother wasn't capable of love. 'We saved this child,' my sister Mary was saying. 'You have no idea how we saved her. We actually saved her life, so that makes her very special to us. And we'll be very special to her too.' I detected a note of hysteria.

'Take it easy, Mary,' I said.

'You don't understand, Joe,' she said. 'You don't know this kind of love. It's like being touched by God.'

Well, I remember thinking, and *touched* is the word.

The first letter from America came in six weeks. It was full of prattle about the new apartment, a nice neighbour, the possibility of getting into a counselling practice, Matthew's job, which apparently required him to go to work in jeans, and the climate, which seemed even wetter than home. But it ended on a different note.

'I know we have always had our differences but I want you to know that I haven't given up hope. God will find a way into your heart,' she wrote. 'Atheism is a barren way of thinking. Nothing worthwhile will result from it. I pray for you always. I go to a prayer-group once a week and I have told them all about you. We are very active on God's work.' She enclosed a press cutting describing the picketing of an abortion clinic in which police were called. A doctor had been attacked as he left his car. His right hand had been injured in the assault; the sentence describing the injury was underlined. In red biro, in the margin, Mary had written, 'Pity he wasn't a surgeon.'

Part 3

13

My father met me at the door, light streaming from behind him. Unaccountably he shook my hand – he was not physically demonstrative – holding it firmly and silently for a few moments, and looking directly at me. 'I should have told you before,' he said. Before I went in I turned and looked back towards Durrus, in the direction I had come. At that time of year, when the trees were bare, it should have been just possible to see a glimmer of it in the distance, but there was no moon to polish silver between the stripped sycamores, scrub-ash and alder, and the sea was sullen.

I could hear someone humming in the kitchen. The smell of roast lamb. Heat when the door opened, like a physical hand on the face. Mary was standing at the sink, peeling potatoes. The rinds lay in perfect spirals on a newspaper. A kind of sleight of hand, a party trick: to peel a potato without lifting the knife. When she turned to look the bright blade winked.

'Hello, stranger,' she said. I could not detect anything American in the fake Americanism. In the window at her back our meeting was reflected; there was no warmth in it. 'Dinner will be served in forty minutes.' She smiled. She was paler, thinner, more shapeless looking than she used to be, as though she had been physically remoulded by America and some of her substance sucked out.

'You got here quickly.' I still could not imagine the process by which she was transposed from Seattle to this farmhouse on a remote sea-coast. So many thousand miles. Time too. Seattle was a different universe happening eight hours ago, indescribably far away.

'It took me almost a week to organise everything. Matthew is taking his vacation to look after Claire. It's amazing how hard it is to get flights. Connections. Seattle to New York was easy. It was the rest of it was the problem, not to mention the cost. You know the way.'

'How are they? Claire and Matthew.'

'Fine. Really fine. And you?'

Something scraped on the floor overhead and we both looked up at the ceiling. Dad was gone before I could turn round. I heard him calling as he went up the stairs, 'Visitors, Eily. You have a visitor.' We listened until we heard his weight on the floorboards.

'You haven't seen her lately?' It was an accusation. I was not disposed to deny it or justify it.

'Since the book. Not really.'

'How long is it now?'

'Five years,' I said. Too long. Much too long if she was past caring. 'You know the story.'

'Claire is going to be ten next week. Her birthday is on Friday.'

'Wonderful.'

'Yes.' She turned back to the sink, spirals of rind turning out of her fist. 'She doesn't seem to care. I don't think it registers with her.'

'Mam? How bad is she?'

'I'm talking about Claire. She doesn't respond to me. I thought I'd better say it. Things are going to be hard enough here without me keeping up appearances. At least if we say it straight out, we won't have to tell any lies.'

'I'm sorry, Mary.'

'You're thinking: I told her so. You're thinking: it's a taste of her own medicine.'

'Mary! I said I'm sorry to hear it.'

'Whatever.' Was she crying? There was something fragile about the set of her shoulders, something unsettled. 'There's a teacher. She talks to her. And she plays with Matthew. Sometimes I think she doesn't even see me.' She pressed her sleeve to her eye. 'Oh dear God, I was glad to get the call to come home. Would you believe that? It was a chance to get away. A change of scene.'

Above the television I noticed a rectangle of brighter wallpaper. Something was missing. Then I remembered the triptych of John, Paul and JFK. Who took it down? Perhaps Mary had seen the irony of the group – the popes and the philanderer, idols of the Catholic Ireland of our childhood. Or perhaps my father. The historical map of Ireland was still there, its glorious battle-sites strangely outdated by thirty years of internecine slaughter in the North.

'I'm very, very sorry, Mary,' I said carefully. 'I wouldn't wish it for the world.'

'No. I suppose not.'

The phone rang once, twice, then stopped.

'They have an extension upstairs now.'

'Dad told me.'

'That'll be the doctor. He rings most evenings if he doesn't call.'

'How bad is she?'

'She's dying. But she's in no hurry. Or at least, the disease is in no hurry. When Dad told me I looked it up. Do you know how the dictionary defines the word *chorea*? St Vitus's dance! Would you believe that? The shakes. That's what she has. The shakes.'

'For God's sake, Mary!' I knew that malevolent gleam in her eye.

'I've had enough, Joe. I'm all out of sympathy.'

The mound of potatoes seemed enormous and was still growing, as though she were feeding an army. I did not dare to interrupt the slow unwinding knife.

'Do you know what I was thinking of this morning? In primary school, do you remember when the diocesan examiner called?'

'A droll kind of character? A Father Kelly, wasn't it?'

He examined our knowledge of the catechism, preparing for Confirmation.

'I was always word-perfect.'

I laughed. 'In everything.'

'First I am the Lord thy God, thou shalt not have strange gods before me. Remember that thou keep holy the Sabbath day. Honour thy father and thy mother. "Well, well," he used to say. "You have it to perfection. Would you ever think of a vocation?" He gave everyone sweets, even the ones who got the questions wrong. Do you remember? He always had toffees that clung to the gaps between our teeth. Scots Clan or something. And then there was the schools inspector.' She started to chuckle, an unlikely, infectious sound. I smiled too. 'He always stood at the top of the class looking at the roll-book. When he asked us questions he gave hints about the answer. "This country here now, this red one. What would the name of that be, I wonder? Would it begin with G?" "England, sir." "Would it begin with Great? Great . . . ?" What I was thinking was, those days there was always an answer, or else there was someone who could give it, a grown-up. Grown-ups gave out hints and sweets. That was their job. Now we're the grown-ups.'

In the evenings our mother did the books, glasses falling forwards onto the tip of her nose.

'Have you a docket for those yearlings?'

'That was cash, Eily. Look, I have a note of it.'

His diary: cattle bought and sold; fodder purchased; land let or acquired for conacre; drainage undertaken; the vet. At the back, the book reversed, weights of fish caught – bass eleven pounds six ounces, small skate nine pounds. I would be reading by the range, hunched over *Treasure Island* or a Sherlock Holmes. Mary's handwriting was beautiful, exact in every detail from the very first letter she learned. 'Look how neat mine is, Mam?' She would spread her books on the kitchen table and form perfect shapes between perfect lines while our mother balanced our lives down to the last halfpenny.

'The mother is the heart of the home,' she always boasted. We had seen it happen to others – father, children whirling out of control in the centrifuge. Jimmy Simpson's mother died of cancer. His father drank himself to death. Where was Jimmy now?

Mary didn't know. 'He used to look over my shoulder and copy my answers,' she said. 'I was always terrified we'd be caught.' When the teacher's back was turned he teased her. Jimmy Simpson's father used to lean his head against the wall when he was urinating, the pebbledash of the Elm Tree Bar and Lounge imprinted on his forehead.

Where had the turning started? When did we first become aware that the world was spinning, and that the gravity of love was not enough to hold us all together? We lived in a house full of second-hand possessions; we could have guessed that the mahogany commode, purchased for a bargain at a house auction, was someone's answer to a sick relative ('You won't have to go out any more'); the antimacassars guarded against a father's excessive hair oil, vanity blind to encroaching baldness; this oak letter-holder once held letters from America that stretched the elastic bond. We could have seen that all of this was the detritus of other disintegrations, the archaeology of family.

She gathered the potatoes and dropped them into a pot. She lit the gas. She folded the newspaper over the skins and brought them to the kitchen bin. When she turned on the tap to rinse her hands the pipes began to hum and judder. We listened for a minute, childhood hammering at the door, the two of us on the outside wondering if it was safe to go in. Then she looked at me and smiled.

'I was in an elevator downtown in the BonMarché once and I heard that sound. Something to do with the cables. I started to laugh aloud. I sure got some looks.'

'It's the sound of home,' I said. 'The ghost in the plumbing.'

The room smelled of stale urine, stale air, sweat, something antiseptic. She was propped up on pillows, a stained towel spread in front of her. She hardly seemed to leave an impression in the powder-blue quilt. The dog-eared postcard of Miss Stella Gastelle was propped against her bedside light. I wondered if either of them had tried to decipher the text.

'Hello, Mam.'

She did not reply. Her eyes moved rapidly from side to side. Her left hand jumped outwards purposelessly.

'They tell me you're not well.' A movement of the face that could have been the beginning of a laugh.

'She won't talk in front of strangers.' He gulped and stared at me for a time. 'I mean anybody but myself. Or the doctor. Sometimes she talks to the doctor. I didn't mean you, Joe. She didn't even talk to Mary and you know the way they were.'

'It's all right, Dad.' I knew what he meant. How long since we had been close? A lifetime. She looked frightened now, staring to the left where her leg was moving in a prolonged rotation.

'That'll pass. That's the way the chorea takes her. That's not too bad.' He caught my elbow and pulled me towards the window. We looked out on black glass with a reflection of ourselves looking in. 'I mentioned that she's inclined to see things. Imagine things. She thinks her mother is moving her legs. She told me that. That's what really put the wind up me. She told me, back along when she was talking still, that she could actually feel hands. Then it got to the point where she could actually see her mother. That's a symptom. The doctor said so.'

'Hallucinations?' My poor mother's restless all-night day full of chimeras, monsters, the walking dead.

'Seemingly.'

'She must be terrified.'

'She won't take anything. She has her mind made up.' Sudden confusion. 'Well, she had anyway.'

'Poor Mam.'

He lowered his voice so that I had to lean close to him

to catch the words. 'They say now that her mother had the same thing.'

All evening I had been troubled by a memory, something close to the rim of consciousness. Now it was clear to me. We never talked about my mother's family when we were children, but once, talking about ghost stories, she said, 'That was why they put my poor mother away.' By accident – I can't remember the circumstances – I learned that she had died in the county asylum, committed by her husband and the family doctor. My mother had never forgiven them, especially her father, for that betrayal – a blackness in her heart that had been turned in time on me. The doctor, her father, those anonymous psychiatrists shared with me my mother's blistering hate.

'The same disease?'

'From what Eily says. The doctor was asking her about it. This is back along now, back a while.' Suddenly he was close to tears. 'It runs in the family, it seems.' He put his forehead to the glass and covered his eyes with one hand. 'Joe, I'm sorry. She's sorry. She said so. She blames herself for everything. And all that about your book.'

'No, no. How could she know? We all thought there was plenty of time to make up! Children think their parents will go on for ever. I was forever making up my mind to come down and talk it over. To sort it all out. It's nobody's fault.'

'She thought she was after getting away with it. She thought it was insanity. What got her mother. Or a nervous breakdown or something. But she was always normal that way herself. She was never flighty or depressed or anything. She was a bit funny after Mary was born all right, but it wasn't this post-natal depression thing or anything. You know the way. The only thing I *will* say is that she was inclined to go overboard on things.'

'The collecting?'

'She was inclined to get into a bit of an obsession about things.'

'I was thinking about that chair.'

He laughed. 'The famous Trafalgar chair! As if that shagger Nelson put his ass in it! Horatio Nelson's commode, complete with his you-know-what, untouched by human hand since eighteen-something!' He was chuckling, a warm low staccato, a stuttering love. 'That's the kind of thing I'm talking about.'

'I suppose we should have paid more attention.'

He shook his head. 'There's no fault. Life slips by.'

I wanted to accept that benediction. 'I wasted a lot of time.'

'That's all water under the bridge anyhow.' We turned and surveyed the woman in the bed. She was bone-grey, white-lipped. Her eyes had a flat, stale look.

Suddenly my father was holding out his hands, walking towards her. 'Eily, Eily,' he was saying quietly. She turned her head towards him and a calamitous seizure began under the quilt, as if her entire body was quaking. I smelled their pain. I could not look. I stumbled out of the room blinded by tears. I had not been able to touch her. I had been unable even to speak to her.

'I'm lucky in a way,' Mary was saying. 'I never told you, Joe. I never told anyone. But I had a miscarriage once. A good few years ago now.'

'I never knew that.' I was thinking that she hadn't put on any weight in Seattle. Her skin had lost that translucence that it used to have; paper-dry now, grey and thin-looking, as though a sudden movement would tear a gap through which her bones would gleam.

'As I said, I never told anyone.'

'That must have been very hard for you. And Matthew of course. But there'll be other chances. Won't there? It wasn't anything permanent?'

'It wasn't Matthew.'

I stared at her.

'It's all water under the bridge now. It was my first year in college.'

'First year?' I had a sudden revelation of all the fatuous judgements I had passed on her; they paraded through my mind the way a dying man is supposed to see his past.

'I got involved. I made a fool of myself.'

Involved? A fool? She had not mentioned sin.

'I suppose I was gullible. I'm not good at controlling my passions. Or at least I wasn't then anyway. Self-control, easy to preach, hard to practise.'

'Amen, oh Lord.'

She looked at me with interest for a moment. 'I don't suppose that means anything?'

'What happened to the man?'

What had happened to Mary between school and miscarriage? Somewhere a normal, passionate girl had emerged briefly into the light, had fallen in love, been fooled, been hurt and had taken wing. Or reversed out of fragile beauty and back into the chrysalis. Now she wore the ugly crust like a badge of honour.

'He left when he found out I was pregnant.'

'A shit so. Better off without him.' I was uncomfortably

aware that this might in time be exposed as another of my easy judgements.

'Let he who is without sin . . . I don't think you would have behaved any differently.'

'The same old Mary.'

'Not the same at all, Joe. We're both different. Do you know who I met the other day? Mick Parfrey. You remember? The singing bus driver?' I shook my head. It was not that I did not remember him, but that I could not see the connection. 'He's retired now. But he's still singing at mass. When I was in the States there was a church choir that had a baritone just like him. Every Sunday I used to think of Mick Parfrey.'

'What about him, for Christ's sake?'

'"Well, Mary Lyons," he says. "Where are you off to now with all your bags?" I was coming from the airport. It was just the same as if I never left home. When I told him, he started to sing "Come Back to Erin". The thing is, he had his granddaughter with him. She had the same nose exactly as Mick.'

'That's a family heirloom.'

'And he told me her mother was raising her on her own. He was embarrassed. He looks after the little girl while she's at work.'

'You think you had a lucky escape?'

'I was thinking about Mick Parfrey's nose. I was thinking that at least I didn't go the full term. The point I'm making is that I don't have children. So I'm spared that.'

'Spared what?'

'Handing it on. I don't think I could bear the thought of passing it on to a child.'

'What?'

'Don't you know? Mam's disease.'

'What do you mean? It's inherited?'

Inherited. Autosomal dominant. A gene in chromosome . . .
Sharp the realisation that I had seen all this, all there before
me in plain English on the computer screen. *An inherited
disorder*. And I remembered some of the other things.
Selective cell death. I had got out of the habit of reading
signs. I had missed my own future. Now, in an instant,
it took possession of me, as painful and all-encompassing
as a plunge into ice-cold waters. I felt my nerves singing,
taut as steel hawsers, blood retreating from the periphery,
confusion, vision contracting to a pinprick. I saw the
same icy cold in Mary's eyes; and then I saw the eyes
themselves, the pale blue, almost green colour that we
had both inherited from our mother's side. *An inherited
disorder*.

'I had a blood test before I left Seattle, but it takes weeks
to come through.'

'Oh Jesus Christ.'

'We could both have it.'

In the silence I could hear the distant rumble of their
voices that had troubled my dreams and soothed my
fears through childhood; night-times when they would
sit talking in the kitchen for hours, going over the books,
reconciling the day, talking, planning, solving our lives
through the famous equation of love, the simple balance
of two people's hearts. And all the time the beast was
in the house, twisting and turning in the labyrinth of
the flesh, letting the household sleep, gulling the household gods.

'The Egyptians believed you could actually see heaven,
in the stars. They believed that if you could orientate a

body correctly the soul would find an easy way to escape. It was all a matter of calculation.'

I stared at her. 'It's a time bomb, isn't it? This disease? It's built into our genes and it's going to blow up one of these days.'

Her calm shattered me. I felt like a swimmer pounded on a rock who finds that even this rock on which he is being beaten is crumbling under his hands.

'They had a star-clock, the Egyptians,' she was saying. 'And they believed in the mystical unity of the universe. Isis and Osiris, the brother and sister. It was like geometry. I find that hard to accept now. That's what's so homely in our Christian teachings about the afterlife – the unpredictability. No one knows what's ahead of them. There are no sacrifices that will insure against eternal pain. There are no easy ways out. There's no alignment of the grave that will point us towards eternal salvation.'

'What am I going to do, Mary? What will we do?'

She took a deep breath, held it for a moment, then sighed and shrugged.

'Pray. Take the test.'

He sat to the table without looking at us. Mary opened the oven door and heat escaped like an exhaled breath. She put his plate in front of him and then folded the tea towel with which she held it, draped it on the edge of the sink and leaned back against it.

'She's asleep now,' my father said. 'She'll be all right for a few hours.' He cut his meat deliberately, stacked peas and potatoes on the fork.

'Tea?' Mary said.

'My tongue is hanging out for it,' he said. 'I thought you'd never ask.'

'I wouldn't mind a cup myself.' I got up and reached the kettle before her. I struck a match and lit the gas. I saw that the trembling in my hands was reduced; the flame barely flickered. Still my hands and feet were cold, nerves searing at the boundary where the blood was repossessing. I forced myself to think of him, of her. I put the future away.

'The pilot light is inclined to go out,' he said. 'I have to turn it off at the bottle.'

'Dangerous.'

'Your mother . . . The memory is going on her. That's the part that gets her. You're nothing without the memory, am I right? We're made of memories, that's what I think anyway.'

'Does she take sleeping tablets?' I was listening to the gathering excitement of the kettle. Its tiny quivering movements. And making substitutions: will there be sleeping tablets for me? How will *I* manage?

'I told you. She won't take a thing.'

'But I saw the bottles.'

He looked at me and blinked once, then looked deliberately at Mary. 'Mary, you're a dab hand at the cooking.'

'We can't get decent potatoes in Seattle. We get organic most of the time, but the farm we get it from was hit by a hailstorm last fall. Over on the Eastside. Hailstones as big as quarters, it said in the *Intelligencer*. They lost a lot of stuff. All the Hallowe'en things. Pumpkins. Stuff for Thanksgiving. They lost it all. I don't think they'll be around next year.'

'Is that a fact? Is organic going well over there?'

'Americans are into it in a big way.'

'Is that a fact? It'll be the same here. It'll be quality instead of quantity. One time it was all quantity. Then we had overproduction. The beef mountain. The butter mountain. That's the EEC.'

'Dad, what does the doctor say? What's going to happen to her?' And me? The words of a childhood song: Will I be happy? Will I be rich? What was the answer? *Que sera sera*. Easily said.

He pushed the plate away and I noticed that he had cut the fat off his meat and put it to one side. He was eating well though, no fear that he would starve.

'I had an offer for the farm.'

Mary looked at me. I could see that she was thinking that I would feel the loss. A writer of modest means? I could expect to inherit the farm in the traditional way, even become a gentleman farmer myself, or rent it out as he had done in recent years, and live comfortably on the proceeds. Was it John McGahern who bought a farm? It stuck in my mind that he took up farming after one of his books was banned.

'Agricultural land is fairly good at present anyhow. There's ten acres over by the village that I've had enquiries about. An auctioneer. Not your man Carey. A stranger. He says he can guarantee planning permission. I wonder who was bought and paid for to get that?' He joined his hands on the table in front of him and placed one thumb against the other, a deliberate, considered gesture. 'Mike O'Leary is the man who wants the farm. The whole shooting match. He said to say he was asking for you, Joe. The two of you were at school together, am I right? Anyway, he's renting from us for the past two years. He's dairy, as you know. He has surplus milk capacity and he says he knows where he can pick up another quota. He's not short of the readies.'

'It makes sense,' I said. Mary took a deep breath and opened her mouth but seemed to change her mind. Instead she turned and tightened the cold tap to choke off a drip. In a moment I heard the drip again.

'You're not interested, of course,' he said in an offhand way. 'Farming?'

I shook my head. 'You know me, Dad.'

'This happened to half of us. We educated our sons and daughters out of a farm. There's hardly a farmer I know who has a son left on the land. Except the O'Learys. Michael is a qualified engineer. I don't know what brought him back to the farm. He's making a go of it anyhow. Of course he draws plans and things. For houses. That brings in the extra bit.' He smiled at us to say it didn't matter and I almost believed him. 'You have your own life, Mary, over there. Yourself and Matthew and little Claire. And there's no use in saying we'll wait for Claire to grow up. I'll be dead and buried by then.'

Mary coughed and covered up by coughing again.

'So all in all, I'm thinking I'll take his offer. It'll make things easier.'

I was careful to control my voice. 'You should, Dad. You have to think about yourself. And Mam. You deserve a bit of comfort.'

'I suppose so.'

The kettle began to scream. I pulled the teapot from its shelf and dropped two bags into it. Mary clattered three mugs. I saw her swing the fridge open to get the milk, the remains of a roast and a piece of steak carefully cling-filmed on separate shelves. Plain cooking. Whatever he might eat,

Mary would not be likely to take up the rest. I had seen her pushing food around on her plate when we were eating together. She drank a lot of water and very little else. The thought occurred to me that there were two dying women in the house.

'I'll invest it. I have advice on that. Good advice.'

'That's the thing. Advice.'

'There'll be plenty left over. You needn't worry about that.'

'Dad!' Mary put his tea in front of him and put her hands on the table. 'That's the last thing in our minds.'

He looked up at her, bewilderment stealing over his face. 'You know the way my health is. I won't be long for the high road.'

'We'll take care of you, won't we, Joe? You'll have plenty of time to take advantage of us.'

'What I'm afraid of is . . .' His lower eyelids had gone slack. They shelved outwards slightly, exposing a pale reservoir that now brimmed with water. Mary folded her hands over his and sat down beside him.

'Don't, Dad.'

'Will she outlive me? That's what I'm afraid of.' He began to shake his head. 'She was right,' he said. 'She was right. There's only one way.'

'We'll sort something out,' Mary said. 'You won't have to fight this thing on your own. We'll be there for you.' I heard the tiny ghost of a voice, a thin, harsh voice, saying the same thing: *We'll be there for you.* The memory was from Oprah Winfrey. It was a tragic chorus – the chant of the guilty and the damned, the false son and the false daughter; a prayer for forgiveness, for the expiation of sins. The point of the whole show was that they had not been there, some family from New York or Boston or wherever the thing was made. And neither had we. It was all I could do to suppress the bleak laughter. Shallow, shallow, shallow, I thought. How sharper than a serpent's tooth it is to have a thankless child. How much had I missed? All the years of pain. My father facing it alone, visiting me and keeping his promise not to tell me. Hinting. *Hinting*. And Mary.

14

Sometimes you read that the publishers have recalled a book. Some terrible error, a catastrophic insult, a danger so great that the very words must be expunged from the world. But the terminology is false. The deed is done. There is no going back. The smallest thing, the tiniest action is irrevocable, for ever beyond recall. The severity of existence is revolting. That we have not the slightest power to undo what we have once done. The *thingness* of our actions mocks us.

My mother received me coldly, dressed in her best slacks, a red jumper with a streak of glitter across the front in the shape of a branch in leaf. I had heard her say: 'Send him into the front room.' My father took me in there, the room that was only used by visitors, cold, furnished in rich mahogany. A mirror-backed sideboard reflecting double the silver and pewter ornaments; the chipped Minton teapot in the shape of a Chinese actor holding a mask; the two crooked candlesticks; the silver snuffer; the pewter mug with a glass lining; the pen holder; the three square glass ink-bottles, one with a pale blue dusting at the end. This was the room I was to apologise in. This was to be the place of abasement. A moment of humiliation, and then all would be well. As in childhood I would be forgiven. Send him into the front room. I knew why.

'Sit down, Joe,' she said. She indicated a balloon-back

dining-chair, uncomfortable, its seat sagging in the centre, a pubic scruff of red horsehair showing underneath. Now that I can name it, I see in memory the weird rippling of her left hand, the jerk of her head, the way she seemed to step from foot to foot like an excited child slightly off balance. I sense the pent-up, demented fury and the restless energy of the chorea. Back then, expecting forgiveness, exercising my right as a beloved child to be absolved, there was nothing to prepare me.

'Do you remember this place?'

'I do of course.'

'How many books will you sell? A thousand? Ten thousand?'

'Two would be OK. It's not going to sell much. It's not that kind of book. What they call literary fiction.' I was hoping she would ask me about it. (*How is it going? What are the reviews like?*) Perhaps, I thought in my ignorance, it may be possible that in the end she could be proud of me. That we could work through the anger and hurt to find the common ground.

'Only two thousand? Well, that's two thousand people who would recognise this room if they saw it.'

'It's not like that, Mam . . .'

'No? Tell me so.'

'It's fiction, Mam. Every fiction writer draws from his own experience, transforms it. The work of art transcends its origins.' How flimsy it sounded even then.

'Liar!'

'Mam!'

'You used me!'

'Not so. I thought you would be pleased. You were the model for that character.'

'You ate me up . . . You spat me out . . . in this!'

She took out a page from a school copybook and spread it carefully on the table, one hand to pinion the bottom end and one to smooth it. I saw my own hand spreading an identical copybook on the same swirling mahogany twenty years before. 'A neurotic collector of rubbish. Bits and pieces, the leavings of other lives. I quote. Gathering a kind of . . . antique dandruff, I quote.' Her voice had a coarse quality that I had never heard before, a kind of masculine rumble.

'That's not you.'

'No. What two thousand people think of me . . . What they believe you think of me.'

'The critics are focusing on the warmth. The affection . . .' They were also mostly unenthusiastic about anything else in the book. 'You're looking at it the wrong way, Mam.'

'My private life . . . in every newspaper. People I don't even know. Passing judgement on me.'

'It's a book. It's the way all writers work.'

'Indecent.'

I noticed a Royal Doulton cup and saucer that I had not seen before and wondered if I could change the subject, slow things down. 'I see you have a bit of new china, Mam. Doulton, I'd say.' I smiled. For a moment I thought she would smile back, but her head jerked upright and I saw that it was not a smile but a kind of grimace.

'I'm sorry you were ever born,' she hissed. 'You Judas.'

She was rising, pushing back her chair. Her hands were shaking. I could think of nothing to say, paralysed by fear. 'Get out! Don't come back!' It was almost screamed.

Dad came, thrusting the door inwards and almost striking her.

'What's happening here? What? What did you say?' He was looking at me.

'Please, Mam,' I called. 'I didn't mean it. I'm sorry.'

'Out of my way!'

She was past him and out in the hall in a moment. My father stared after her, his hands held out towards her like a card-sharp showing that he did not have an ace in his palm. 'Eily! Come back.' But she did not turn. She seemed to draw the air of the room with her.

'I have to go,' I said. 'I have to get out of this.'

He caught the sleeve of my jacket and slowed me down, led me to the door and across the yard, out through the wicket gate into the boreen. 'She's not well at all,' he said – even then there was the code if I had had the heart to break it, but I thought it was an excuse – 'She's not herself. She doesn't mean it.'

'She's totally unreasonable,' I told him. 'A raving lunatic.'

'She always loved reading. Remember when she used to send you down to the mobile library? There was always some book she was after hearing about.' The secret code. She used to write a tiny X in the gutter of the same page each time. Page 59 – the year I was born. I never needed to remember what she had read. Once, flicking through some books in a barrow outside a shop, ex-library stock still with their battered plastic covers, I discovered the X of the code and my childhood flooded back, drowning me in yearning.

'Well, she certainly doesn't know how they get written.'

'She was like a child. Looking forward to your book. When she saw the cover . . . ! She couldn't believe it. She thought it would be a *nice* book.'

'It was all a mistake. I was so wrapped up in it I didn't notice. That's all. I couldn't help it. If I thought she was going to be like this I would have changed it.'

'Ah, but it's past all help now.' His voice was gentle. 'You can't take it back.'

The first opening buds of whitethorn were luminous in the gloom. We turned and I saw the light of her bedroom. 'I'm going home, Dad. I'll phone when I get back to the flat. Maybe she'll have cooled down.'

'Do that. She's upset. Whatever it is has got into her, she's inclined to fly off the handle easy these days.'

I saw her shadow fall on the bedroom window, a Gargantua blinking at me, and then it was gone. So often I had watched that light, coming home by the short cut from school; it marked the safe pilotage in the chart of childhood.

I took a glass of milk and a battered first edition of *Henry Esmond* to bed but they failed to put me to sleep. I could hear my father knocking around downstairs, opening and closing presses, doing something with cups and plates. After an hour the house fell silent. I got up, pulled on a sweater and socks and began to write, mechanically, unconvincingly, knees jammed uncomfortably against the wall under the small table that had been big enough when I used to live here. I was attempting to build a fictional version of St Keelin's stone by stone: the boys and their ways, the arcane rituals by which they survived together; the priests and their mannerisms; the mundane business of classes for which the school ostensibly existed. I was con-stantly being overtaken by the facts, sometimes too crass or commonplace for the telling – the boy who was me, years before, a million years before, a prehistory of the writer scrabbling in the dark in the house of his childhood. I was conscious of a tendency to write a testament now, a justification, a bid for immortality. I had to consciously control the prose. Slowly I was sucked in, sucked out, absorbed.

In time I would look outwards at the world from inside the story, with the jaundiced gaze of one who had swallowed poison and metabolised it so that his normal reaction to the world was malevolence. I knew the feeling, loved it, lived for it even; but tonight it was joyless, pointless. I knew that no careful revision could penetrate the past. The story I had begun weeks before now had its own irrevocable logic and in my weird disorientated world of anguish and foreboding I felt that I was writing my own future, yet at the same time I felt that I could use the fictional past and present as a shield against catastrophe, not like a prayer but like a prophecy, something that had nothing of the invocation and everything of the certain prediction.

In the end, when my scrawl was running off the edge of the page, illegible even to me, I threw the pen down and went back to try for oblivion in the damp sheets.

My father was never a man to squander food: waste not, want not, he used to say. Or was that my mother? At dinner he had eaten heartily and when he dozed off, Mary tucked a rug over his legs. In sleep he looked slightly collapsed, filling and emptying with each breath. Mary wanted to tell me her favourite memory of childhood. She drew her chair up to face mine and deliberately held my eye.

Other people's recollections can be dangerous things, but this one was mine too: I remembered it well. We were very young and my father took us down to the beach. While he fussed along the tideline, she and I went too far out along the rocks. She was caught, turning up stones and poking at shells, across a shallow bay where the tide swept in behind her, and I had to carry her to safety on my shoulders. My legs were sinking into the sand under the water. 'Hold on tight, Mary,' I cried. 'I'm sinking.' She recalled screaming, feeling the sucking-yielding-sucking of the world transmitted through me, the crazy giant lunging movement whirling her from side to side until I fell forward onto the rock face and she scrambled up. Looking back now I realise the water had been scarcely knee-high, my short pants just wet to the gusset.

'Daddy, we got stuck,' she shrieked. Three years old? Four? He had found a metal pot-buoy tangled in the masses of spindly kelp and he rolled it towards her. She remembers the wobbling curling roll, like a globe orbiting out of kilter. Thinking it was a football she kicked it back to him. It had almost broken her toe.

'It taught me never to trust things, Joe. You probably think that's trite, but it taught me a lesson too.'

But now I was remembering those desperate panicked steps when it seemed that something was sucking us down. I felt the quicksand pull of time, remembering what my father had said about the sea eating the land, the gable of the empty cottage on the cliff that once had sheltered decent people, the temporary safety of six feet down, and how the whole world was becoming sand on the seashore in infinitely small exchanges but irrevocable haste. I dozed and dreamed about death and woke with a start thinking how Mary never trusted people, but she put her whole trust in a Being who never made any kind of restitution.

*   *   *

I twisted and turned, trying in vain to warm myself. I heard the house cooling down, the ticking and clicking of slates and timbers and stones adjusting themselves to their shrinking world, the minute alterations of the universe that is a home. By four o'clock I had thought of everything, seen myself die in every conceivable setting.

Always alone. That was the fact now. The new irrevocable.

Suzie was impossible.

It was as if life moved forward in increments, at each step a new set of realities was established. For a time, moments only, the realities were malleable, plastic. Then, in the blink of an eye, before we can put a hand to them to make adjustments, they have set diamond-hard.

I heard sounds from my parents' room. Someone coughing. The creaking of springs. Feet on the floor. I heard him thread across my darkness and back again – the murmuring of the guard, the night-watch at the door of death. I knew that sometime it would be the same for me. Everyone knows it with certainty, but I knew the manner and the time. *This disease is most common among forty-to sixty-year-olds.* I had my father's nose, his way of standing, a certain trick of speech. My grandfather's hands, they used to say. But I had my mother's death.

15

'It's not the end of the world,' Mary said. 'We have a nice house. Matt has a steady job. Millions of people cope with troublesome children every day of their lives. You know how people say that a child enriches your life?' She took up the teacup and drank from it, then put it down with an expression of distaste. After a few moments she said, 'I only wish it was true.'

The morning sounds. A house waking. Something was going on in our parents' room. Two people facing the day together.

I saw a wren moving among raw branches outside the kitchen window, a nervous flitting down some invisible corridor. It is all a matter of perception. To the human eye the wren was wandering aimlessly; but the wren himself saw the tracks, the ley lines, the great circles, not rambling but travelling purposefully. How small or how great a place is home – a skeleton of branches in a hedgerow, a townland, a seaside village. Migratory birds flew a thousand miles. One pair of swallows could inhabit the same nest in two places. Mary had flown home across a continent and an ocean because her mother was dying. I had my own odyssey, although the distance was no more than the silence between two heartbeats.

'I'm sure Claire will be wonderful,' I told her. 'You know the way – the terrible twos or something. Or nines. Kids are like that. She'll come out of herself in time. Before you know it she'll be wanting to go to the high school prom, or whatever they really call them over there.'

She laughed. 'The prom? Not Claire. I have this feeling that she's never going to come alive. Not when I'm around anyway. I saved her from being killed and she punishes me by playing dead.'

'Are you keeping busy?'

'I do a bit of counselling and I'm involved with some local groups.' She grimaced ruefully. 'You mightn't approve of them.'

'We're too old for that, Mary. You went your way and I went mine. To tell the truth, I don't know which of us is better off.'

'I shouldn't have done it.'

'What?'

'The adoption. You know it was illegal.'

'I guessed.'

'Somebody could take a case now. Challenge it. The mother could. We're not the only ones, you know. There are others in the movement. We were so riled at the abortionists. We made a lot of rash promises. I wasn't the first to adopt a baby to save its life. Or the last.'

'You did it for good reasons.'

'That's a trap. The end justifies the means?' She laughed. 'But it's more or less right.'

'That's what Youth Defence says too. They picket politicians' houses. Shout slogans all night.'

'I don't blame them.'

A strange staccato rapping had begun upstairs. I wondered if it was an emergency. Did they need help? Mary ignored it.

'Did you get my letters?'

'With all the clippings? I did.'

'You never replied.'

'I never had anything to say.' Other than to say: stop. At least I always believed I would say stop if I could. In that case why did I never write? *Dear Mary, stop sending me this Christian shit in the post. It's not going to change my mind about anything.* In fact I would have missed it. It was like watching a story told in metaphor, in symbolic form. The way a cubist extracts the essential shapelessness of human existence and leaves behind the unchanging forms, or perhaps the true process is the reverse and what we are left with is an illusion of shape and structure. Each of Mary's postcards, each newspaper clipping was part of the parallel story of her life.

'I haven't changed my beliefs, you know. I still believe the same things. Don't mistake bitterness for lack of faith.'

'I'm very sorry to hear it.' I tried to prevent the note of sarcasm from sounding – with limited success. She gave me a sharp look and then busied herself at pouring more tea for the two of us. I buttered a second slice of toast and ladled honey onto it.

'Did you think about what we said last night?'

I swallowed hot tea and wondered if I had scalded my mouth. I picked up the milk jug and drank the cold soothing liquid. When I was finished I saw that she was looking at me enquiringly. I explained that the tea had been too hot.

For a moment longer we sat staring at the milk jug, my hand still clasping the handle. Somewhere outside a dog was barking, fields away, normality yapping in someone else's life. Even more faintly the sound of a tractor working.

'I thought about it all night. From what you said, correct me if I'm wrong, you and I have a fifty-fifty chance of inheriting the disease.'

'And if we have it our children have a fifty-fifty chance of inheriting it in turn.'

'Yes. Well, the way I see it, there's not much point in knowing, is there? All that happens, if I find out, is that I spend the rest of my life waiting for the first symptoms.'

'And if you don't find out, you spend the rest of your life wondering.'

'Mary, I don't see the point. Knowing is worse than not knowing.'

'At least you can prepare. Eat the right foods. Try to be strong.' She shook her head as though to clear it of something. 'And you could make your peace with God. Prepare spiritually.'

'What about them?' I jerked my thumb at the ceiling. 'We should be talking about what we can do to help.'

'I can't stay here.' It was sharp. Too quick. This wasn't an idea that had just come to her. Yet there was pain in her eyes. 'I have to go back. Matt isn't coping very well.'

'I know, Mary,' I said softly. 'You have your own life. Your own troubles.' She was surprised. 'I've thought a lot about it, Mary. But I still don't know what to do. The truth is, I'm frightened. I don't think I can manage this.'

We heard my father whistling along the upstairs landing. The sound of water being emptied down the sink. The clanking of an enamel basin.

'Talk to him,' she said. 'Get him to talk.'

'I'll try. You know the way he is.' She smiled. 'Sometimes he won't say a word and the next he's reciting poetry.'

She picked up the cup she had set for him and looked

at it from several angles. She brushed something off the underside and put it back down again.

'The funny thing is, I met him again over there.'

'Who?'

'The boy I was in love with. The father. I told you yesterday evening. I told you I had a miscarriage.' She stopped, surprised by the words. She coloured quickly and twisted slightly away so that I could not see her face. 'That's true, I suppose. I was in love with him. I should have had more sense.'

I shook my head. I was thinking of Suzie.

'I met him in Seattle. Isn't that incredible? A population of millions.' She picked up the cup again. 'I didn't tell him. About the miscarriage. I didn't think he deserved to know that.'

'Jesus,' I said. 'He thinks he has a son or a daughter walking around over here someplace?'

'He didn't deserve it.'

I whistled. 'You're a beauty, there's no doubt about it.'

'He asked me all right.'

'And?'

'It was in a restaurant. We went there to talk. I just walked out and left him with the bill.'

The kitchen door opened and my father came in carrying a plastic tray. 'Good morning, all,' he said. 'Great day for a fish.' He gestured at the window beyond which a low sky brooded over the fields. 'There's a gale of wind forecast for tomorrow. From the south. That'll mean there'll be a nice bit of a lop on Durrus Strand today. A day for a bass.'

I looked at Mary and she smiled.

'I'm up for it anyway,' I said. 'A bass sounds good.'

'How's Mam?'

'You know the way it is, Mary. She's a day up, a day down. But she's up today.' He put the tray down by the sink and I saw a watery porridge in the bowl, still almost full. A plastic cup with a drinking spout, two tiny holes in it. There was a Donald Duck cartoon on the side of the mug.

Mary said: 'Take your time coming home. I'll manage her fine.'

Suzie was on the phone. How was I? How was my mother? How was everybody taking it? I told her that we were doing fine, that my mother hardly recognised me, that she was bad. 'Poor Joe,' she said, as if I were the suffering one. The line hissed and crackled and it occurred to me that the weird effects that obscured my father's calls originated in his telephone. 'I love you, Joe,' she said and I knew that my echo was a lie. It was not that I did not now realise how much I loved her, but that love might well be impossible for me. My silence cheated her.

'Joe,' she said. 'I used your key. I wanted to be close to you.'

'Where are you now?'

'I'm in your flat. I slept here last night.'

'Is everything all right?'

'Joe, I decided to look up the disease on the Internet for you. I thought I'd surprise you with all the background info. I used your Mac.'

'And?' My legs felt suddenly weak. I looked around the hall but there was nothing to sit on. I sat down on the floor and propped my back against the leg of the table.

'I noticed that you marked a site. I just clicked on that.'

'And?'

'I'm so sorry. Joe? I'm sorry.'

'What did you find out?'

She was crying now. I could hear the snuffling and coughing above the static.

'You couldn't have it, Joe. I'd know if you had. Wouldn't I?'

I had not slept all night. Hour after hour I had imagined the words. I saw myself standing in a surgery and hearing a doctor say it: you don't have it. Then I saw myself opening a brown envelope and seeing the words in black and white, a death sentence passed in the most casual of terms: you have it too. A fifty-fifty night of hope and despair, but the certainty that every positive thought was matched by an equal and opposite one of despair made every hope hollow.

I put the phone down and went out into the yard. The breeze had broken up the clouds. The air was crisper. Down the hill towards the sea I saw Mike O'Leary's cows make their slow way back from milking. They swung their heavy bodies through a distant gate and scattered over the field. Then the phone began to ring again, muffled by the door, but still audible, punctuating the insistent thought: I have it too.

I opened the wicket gate and stepped out.

We went first to the little neck of land that juts out to the east of Durrus. I pulled on a spare pair of boots, the inside damp and cold, smelling of old socks. Between the stones he jammed the pike into the mud and opened holes that revealed buried shells, stones, the aimless tunnellings of unknown creatures. The wormholes followed their own logic, the worms pulsing in the air like exposed intestines. He dug the holes, my job was to pick them out and drop them in the can. Sometimes, in my grasp, a worm shortened itself and hardened in rapid muscular spasm like a tiny prick; sometimes, turning over a stone, the flat frayed shape of a ragworm; sometimes a tiny crab, its carapace pliable as cellophane. We progressed in silence, and when we were ready I straightened my aching back and saw that we had turned the muddy stony waste into a no-man's-land of shellholes and craters and the flood tide was advancing through the weed and rock, ticking and whispering at our backs.

We crossed the headland and walked down to Durrus. The sand was hard and wet still from the night's dew and the low sun gleamed coldly on it. Our boots made dull reports that carried away in the breeze. We spilled the worms onto a sheet of plastic and sorted through for the best ones. He baited according to a favourite pattern: a soft crab on the lowest hook, a ragworm next, the top hook trailing the loose tail of a lug. I stuck on whatever came to hand, threading the yielding bodies, trying to prevent the hook from breaking through before the whole worm was hooked. Then we waded out, the traces swinging just above the water. We held the rod behind us, finger on the line, the clutch free, and, fixing our eyes on some vague target on the shifting face of the sea, swung it outwards and upwards with what force we could. We watched the traces whirl against the horizon, the distant splash, and then the spinning clutch engaged and the line took up the burden of the ocean. We retreated slowly to the beach, paying out as we went, and settled down for the long wait.

Behind us a car pulled into the car park. For a moment

it looked as if the occupants would not get out. Then a father and daughter slammed the doors and rushed onto the strand. The child wore a bright red coat and a striped knitted hat. Their feet made giant and midget tracks in the sand. Water oozed into their footprints, smoothing the edges out. From a distance it looked as if the earth were erasing their presence. They raced each other by the water for a time, then went slowly back and drove away. When they were gone the beach felt bereft.

After an hour we opened the pack of sandwiches and the flask. Hot tea warmed our tongues. We stared out to sea because we could not look at each other.

'How long, Dad?'

He drank from his mug and did not reply. A flock of seagulls had settled on the edge of the tide. They stood insouciant in the face of time, shifting their base when the ripples almost lapped their feet.

'Weeks? Months? Years?'

'Do you believe in God, Joe?'

'No,' I said. 'Certainly not a God who could create that. Not the God of disease.'

'Yes, but he's not the God of disease. He's the God of forgiveness.'

'A cruel mind that could invent so many ways to make people suffer.'

'But Mary believes, though?'

'She does. To the power of ten.'

He began to whistle. I could not make out the tune. He stopped to adjust the line, tightening it a little. Our leads were being carried in by the flood. 'The hallucinations get to me,' he said. 'I was telling you that, wasn't I? She sees things. In the beginning that used to frighten the living daylights out of me. Ghosts and so on. I was inclined to think she could see something that I couldn't. I was always a bit superstitious.'

A breeze rose like a sigh and died again. I heard it rustling through the rusting bracken on the hill behind us. A sudden longing for Suzie. I saw her propped against the wall of her grandfather's house, one boot against the other.

'It goes with the disease, you told me.'

'It does. But, you know, after a bit I started to think how frightened she must be. She doesn't say much. She can't. But sometimes I can see it in her.'

'How much understanding has she?'

'Dementia? That's part of the whole thing. In the old days they used to lock them up in the asylum. You can imagine. They thought they were mad.' He swallowed hard. 'I thought so myself.'

'It's not a good death. Is it?' I knew the answer to that. I had seen it in the room yesterday, saw it in my mind's eye all night. Still it was the thought that haunted me. To make a good death. The irony of that old phrase.

'We know all about that. We went into that with the doctor. A while ago.'

'I have to make up my mind, you see. For myself. Whether I want to know or not.'

'And there's that nice girl. Suzie, is it?'

'I don't know what to do.' I didn't want to tell him that I had been watching his pain. That I knew I wouldn't have the strength of either of them and that I didn't want Suzie to waste her life on me.

'And Mary has to tell Matthew. I don't think everything is right there. I hope I'm wrong, but I think they might be in a bad patch.'

'It's like a death sentence. Having a death sentence hanging over you.'

He started to reel in the line. The seagulls rose with the sound, a sprinkling of tinfoil against the clouds. I remembered summer days paddling with him along the water's edge, how we felt the skittering of tiny flatfish under foot. Mary and I had made a game of counting them, the camouflaged penny-shapes that dozed in the sand at the water's edge. The excitement when I felt one flicker out from under my toes. Shrimp too, tiny, transparent, unlikely forms lingering and jerking out of my grasp. I sometimes netted them for bait, although worms were my father's preference.

'Your mother has made her mind up. You know the way she is. She was always obstinate. She wants to see the two of you this evening. Together. Early because she gets worse as the night goes along. Before tea. She made her mind up a long time ago. This is all organised. I was the one who had to decide when the time was right. Before things went too far, but not too soon. She wants to put things right between us all.'

His trace was dragging up towards us, scoring the sand as it came, and he began to walk down towards it, his right hand twirling as he went. We had caught nothing. The clouds had come down again and the bright breeze was gone. The afternoon was growing cold over a leaden sea.

'Your girlfriend called. She was very upset. She said you hung up on her.'

'Did she say she was my girlfriend?'

'I put two and two together.'

'What did she want?'

'She's coming down tomorrow to see you. In a van, I think she said.'

I laughed. 'Allie's van!'

'She seemed like a nice girl.'

'Mam wants to talk to us.'

'Is that what he said?'

'He didn't say much. To tell the truth I'm not in much shape for talk myself. Anyway he said Mam wants to see us.'

'Are you planning anything with your girlfriend?' She wanted to know if I was going to get married. She'd like to be matron of honour, she said, even if it was in a registry office. She told me an irrelevant story about a wedding she had attended in America, with recorded organ music. The bride was given away by her ex-husband. 'It was like a Frank Sinatra comedy,' she said. But I recognised what she was doing, this backhanded rite by which our family absolves sins. I was grateful for it.

'You'll be the first to know,' I said, winking. 'So you can get the dress in plenty of time.'

'Are you going to tell her?'

'She knows already. She looked it up.'

'She must love you very much so.'

'I don't know why.'

She looked towards the ceiling. '*They* were always happy. The perfect couple.'

'How was she today?'

Mary had tried to feed her, but she would take nothing. Coughing and spluttering on every mouthful, spilling more than she took in. The trembling and the involuntary gestures were worse than ever. She hardly spoke more than five words. 'How was Dad?'

'There's something weird,' I said. 'He doesn't seem too upset. He's almost . . . almost content. I don't understand it. He's lonely but he doesn't seem upset.'

'There's no such thing as happiness in this life. There's always something else. Somewhere else. I read somewhere that the pyramids of Egypt are arranged to mirror the heavenly Paradise. They thought they could create heaven on earth. As if people could make anything that was perfect.' She looked blankly at me, not seeing me, seeing something else. And then, bitterly: 'Nobody knows what's happening in other people's lives.'

16

'Will you answer the door?' my father shouted. He was upstairs somewhere, somehow involved in the sound of the pipes throttling back – in the late afternoon he bathed her, after her rest. It was a priest, a young man. I remembered my father telling me that they had a new curate. His face gleamed as though his mother had just scrubbed it and sent him out to meet the world. He looked at me for an instant and then stuck his hand out. A smile.

'You must be Joe,' he said.

'Come in, Father,' I said. 'What can I do for you?'

'No, no. I'm on my rounds, that's all.'

We stood in the hall for an awkward five seconds.

He smiled again and said, 'How is she at all?'

The thought struck me that he would know the answer better than me. So far I had stood at the end of her bed and watched as my father spoke to her. Her eyes did not meet mine. She had not uttered a word in my presence, although from time to time small sounds escaped her, little grunts and starts of pain or displeasure.

'As you know, I haven't seen her much lately.' An obvious evasion, but he let it pass without as much as a raised eyebrow. 'But to me she seems very low.'

'She is. I know what you mean. But we have the spring to look forward to. The sun makes a great difference to people.'

'Dad is taking it fairly well.'

'I read your book. Oh, a good while ago now. The time I came to the parish. I was interested, you know, because of the association. With the place. I must say I enjoyed it very much.'

'Thank you.'

'The descriptions and everything. You have a wonderful talent.'

'Thank you.'

'Are you going to bring out another one?'

My father came down the stairs. 'Father John! You're early. I wasn't expecting you for another hour.'

'I'm a bit early this evening, Mr Lyons. There's the Ireland match at half-six . . .'

'Will you have a cup of tea? Herself is only waking up.'

He sent us into the front room. The priest sat at the table. I stood by the window. I could see Mary coming along the side of a distant field. She seemed to have a dog with her, an errant speck at her side, though where it could have come from I couldn't guess. The dog trotted ahead of her, stopping now and then to make sure she followed. Hard to tell at the distance, but he looked like a farm dog, a sheepdog maybe.

'She has odd notions,' the priest said. 'I don't know if your dad mentioned it to you.' I turned and saw that he was fiddling uncomfortably with the shell-feet of a silver cruet stand that we bought at the auction of an old Protestant neighbour's house. Mrs Prendergast, my mother called the stand in her memory. Polishing Mrs Prendergast.

'She thinks she's going to die . . .'

'Knows. Knows she's going to die.' I was abrupt. I saw

him hunch his shoulders slightly, as though anticipating a blow. 'Let's not beat about the bush now. I know and you know.'

'Yes. She knows.'

'She knows she's going to die. It's not a nice end, they say.'

He nodded. 'The specialist told her that. He went into all the details. I don't think he was right to do it that way, but that's the way nowadays. The patient's right to know. I see a lot of that.'

'People have a right to know about their own death.'

'Do they?' He looked at me curiously. 'That's not the way I see it. God didn't give us the gift of seeing into the future. Whenever someone had that gift, now if you look back at history and so on, they always thought it was a bit of a double-edged sword. Tiresias, for example, in the play. He didn't want to tell the truth to the king. And all the prophets suffered for their knowledge. Our Lord knew how he was going to die and he asked that the cup might pass. What right have we out of all creation to foretell our own death? Did you ever read the poet Patrick Kavanagh? We studied him in school. There was a line there about "the knowledge we stole but could not use". That's science as far as I'm concerned. A lot of it anyway.' I had the feeling I was listening to a sermon in the preparation. 'And we have no right at all to have a hand in it. In our own death.'

'The Church has always had a down on suicides.' It was intended to be sarcastic. 'If they won't put up with the hell God gave them in this life, He makes sure they get it in the next.'

But he was not listening to me. He picked up the cruet

stand and rotated it in front of his face, a silver twirling merry-go-round. 'Or euthanasia,' he said.

'You'd like my sister Mary,' I said. 'She's so pro-life it'll kill her. It's eating her up.'

'We met already,' he said dryly. 'The day she arrived. We thought your mother was a goner that day. I gave her the last rites.'

'She was always very close to Mary.'

'So I'm told.' He swivelled round to face me. 'You're very bitter, aren't you?'

I laughed. 'That's the direct approach anyway.'

'You should put it all behind you. For your mother's sake. You can't get over something unless you let it go.' He made a small gesture with his free hand, enough to indicate something being released. A seed on the wind? An insect brushed from the face?

'The sacrament of reconciliation. That's what you call it now, isn't it? But it used to be called confession.'

'Reconciliation is a better word. It changes the focus.'

'Well, I'm against confession. For reconciliation purposes anyway. Talking only makes things worse. The least said the soonest mended is my principle.' I felt the next words choking in my throat, a great glob of pain blocking the cords and choking the airway. 'Trouble is, she doesn't talk to me at all.'

'She will.'

'Is that an act of faith?'

'You feel hurt and rejected. But your mother doesn't hate you. She'll talk to you in good time.'

Was there, in the blind tunnels of her dying brain, a place still where I was a child, a happy boy playing with a wooden tractor in the yard, a place where I could find her in time, before the last doors closed and I was left outside for ever?

'You know, Father, my problem with people like you –'

'People like me?'

'– is the way you always think you can solve other people's problems. You should face up to the fact that some people prefer to solve their own. And that you're not necessarily invited in to help. You're blundering around in my life and to tell the truth I'd prefer if you left.'

He didn't answer for a moment. When he did his voice was low, almost inaudible. 'It's not your life I'm blundering around in.'

He came downstairs some time later and shook my father's hand. I heard them muttering in the hall, the front door open and the warmth of the house escaping into the early evening darkness. No chance now of catching the first half of the Ireland match. Whatever was being said, it was intense, more than just a casual benediction. I heard a dog barking and Mary's voice sternly telling him to go home, then she too was in the hall, wind scooping in after her, not the predicted gale but a dry buffeting that rattled trees and shook window-sashes. I heard them greeting her, the voices louder for a moment.

'Well, Mary?'

'Hello, Father. How did you find her today?'

'Where did you find that dog of O'Leary's? He'd follow anything that moves.'

'Mike O'Leary was asking after you, Dad.'

Then the noise dropped and I could no longer make out individual words. When she came in her face was flushed from the walk.

The priest's car did a three-point turn in the yard,

the lights tracking over the house. My father went back upstairs.

'I was over at O'Leary's,' she said.

'I saw you coming across the fields.'

'The dog followed me.'

'I saw that.'

'That was Father O'Shea.'

'I know. I met him.'

'He says he read your book. He liked it.'

'He should have brought a copy and I'd sign it for him.'

'What's wrong with you? You sound like something bit you.'

'Nothing whatsoever,' I said. 'I'm not keen on priests is all.'

She pulled off her scarf and jacket and threw them on a chair. 'I can't get any sense out of Dad,' she said.

'Why? What's he saying?'

'Father O'Shea was talking about something. He was being very shifty. I guess he knows something from her confession but he won't say what it is.'

'Naturally.'

'Dad knows too. The two of them were practically fighting out there in the hall. It was all over my head.'

'He's a busybody. That's the way they all are.'

'It's something about Mam. I have my suspicions. I'm afraid she's turning against God. I wouldn't blame her. She probably blames Him for all the suffering. That's natural. She could be turning against Him now. She might be refusing the last rites.'

'Ten-dollar question. Who said: I never saw the hand of God so clear in anything? And what did he say it about?' Actually the question was purely rhetorical; I could not myself remember where the quotation came from, although I knew it was a play.

'Father O'Shea would be worried about that. He'd want to see her reconciled. He said my father should try to talk her out of it. Try to get her to accept the will of God. They were his words.'

I gaped at her. This was a woman who was a qualified psychologist, who had counselled in Ireland and America, who had lived more in her own narrow way than I would ever do. I was amazed at her blindness. Did she think that in my mother's state rational argument, or even persuasion, would have any effect? Did my mother even register our presence? The sounds? Did words have meaning for her? 'Jesus, Mary! Will you ever grow up!'

'There's no need to swear at me, Joe.'

'Look, I'm sorry. The whole thing is too much for me. That's all it is. One shock after another. My head is spinning.' And I did feel dizzy, as though I had suddenly become aware of the rotation of the planet beneath my feet, a giddy uncertainty that threatened to spin me sideways onto the furniture. 'It's just that your worries look so bloody trivial beside what's really happening. She's dying. She's in agony. If there's a God she stopped worrying about him a long while ago.'

'You're wrong. You're all wrong, Joe.'

'I don't care.'

'Some people do.'

I shrugged. 'None of my business.'

She picked at her sleeve and then, drawing a deep breath, wrapped her arms tightly across her chest, cocooning herself in her cardigan.

'Since he came back from the fishing he hasn't left her. Did he say anything to you?'

'Nothing much, Mary. Just small talk.'

Later I found that the priest had left a small blue card on the table in the hall. 'A group of Catholic organisations and prayer-groups had come together,' it said, 'to promote the saying of a daily prayer to St Oliver Plunkett.' I turned it over. The prayer began, 'Glorious Martyr, Oliver, who willingly gave your life for your faith, help us to be strong in faith.' I stuck it between the bars of the grate and watched the glowing coals consume it.

I heard my father calling from halfway down the stairs: 'Joe! Mary! Let the doctor in.' I saw the glow of the car lights beyond the hall door. He was a small man, balding gently, the classic kind of country doctor. He walked into the hall and shook my hand, waved to Mary who waved to him from her chair in the kitchen, and then went upstairs. There was a nursery rhyme my mother used to sing: *The doctor came with his bag in his hand, where is Teddy? Yellow little Teddy?* How did it go from there? Did the doctor cure the teddy bear?

Afterwards he sat with us for a time, drinking tea. He was awkward and embarrassed. Mary prattled on about the things my mother was and was not able to do and he nodded his head and tut-tutted at all the right places. Then he said, 'The two of you know, I suppose? The details?' He cleared his throat.

'Of course we do.' Mary seemed to be determined not to show any emotion on the possibility of having it herself. I had noticed it before this: whenever the disease was mentioned a steely determination came over her.

'And the background? The family?'

'Look, doctor,' I said. 'We know it's hereditary. That we might have it. There's no need to go into it.'

He looked relieved not to have to break the news himself. 'You're not married, Joe? It's a consideration. If you're ever thinking of getting married ... The children of course. You'd want to know for sure. There's a test nowadays. The lab is in Dublin. They'd have to take a sample at the University Hospital and send it up. By courier, I believe.'

'By courier?'

'The bloods have to be taken before eight in the morning. It's a sensitive procedure. To get it right. And it's a long trip up to the lab. So I'm told.'

'What are our chances?'

He shrugged. 'There's two ways of looking at that. You heard the one about the half-full glass? The pessimist and the optimist one?'

'And if you have the gene? The actual gene?'

He shook his head slowly. 'Not too good if it turns out you have that. You will definitely get the disease if you have the gene. Early or late. There's an interesting study that suggests that if you inherit it from the female side you get it later. I'd say if you're not showing symptoms by forty-five or fifty you're in the clear. What age are you?'

'Thirty-six,' I said.

'The next few years will tell a lot.'

'I had the test done in Seattle,' Mary said.

He nodded. 'No result yet? It takes time.'

'Not yet. I haven't heard. Matthew is going to call me.'

He nodded again. 'And there's the matter of family planning. Now I'm not your doctor of course, but I'd have to advise you both to look into the family planning issue. You wouldn't want to take any chances. Not until it's all cleared up.' He winked and me. 'None of this Vatican

Roulette, as they call it.' Mary coughed. 'I know, I know. I'm a religious man myself, but you have to be realistic. You have to use your head.'

'How do you find my mother?' I asked.

'She's a very strong woman. But you know, the brain is going very fast now. She's not really in control any more. Your father says she wants to see you tonight. It might be difficult. It would take all the equipment of a research hospital to know how much is gone. We don't know. We can't be sure. But she's still the same person. So don't be upset. She knows what's ahead of her. She worked it all out.'

'I won't be able to stay much longer, doctor. My husband took his holidays to look after our Claire. I'll have to go back soon. Do you think he'll be able to manage on his own?'

'He's a tough old bird. He'll be fine. Don't worry about him.'

'I don't know what I'll do if I find the test is positive. There's Claire to think about. She has to be looked after.'

'And they're making strides towards a cure all the time. All kinds of new therapies just around the corner. Genetic modification and so on.'

'Mam's case was very quick,' I said. 'That's unusual?'

'A small percentage, I believe. This is my first case. It's very rare, so I had to look it up and make a few phone calls when the diagnosis came in. But the consultant was very clear about it. Very helpful. I saw it in my internship, of course.'

'She never stops moving.' I could see the writhing body under the duvet, the ceaseless twisting, rippling, swaying, jerking torture that was consuming her. Suddenly an image from the television news came into my mind, something I had seen days ago, weeks possibly: an Arab woman kneeling in the open, her hands and upper body rocking and flailing, her face contorted in anguish. The universal sign language of pain.

'That's it,' he said gently. 'That's the chorea.'

My father led us up. Out of the freezing hall, past the picture of the Sacred Heart on the stairs, past the window on the landing where we used to put the crib at Christmas. We paused at the door. I could hear the low hum of the electric heater. The door itself seemed warm, the only warm thing around. A kind of damp cold had invaded the house, as if the sea had undermined it and filled every room with its sharp, salt air. 'Don't be frightened now,' my father whispered. 'We're a bit late because of the visitors. This is her bad time.'

There seemed to be no part of her that was not in motion. Under the pile of blankets and the thick quilt her body was straining and twisting. Her face blinked and squinted, grinned and coughed and nodded continuously. Her eyes moved. A hand that had been left outside the blankets made bizarre signs, half-realised gestures, as though in the possession of an outside force. The demented, unceasing dance of death.

He had drawn two chairs to the bedside and now he motioned us to sit down. I saw that Mary was crying. He sat on the end of the bed and placed a hand on her right foot. The spasms seemed to subside a little. A hand calming the waves.

'Eily, I brought the children,' he said. She had been twisted away from us towards the window. Now she adjusted herself so that she could turn her head towards us.

'Mary?' she said.

'I'm here, Mam.'

'Joe is here too, Eily.' She opened her mouth and closed it again. I saw her grinding her jaw as if she were trying to control a spasm.

'Take it easy now,' he said. 'Take it easy there.'

'Joe,' she said. It was barked, gruff.

'I'm here, Mam.'

'Good. Glad.'

'Didn't you want to talk to them, Eily? The speech is very poor with her tonight. Some nights she's better.'

Her hand lifted off the quilt and moved towards me. I reached out and grasped and felt the involuntary with-drawal, the disease subtracting her gift. I let her carry my hand back to the quilt. I did not intend to let go.

'So much . . . pain,' she said.

'I'm sure the doctor will give you something for that, Mam. They have wonderful things now.'

'Forgive!' she said. I did not know whether it was an order or a request. I held her hand to my face and felt the pluckings and tappings of her nerves, the cells firing and dying deep down in the sea of her brain. I thought I could read the signal.

'Thank you,' I said.

The shaking became worse, a squall, brief but violent. It passed through her body and out into the air. We all felt it. It shook us. I felt panicked, beaten.

'Mary. Love.'

'Yes, Mam.'

'Someone at me. Stop.'

She was staring away. Her eyes seeming to follow a movement in the corner of the room. We all looked. Then my father stood up and whispered, 'Time to go.' Her left leg bent at the knee and rose up under the blankets.

'Stop!' she said.

'Come on.' My father was agitated. 'Out now.'

I disengaged my hand. 'I'll be back in the morning, Mam.'

'Bitch,' she hissed. But it was directed across the room. Not at me. As I watched, her entire body arched, curved and rigid. Her eyes were dry and blank. The beautiful body of the mackerel frozen in the act of evasion, death's sordid rictus making a mockery of tenderness.

17

We descended the stairs in silence into the dark pit of our own despair, the Sacred Heart glowing at us as we went down. It is not the heart but the brain that is sacred; the true conflagration is in the head. Suppose each neuron firing in the darkness could be predicted, the dry lightning of the brain; suppose every conceivable thought could be traced to its components, broken down in terms of chemicals, electrical charge, paths and forks, difference and potential. Suppose then that a single human sentence were analysed.

But no structure exists within which the computations could be carried out. The backward track from each word falls into disorder, a vast soup of waste and pointlessness. And yet this desert, this chaos is the source of all meaning.

My mother's brain was burning out. No formula to distinguish what was meaningful and what was not. Every trivial or important movement and sensation spiked up into consciousness, calling for a response. She was flooded with desperate demands, a global catastrophe in one head. In so many significant places, my subtle mother was lost. No guide. No track.

I saw into her head, saw through her eyes, the improbable flaring and fusing wires.

*   *   *

The night settled down, cold and clammy, as the heavy sky had foretold, and we struck up a fire of turf and coal in the front room. Flames gleamed on the confusion around us, and we huddled close for the warmth, stretching our hands out, leaning forward, faces to the blaze.

Mary talked about her miscarriage. She told me also that she had tried, in the early days, all the tricks that pregnant girls have tried. 'To murder my child,' she said. 'And then the child died of its own. It was a judgement on me. Or so I thought.'

As she talked about the boy – the man – her voice filled with disgust. 'He was an engineer,' she said. 'So is Matthew. It's a cold kind of knowledge. Just numbers. Everything is a number.' She used to attend his lectures and they impressed her. How numbers turned into geometry – vectors and tangents and sweeping parabolas – the abstract becoming solid or plane. The purity of it. But at night he snuffled between her thighs like a pig rooting for food in the undergrowth.

'Partly I liked his coldness,' she said. There was something professional in her tone. I could imagine her sitting at a desk, listening, assessing. 'Engulfment. It's a term from R.D. Laing. The schizoid is terrified of love because he thinks that to love someone you have to understand their condition. He has no real grasp of his own *self* and so he thinks you're going to engulf him. He sees love as an invasion, a form of hatred.'

She was looking at me now.

'He often rejects loved ones or deceives them. Fear of engulfment is described in terms of being buried alive, drowning, being sucked into quicksand, being burned alive.' She actually joined her hands in front of her face in the classic pose. 'It's a strange set of images, isn't it? *Both* burning and drowning?'

The television was still playing in the kitchen although there was no one there to hear it. I could hear a game show prattling about fortunes won and lost. I wanted to turn it off because the silence and the fire had imposed some kind of sanctity on the house. It brooked no violations. There was a hollow, a short-lived thing, a scoop out of time that made a sheltered valley where our words had time to grow. A place to be out of the wind.

'Sometimes I think I saw Matthew as a refuge. Oh, I know all about physicians healing themselves. I shouldn't think too much. Call on a colleague, all that. But Matthew is so different. *Was* so different. Safe. Dull, I suppose.' She hesitated. 'He has no interest in other people. At least, not in me.'

She stared at her hands for a time. 'After the miscarriage I thought I never wanted to do something like that again. Any of that. But we're programmed to forget, did you know that? We forget the pain. We retain an objective memory of it, but we have no grasp of the extent, or the depth. Otherwise the human race would die out over a bad weekend.'

I laughed. 'I thought our problem was that we remembered too much. That memory was our punishment.'

'No. The punishment is in repeating the pain. And remembering too late. Matthew was really a mistake. I was well equipped to be aware of it. Even at the time. There's a terminology even. Yet I walked into it.'

Suddenly she snapped out, 'I didn't think I'd need anything more than affection. But I do. But I haven't got it and I never will.' She looked at me, hurt and defiant, challenging me to laugh, to sneer, to betray her honesty. 'I'm so guarded,' she said. 'I just can't say it out.'

'I'm human too, Mary. I understand.'

She loosened. I could see tension draining from the muscles of her shoulders, her face, her hands. 'The trouble is I remember the good things.'

'How about counselling? These things happen.' The faint sound of applause from the kitchen, a tiny chorus weakening me. 'I wouldn't have thought it would bother you. You know, with the religion and everything. With your religious beliefs.'

'I shouldn't care about it. I should be happy with what I have. I should focus on Claire and helping her.'

'You need to think of yourself too, of course.'

'Now there's all of this. All of the problems. I don't know where to turn.'

She had phoned Matthew two nights ago, she told me. His talk was full of the riots downtown at the World Trade talks. She found herself tiring of his bile, wondering if *all* the protesters could be communists and crackheads and environment freaks. She had heard that one of the groups protesting was a hillwalkers club. She suppressed an urge to laugh as he ranted, her mind idling on the thought of elderly couples tanked up on crack, rushing around the foothills of the Olympic Peninsula in the perpetual rain.

'We were over there once on our only camping expedition,' she told me. 'We came home after two days. We were defeated by the outdoors. Americans have grown up with the wilderness, but Irish people think of the outdoors as a view.'

'Listen what Thomas Friedman wrote,' Matthew had told her on the phone.

'I could hear paper being straightened. The *Intelligencer* is printed on real flimsy stuff. He reads the newspaper in bed!' His hands revolted her afterwards, she said. She never wanted him to touch her. 'Thomas Friedman called the protestors "A Noah's ark of flat-earth advocates, protectionist trade unions and yuppies". I remember the words because he said them three times. On an international call! He believes every word that man writes.'

Then he told her that he had gone back to work. Had to. The boss had called him in personally.

'He left Claire.'

Her eyes were big with the enormity of his sin. He had hired someone from an agency, she said, some anonymous half-trained semi-professional nanny. 'You need to get back here as soon as possible,' he told her. 'I can't handle all this on my own.'

'I told him Mam was dying,' Mary said. 'He said he knew it, that I had told him before. What he wanted to know was, could the old man cope? How soon could I get back? And all this time I'm wondering whether I'm dying too, and that bastard never even asked me how I was! Not once!'

Later I told her about Suzie's van, the trip to the island, the music. Suzie was my charm against despair now, in opposition to the bleakness of Mary's life. Suzie, I told her, was connected to something that I hardly knew existed. I was thinking of the way she often sang as she worked, and thinking that maybe the song had a healing power. In my mind's eye I could see her taking her fiddle-bow from the case and that elegant gesture as she tightened it, the choreography of the rotating wrist and the twirling tip of the bow. She could do it comically too, with the fiddle tucked under her chin. The different meanings of action and sound.

'You're getting on,' Mary told me. 'Are you going to marry her?'

'I don't know. I have to think about it. All this . . . everything complicates it. I wouldn't want her to have to go through this.' Afternoons when she would have to wash me, the basin of warm water balanced on the bed, the chorea rippling in the water in diminishing circles. The thought was unbearable.

'On the phone she seemed nice.'

I stood up and turned my back. 'You'll meet her tomor-row.'

I went to put the kettle on. The late news was talking about a bus strike. I turned it off, waited while the kettle rumbled. I put some cups on a tray, shook biscuits onto a saucer. I wondered if I should call Dad. 'Leave him be,' Mary said. 'He's probably asleep himself. He's worn out. He'll come down if he wants anything.'

I wondered how long it would last. Mary guessed six months. 'She's getting weaker even since I came and that's only a week. I guess she's not managing to get much food down. Did you see how thin she is?'

Mary had helped bathe her. So far I had got no closer than holding her hand. Shame made me babble about how long a person can live without food, how important fluids were. I talked about the hunger strikes, IRA prisoners struggling on and on for weeks at a time.

'But there's a difference.' That professional tone. 'A hunger striker has powerful motivations. He wants to survive. He wants to punish. There's the Cause.'

'I don't know how you can be so calm.' I felt it bubbling

up in me again – the future. A coin flipped in the light, the possible glimmering briefly; snap, a hand covers it; when the fingers open what will it show? Heads I win, tails I lose. 'I think I'm going to crack up.' I felt the lump in my throat, not the metaphor I always took it for, but a hard ungovernable mass. 'It's too sudden. There I was a week ago planning . . . I'm working on a new book. Was.'

'I feel like screaming,' she said. 'But I know if I start I won't stop. I feel like a pressure-cooker and the relief valve is jammed. Remember?'

I remembered all right. When we were kids an elderly bachelor, a neighbour, was killed. His niece gave him a present of a pressure-cooker. He was used to warming a plate for his dinner on top of the pot but the plate jammed the relief valve and the cooker blew up in his face. It took him a week to die. The inquest found the secondary fail-safe valve was faulty, made of a metal with too high a melting point.

We stared at the fire. I took a poker and rattled it and the fragile architecture collapsed, heat surging out.

'Mary, did you ever enquire about the father? About Claire's father?'

She drew back as if she had been burned. 'Why?'

'Who it might have been? I mean, you met the mother, you told me that. And she was planning to have an abortion. That's it, isn't it? And you talked her out of it with the promise of fast adoption, no questions asked? But did you ever wonder about who the father might be?' I was thinking of Suzie's reaction. Who was the father, she wanted to know, and did he consent to the adoption? And why? 'Did you ever try to find out who it was, Mary? What the circumstances were?'

She didn't look at me. 'There's a certain amount of stuff we were able to track down.'

'Before or after? Before the adoption?'

'Afterwards. When I was in Seattle.'

'You got in touch again?' I could imagine the ferocity of pain that drove her to that.

'I got in touch with the people in my old agency.'

'They made enquiries?'

'They were able to source some information. Because it was me. They did it as a favour. There's the confidentiality problem. They got round it by regarding me as a professional in the field. Rather than a mother. Because at the time of the birth she put down "Father unknown". But we have contacts.'

'It was . . . consoling?'

'No,' she said coldly. 'I would not say it was consoling.'

'Did you ever think of giving her back? Bringing her back to Ireland and handing her over to the authorities?'

She turned away.

'Don't cut me out, Mary. I'm just thinking, how many lives have been fucked up now? Claire's mother's? Yours? Matthew's? Now it looks like Claire too. What if you have the gene? If we have it we'll get it, that's what the doctor said. Maybe you'd be better giving her up.'

'I can't,' she said. Her voice was choked. 'She's my responsibility now.'

Mary talked about miracles. 'We should take her to Lourdes,' she said. 'I could try to persuade Matthew but he'll say we can't afford it. Especially after flying over here. I couldn't get a good deal because of the short notice. They really rip you off on short notice.' She told me about someone she knew who had been cured of something, eczema, asthma, cholera – she couldn't remember.

'I don't believe in miracles,' I said. 'I believe in chance.'

'We have to believe in them,' she said.

I told her about a news story from the year of the moving statues – concrete casts of the Blessed Virgin weeping, waving, taking a step forwards or backwards, smiling, all over the country in the luminous gloom of a bad summer. 'Remember, people used to come from everywhere to see them? One woman phoned a radio show to say that she had prayed all the way down from Donegal or someplace. All the way down in the minibus, the rosary, over and over again. And then she prayed all the way home. When she looked at her rosary beads the next day they had turned to gold. It was a miracle.'

'I don't remember this.'

'The guy on the radio, Kenny I think. He got the beads analysed. It was electrolysis. The sweat on her fingers had taken the nickel plating off and what was left was brass.'

'The miracle was in that woman's faith.'

'It was an anti-miracle. Prayer turned nickel into brass.'

'What are you telling me?'

'I'm telling you that God won't save her. And he won't save us. It's a fifty-fifty chance. A flip of a coin. He loves me, he loves me not.'

'He loves us.'

'He's making a very poor show of it.'

I went out and stood in the silence of the yard, staring at the stars. A plane went west from the airport twenty miles away, three lights, green, white and red; its rumbling filled the interstellar void.

*   *   *

My father came slowly down the stairs. I was washing the
mugs at the kitchen sink and Mary was drying them. The
television was on again. There was a film. Some mindless
comedy. A man and a woman in a room that could not exist
but was intended to represent the American way of life. 'I
think I'll catch a late movie,' Mary said, Seattle coming
through in the casual phrasing, proof if I needed it that
she had really left. She would sit up, she said, and maybe
later call home. The hall door was closed but I heard the
creaking steps, the steady tread.

'He's coming down,' I said. Why I should have whispered
I don't know. We both stopped and waited. He came in
without looking at us and went to the wall-clock above
the table. He opened the case, reached in and caught the
pendulum in its flight. The ticking stopped.

'Turn off the telly,' he said. Mary flicked it off, the
light of a New York apartment dying to a pinprick. 'Your
mother died about five minutes ago,' he said, his eyes
on his feet. 'She passed away peacefully in her sleep. It
was the best thing that could have happened to her.' He
stopped.

Mary said, 'Dad.' A question? An involuntary cry?

I found myself swallowing something that wasn't there
again, an appalling float that surfaced and resurfaced,
threatening to close my throat, choke me off.

'Will you join me in a decade of the rosary? For the
repose of her soul?' He looked up at us and down again.
'And then we'll go up.'

Mary looked at me. I said, 'She died? She's dead?'

'She passed away in her sleep. She was peaceful. God
rest her soul.'

'But how? You said . . . It was going to be slow.'

'She's gone to God anyhow.'

Mary said, 'Did she say anything? Before she went to sleep?'

My father sighed and looked at the blank window. 'She made me to understand that she was glad the two of you were here. That she . . . that she loved us all.'

He kneeled painfully against a kitchen chair and joined his hands in front of him. 'Are you going to join me in a decade of the rosary?' He looked sideways at us, angry, daring us to do anything else. 'The sorrowful mysteries,' he said. 'Our Father who art in heaven, hallowed be thy name . . .'

I was thinking that the last word she had said in my presence was 'bitch'. Before that? 'So much pain.' How much of the pain was of my making? I could almost feel the dry skin of her hand in mine, the ticking or trembling of her nerves. I was thinking of the tug on a fishing line, the coarse sand. Her nerves had signalled to me but it was too late now to record the syntax. No cryptologist could break the code. Not until we have the gift to read what the future is sending back to us, the sight to see beyond the speed of light.

Mary's face was wet. We see the other's grief as the simple thing, the uncomplicated dragging of loss; not this tangle of memories and mirror images, chance phrases and misunderstandings. But once in a while the chaos that surrounds us, that separates us and keeps us in ignorance, will coalesce; a pattern arises, a strange and beautiful shape, and following that pattern we are led to understand the complexity of someone else's loneliness.

My father kneeled and prayed, lost in the meaning-less drone, mysterious in his sorrow. Mary kneeled too, answering to his bidding. My mother was upstairs, temporarily detained, busy with something else. A thousand nights had found me here, kneeling in short trousers, my father giving out the Joyful or Sorrowful Mysteries, the upstairs busy with the finishing of necessary things: putting clothes away, making up beds, polishing. The house held our pain, releasing things from time to time – light, warmth, voices – but never changing the night outside. I was losing my innocence. I discovered the compound from which our lives were fabricated, and that the strange attractor that held us all together, despite the things that threw us apart, was love.

18

There are ceremonies to fill the darkness. I watched the lights of the car slipping past gates, a silent movie behind bare whitethorns, following the crooked line of the road to our yard.

Mike O'Leary came up to me and took my hand. 'I'm sorry for your trouble, Joe.'

His wife Helen. 'How is the dad?' She was a nurse. Even at this late hour she would leave her bed to minister to a neighbour at the dark door. She had come to wash and dress the dead woman, to make her ready for the journey.

'Mike,' she told her husband, 'put on the kettle for a cup of tea.'

She and Mary did the ministry of death. No place here for men. We have no subtlety.

Afterwards my mother lay in her best blouse, flatter on the bed than I had ever seen her in life; her eyes weighted with silver, hands folded on her breast.

It was the hands that held me, marbled with veins, bone-branched, immobile.

Touch wood, she used to say.

It meant – let's hope for luck. It meant feel the strength of the grain, the comfort of growth, the life of the land that went into the wood. It meant never buy something you have not touched.

The hands that rested on my fevered head, wood-dry,
full of restless dreams: 'That boy has a temperature.' Cool
hands. The hands that hugged me after a fall: 'You'll
be better before you're married, child.' The hands that
counted out the coins, bright faces gleaming on the table.
'There's something for the shop tomorrow,' she said, slipping me a silver sixpence.

It was two in the morning when we all sat down. Mike and
I talked about our schooldays. He knew which teachers
still worked, which had retired. He seemed to me to
be connected to a vast primitive network, a subelectric
world of people met at weddings, funerals, Irish Farmers
Association meetings, on holidays even. He had been on
the blockades in the beef dispute and met people from all
over Ireland. 'Winker Walshe, remember him? He cracked
up, the poor bastard. He put a young fellow's head through
a partition. He took early retirement there last year.'
'He was always a mad bastard.'
'He was. He was. Do you remember that time he went
for you with the steel ruler over something you wrote on
the blackboard?'
I chuckled. 'In Latin.'
'You knew he was the only one could read it.'
'Bog Latin too.'
'He gave you some lashing.'
'I don't know which got to him most – the joke about
the winking or the bad grammar.'
Mike had stoked it up, coal and turf; a half-year's fire
in the kitchen range. A small log crackled and spat on top
of everything else, the king of the castle, loosing a fusillade
of sparks through the grille. The heat was overpowering.

My father dozed in an armchair with his head thrown back, mouth hanging open. Earlier, a little dazed, a little surprised at himself, he made sporadic small talk about old times. Nursing a wife, a mother, a lover was a struggle to postpone his own death as much as hers. As long as she was alive she was a ward against mortality; now that she was gone his own end was before him. His face was naked with grief and fear. In sleep he was already halfway there.

Mike O'Leary nodded towards him. 'Himself is wrecked.'

'He kept it all to himself. We never knew a thing.'

'I was thinking that.' He looked embarrassed. 'I knew there was the falling out over the book. But I knew you wouldn't be that black. Oftentimes I said to Helen we should give you a ring. Let you know.'

'Dad says you were a great comfort. The two of you.'

He shrugged. 'What else are neighbours for?' He took a deep breath. 'Did he mention my offer?'

'I know about it, Mike. He took me by surprise, I have to say. But it was just surprise. The more I think about it the more I think it's the best thing. Mary is in the States. I'm no farmer. He'll need a few bob to live on. And then, you're neighbours, it won't be like some cattle-rancher or beef-baron buying it, the way I hear half the country is going. I wish you every good luck with it.'

He held his hand out to me, relief lighting up his face. 'If I have half as much luck as your father had, I'll be happy enough.' We shook hands on that, me wondering which half he would inherit and hoping it was the youthful part.

A few minutes later Mary and Helen came in. 'I'd murder for a cup of tea,' Helen said. 'Did you ring the doctor, Joe? What did he say?'

'He said he'll be here on his early rounds in the morning.'

'Was he surprised?'

The thought had not occurred to me. 'No. He wasn't surprised. At least I don't think he was.'

'Well,' she said. 'Sometimes people do give up the ghost.'

Dad woke up and straightened himself on the chair, loosening his bones. He looked at us for a bit. I could see that he was trying to put order on what he saw, working out what it was that brought us all together. Then I saw memory come over him. I could almost hear him saying her name.

'Cup of tea, Mr Lyons?' Mike said.

'I will, Mike. Thanks very much.'

Helen looked closely at him. 'How are you feeling, Mr Lyons?'

'I'm a bit shook, to tell the truth, Helen. A bit washed out.'

'You're bound to be. After all this. You should have a lie down. In Joe's room maybe.'

'No. No. I'll sit up now. Tonight.'

'How did she go, Mr Lyons?' Helen asked quietly.

'She just slipped away,' he said. 'In her sleep.' Mike handed him the cup of tea and he took it. The spoon, lying sideways in the saucer, shook like a tiny engine. The noise worried at my mind.

'Had she breathing trouble?'

He looked from one to the other of us, then gulped a mouthful of tea. 'No,' he said. 'She had no trouble at all.'

'I was only wondering,' Helen said. 'Because sometimes the breathing goes astray on a person with chorea. And if the heart is weak it goes. Just like that.' She snapped her fingers, the report echoing around our faces, sharp, unexpected, startling.

My father recovered first. 'That must be it,' he said. 'The heart gave out after all.'

Mike O'Leary was moving the sugar bowl in concentric circles on the table, watching its movements. Mary was looking at Helen. My father said, 'She was a very strong woman.'

'She was.'

Mike said, 'I remember her back along when I was a youngster. I remember meeting her one day on my way home from school. She gave me threepence. I thought I was made.'

Quiet laughter.

'Oftentimes I think what kept her going was the collecting. She was always after the next thing. The next thing on her list. It kept her mind off the other.'

'You were the teacher's pet,' Helen said to Mary. 'You were always getting ten out of ten. I never heard the end of it at home. Why can't you be like Eily Lyons's girl, my mother was always saying.'

'Only for that, I don't think she'd have lasted this long,' my father said. 'She never wanted to get this far.'

The last part was almost lost in the sound of Helen and Mike standing up. 'God almighty, Mike, those children of ours are all on their own.'

'They're only behaving when they're asleep.' Mike's apologetic smile, as if his children's behaviour was something that he had never understood. But I remembered Mike himself kicking a football through the sacristan's window.

'You'll be all right now, Mr Lyons. Mary and Joe will look after things.'

'Fine, fine. I don't know what we'd do without you. The very best of neighbours.'

'You were saying about the gate in the yard. I'll take a look at it in the morning.'

'Say hello to the kids for me.'

'Sullivan's said they'd come early. They'll take over the whole thing. They were saying they'd have the new hearse.'

'Well, at least we won't have it breaking down halfway!' Mike had told me the story earlier: Sullivan's old hearse coughing smoke and stopping dead a mile and a half from the graveyard; the family and friends shouldering the coffin of a seventeen-stone local publican the rest of the way; the heart attack of a relative. It was like an episode from a B-movie.

'And Father O'Shea will give you a ring about ten o'clock.'

My father looked bewildered, as if for a moment he had forgotten the purpose of all these arrangements, as if he had slipped temporarily into thinking that things were as they always had been, my mother asleep upstairs, neighbours going home after tea and talk about the price of dry cattle, what the Co-op was charging for compound feed, the chances of growth starting early.

My father slept in my bed after all and I slept for an hour or so in the chair he had vacated, my head full of strange dreams about boarding school, of all things, about priests and the ordinary patchwork by which cloistered boys survive. Strange that on the night she died I should dream about the times in childhood when she wasn't there. In the zigzag world of unconsciousness I saw the high windows that looked out on the school gardens, the fingerprinting of a thousand grubby hands made visible in sunlight, the loom of a flashlight in the dark corridors where we slipped between dormitories. The priests used lights too – how to know which sweeping beam was a raiding priest, which a friend returning to his bed? The pharology was complex: instant subliminal calculations about the height of the beam, the speed of the sweep, the intervals of darkness.

I woke a few hours before dawn and stoked up the Aga again. I went out into the yard and got blocks from the pile against the shed. The sky had cleared in places, glass stars hung against the smears of indigo. Later I fell asleep again in the heat and dreamed I was a child running from some frightening pursuer towards a home and safety that I could not reach. Lost in the labyrinth of the dream I twisted and turned and eventually woke myself by knocking my knee on the chair arm. Daylight was in the kitchen window, a watery dawn. Someone else was moving in the house. I could hear the floorboards creaking. I got up and filled the kettle.

The doctor came. He sympathised. He went upstairs with my father and came down again shortly. He sat at the table and filled in the certificate of death. 'I'm putting down cardiac arrest,' he said. 'Heart failure due to breathing difficulties.'

'That's it,' my father said. 'Her breathing was inclined to go against her. With the chorea.'

'Technically,' he told me, 'I'm not required to view the body after death. There's a place in the form for that. Not if I've been attending regularly and so on.'

'Mary is still asleep,' my father said wonderingly. 'The sleep of the just.'

'A coroner here would only require you to put down a best diagnosis. I worked in Canada for a bit, years ago, and out there you have to attend to certify the cause.' He told a story about being called out for the first time in a strange country, in the dead of night, to drive twenty miles to certify the death of an elderly man. 'I couldn't see the point of it,' he said. 'He had been dying for weeks. But I'll tell you what, that was the first night I saw the aurora borealis. Out over the plains. Different shades of grey. It was a pretty strange sight. I stopped the station wagon and got out to have a look at it. I couldn't believe my eyes. It felt like it was directly above my head. A hundred feet away.'

My father had not been listening. 'There won't be a coroner involved?' he asked.

The doctor shook his head. 'Don't worry about that. There won't be any of that.' When he said it he put his hand on my father's arm, a simple thing, but I saw that my father had been trembling and now the trembling had stopped.

'Would I give you something, Mr Lyons? Something to relax you a bit. This is a hard time.'

'I never took anything like that.'

'You're right. It only postpones things. You still have to face it sometime. The grieving,' he added for my benefit, nodding towards me. 'You still have to face up to the grieving in the end.'

He shook my hand at the door. 'I hope we'll see more of you, Joe,' he said. 'Your dad will need a bit of help.'

'I'll be around,' I said, irritated. 'Goodbye, doctor.'

*   *   *

Father O'Shea said, 'So. It happened after all.' He was glaring at me. 'Would you expect your mother to die so quick?' I shook my head. 'Will you be coming to the mass or do your principles get in the way?' I said I would be coming.

There was an aggression in him that was out of proportion – our quarrel over confession hardly seemed to warrant the imputation of that last question. That I would not attend my own mother's funeral. 'You went fishing yesterday morning?' the priest said. 'Durrus Strand?'

'I did.'

'You and your father. You must have had a heart-to-heart talk?'

'I can't see that it's any of your business.'

'I suppose you didn't catch anything?'

'Not a sausage.' It was a favourite joke of my father's. Someone would say: Any luck? 'Not a sausage,' he would reply, and together we would imagine the lucky day when he would pull an enormous sausage from the sea, hold it up by the hook and pronounce it a national record.

'I suppose you weren't trying very hard?'

'Look, Father, you came here to see my father. What I did yesterday or today, or what I'm going to do tomorrow is none of your business. I'm trying to be polite to you, but I didn't sleep much last night and I'm on a very short fuse.'

'Actually I came to give the last rites to your mother.'

'All right. I'm not in your way.'

'What I want to know is, putting it bluntly, how much do you know about the state of mind your father and mother were in these last few days? How much did you go along with?'

For a blunt statement, these questions seemed rather cryptic to me. I could hear the pipes shuddering and guessed that Mary was in the bathroom. I wished she would come out.

'We can only imagine what they've been going through,' I said.

He made a dismissive noise, a small sputtering explosion of air over closed lips. The toilet flushed upstairs and at the same time the telephone began to ring. 'Excuse me,' I said, glad of the excuse to move. It was Helen, wanting to know if Sullivan's the undertakers had phoned about the time of the removal. The priest lingered for a moment. I thought he would try to say something else to me. I turned my back slightly, as though the call were private. In a moment I heard him going up.

Afterwards I went into the front room and wandered around staring at the ornaments. I tried to remember the occasion of each purchase but memory could not be commanded. The furniture stared blankly at me. I noticed the dust that had settled on everything, a grey film glowing in the low winter sun.

Islands of grief form in the house of the dead. People gather in unaccustomed places, hold conversations strained by concealment or disclosure. Mary and I met on the stairs and retreated as we spoke until we were standing just outside the front door in a cloudburst of words and memories. She seemed to be worrying something through, or explaining it. 'Durrus means door, Joe. In Irish? Doesn't it? Durrus Strand – an open door. Was it for you? It's funny, when you used to go fishing, I always thought of you as a series of lines like a diagram in maths. You were the vertical, then there was the fishing rod, the angle subtended at the centre, the sand was the horizontal. Do you remember all those definitions we had to learn in school? And then the line of fishing-gut was drawing you out to whatever was beyond the door. The line was invisible just like the definition of a line in geometry, you remember?' She paused. 'I thought you were some kind of oracle. I tried to keep away from you because you were connected to all kinds of uncertainties.'

'Uncertainties,' I said. 'I knew nothing.'

'No. You believed in nothing. That's different.'

I laughed. 'Now I don't even believe in that!'

What if I were right? she speculated now. What if the door opened on emptiness? What if the wind that blew out there was chaos? She told me about an article she had read once about what happened when a window broke in a jet-plane. What struck her was the way the passengers would be spat out into the void, big and small, fat and thin, ripping through that rectangle, vanishing. Rich men through the eye of a needle, she said. The modern equivalent. What if death was like that, so many passengers sucked into nothingness? 'There has to be something, Joe. There has to be a purpose.'

When Suzie phoned I was shocked. I had forgotten that she was coming down. 'That bloody van,' she said. 'It dropped dead in Four Mile Bridge. There was a fellow in a truck flashing me for ten minutes. He pulled over in front of me. "Jesus, girl," he says to me. "You were on fire." There was smoke coming out of the back wheel. I could feel her pulling to the right all the time but I thought it was the rack and pinion again. Do you remember the rack and pinion went last year? But that time it was wobbling not pulling. The lorry driver told me that the brake-pads on that side were seized. I was lucky the engine packed up. He gave me a lift. I'll have to get someone to tow the van.'

'Where are you now?'

'A place called . . .' I heard her put the phone down and call to someone else then pick it up again. 'A place called the Elm Tree Bar.'

'I'll come down for you.'

Her voice became husky, whispering. 'I missed you. I want to talk to you.'

'Suzie, Mam died last night.'

I thought she had hung up, the silence lasted so long. Then I heard her breathing and the sound of a crate of bottles being moved somewhere else in the Elm Tree Bar, a man's voice in the distance, talking rapidly. 'Suzie?'

'I'm still here,' she said. 'Joe, I'm so sorry. I'm sorry.'

'It was the best thing that could happen.'

Weirdly, there were raised voices coming from upstairs: my father and the priest. Did he want her buried someplace else? Some row about the arrangements? Had she become a Protestant in her last minutes? A Jew? An atheist? I looked up and saw Mary standing at the head of the stairs, paused in the act of knocking, staring at the bedroom door.

'But I wish you had had more time. More time to catch up. You know what I mean?'

I forced myself to listen to Suzie, shut out the noise. 'It was too late to catch up anyway. She was way beyond me.'

'Joe, I have no business being there. I'll be in the way. Look, I'll come back for the funeral. I'll head home again. I'll thumb a lift. I'll get a taxi. I'd only be intruding.'

'No. Please, Suzie.'

Upstairs the bedroom door opened and the priest came out onto the landing. His face was bright red. Mary stepped back without a word and he came down the stairs. He did not look at me. The front door was open and he went straight through. I heard Mary call, 'Goodbye, Father.'

Suzie said, 'I'll walk up.'

'No,' I said. 'Stay where you are. I'll come down for you in about half an hour.'

The priest drove out of the yard and my father came out to the top of the stairs. 'I'm dying for a cup of tea, Mary,' he said.

'I'll be here,' Suzie told me. 'I'll wait.'

'You'd better know about all this,' my father said. 'I don't know if Father O'Shea will keep his mouth shut. Not after my performance this morning. I lost the run of myself a bit. I was never the best at holding the temper. Although, God knows, the secrets of the confessional are supposed to be sacred. Still and all, he's mad enough about it. Did you hear the way he was shouting at me?' He made a rueful face and ducked his head a little, like a child avoiding a blow. It was one of his ways of making light of things. He'd forget some necessary message on his way back from the village, and Mam would scold him, and he would grimace and duck his head and wink at us.

'What's happening, Daddy?'

'Mary, I don't know where to start. This is going on so long now I can't remember the beginning. The doctor knows about it too. He can't say, of course, but there's a nod and a wink. He respects the decision. The man is a saint. Do you know that I could phone him up at any hour of the day or night? There's not many doctors of his age would let you do that now, is there?'

'What was Father O'Shea saying?'

'I don't blame him either. He has his principles and I have mine and Eily had hers.'

'Oh no!' Mary said. 'She turned against God, didn't she? She lost her faith.'

'No, Mary, she did not.' He said it quietly. He pitied her. 'The thing is, Eily knew what was in front of her. The two of us did. We talked about it many's the time. Don't forget we both saw what happened to her mother. I'm a few years older than Eily. The whole thing – it's like it was only yesterday to me. What happened to her, you wouldn't do it to a dog.'

'What? What wouldn't you do?'

'If you had a dog that was going in the head you'd put it down. It would be a mercy. That's the way you learn to work around animals. You have to be merciful. It's the natural way. You're not meant to leave things in agony just because you can keep them alive.'

'What are you saying, Dad?' I was thinking of what he said yesterday, on the strand: he's not the God of disease, he's the God of forgiveness. It looked as if we all needed forgiveness now. Forgiveness more than anything.

'What I'm trying to tell you, Mary . . . I don't know the words for it. I don't know how to say it. But you're her children. You have a right to know. I can't keep it to myself. I can't keep it in.'

'Just tell us, Dad,' I said. 'Just tell us the story.'

He shook his head. His eyes were wet. 'She was in so much pain,' he said. 'Exhausted. She never stopped moving. Wriggling and twisting and waving. You'd set her up in the bed and in five minutes she'd be all twisted sideways, half falling out. I bought half a dozen extra pillows to put alongside her to keep her in. And you know the way she used to be. Sure, if it wasn't for her I'd never have managed the farm. She had the business head. She had more brains in her little finger than I had in my whole body. And then she was getting simple. She couldn't remember things. Oh,' he cried, 'you should have been here! You had no right to leave us alone!'

'We didn't know, Dad.'

'God almighty, didn't I drop enough hints! She made me swear not to tell you, but I dropped enough hints.'

'I was deaf,' I said.

'Easy said! Wrapped up in your own bloody world!' he said. 'The two of you!'

'We didn't know.'

'She was so ashamed of it.'

'No,' I said. 'There was no shame. What shame should there be?'

'Losing her mind. Losing the use of her hands. Talking like a child at times.' His voice came roughly through clenched teeth. 'Seeing things at her, poking at her, moving her around, dead people. People that she knew were dead coming into her room and doing things. Oh Christ.' His face dissolved into crooked lines, a down-curving mouth, water on his cheeks.

Mary, standing beside him, put her arm around his shoulders and he wept openly. I reached out and closed my fist over his. It was a rock in my grasp.

'I killed her,' he said.

'No, Dad,' Mary said. 'Don't blame yourself.'

'I did. I killed her myself. I did it.'

Mary gasped and stepped back.

I stared at him.

He looked at us. 'That's what the doctor was talking about. What he said about there being no coroner involved.'

Mary said, 'She died of a heart attack.'

'Look.' He reached into his jacket pocket and took out a fistful of plastic bottles. He threw them on the table. Amber bottles with screw-on tops, computer-printed labels; Medicine, Keep out of Reach of Children, Take as Directed, Drink Plenty of Water. They were empty. They scattered over the table like a fall of stones from a cliff face.

'Sleeping tablets,' he said. 'Tranquillisers. That's what we agreed. Years ago. When it got to a certain point, we agreed. She hasn't been taking them for weeks. Only the occasional one when it got too bad. Getting enough together. The trouble was to get her to swallow them. She hasn't been able to swallow properly for many a day.'

'Jesus Christ.'

'I mashed them up and mixed them with 7-Up. Flat 7-Up. She liked the taste of it. I tell you it didn't taste too nice by the time I was finished with it.'

'Stop,' Mary said. 'Don't tell me.'

'The doctor gave plenty of hints about which ones to use. A few of those, he used to say, are enough to kill a horse, so be careful with them. He didn't need to tell me. I could see what he was saying.'

A memory as clear as a photograph, as instantaneous: I saw him drawing liquid into a syringe, years ago. Holding the bottle up to the light of a torch I held. A heifer was shuffling uncomfortably somewhere in the darkness. 'Five ml, the vet said.' He was always careful about dosage.

'Hold up the torch, Joe,' he said. 'I can't see the markings.' I must have been five or six, standing shivering on the outside of his light.

Mary was backing towards the door. He turned around and faced her. They looked at each other for a moment, and I thought she was like a woman meeting a stranger on the road and recognising slowly that it was not a stranger but some terrible figure from her own past.

'I wasn't going to tell anyone. But you have a right to know.'

'You shouldn't have! You should have kept your mouth shut!'

'Mary!' I was shocked.

'Only I couldn't keep it to myself. She's at peace now, but I have to live with it.'

'She's in hell,' Mary said. 'It was a sin against God.'

'Jesus Christ, Mary! Don't say any more.'

But my father was shaking his head. 'Against your God maybe. But not mine.' His voice was strong, declamatory; here was a father I had never seen. His strength.

'You had no right to murder her,' Mary shouted. She was visibly shaking. 'You took it into your own hands. You were playing God yourself.'

He lifted his palms and turned them face upwards to her. 'You'd have left her in pain. You're the kind of one that'd keep a sick animal going because you couldn't part with it.'

'And you'd kill it.'

'She wanted it herself. She knew she wouldn't be able after a while. I had to be the one to do it.'

'My own father!'

'Your own father and your own mother.'

'Mary, sit down. Don't be hasty.' Words were flying like bullets. Final things were in the air. Words never to be retracted. There would be no forgiveness.

'Euthanasia!' she spat. 'You killed her.'

'And you were as far away as you could get!'

Mary was about to say something, but instead she opened the door and stepped out into the hall. I stood up. 'Mary, come back.'

She slammed the door.

My father stared at the closed door for a second while Mary's steps hurried in the hall outside, then he turned back to the table and put his head in his hands.

I sat down. I was trying to think, to put some shape on what I had heard, what I was feeling. But I kept seeing him draw five millilitres from the translucent bottle and hearing the restless shuffling of the beast just outside the scope of the light.

After a moment he said, 'I'm worn out with it.'

I heard the front door slam.

'You have a right to know,' he said. 'That's the way I see it.'

I took a deep breath, my heart thundering in a hollow trunk.

'When did you plan it?'

He rubbed his hands over his face and then sat back. 'Years ago. When she found out. The doctor went over the whole story with her. It struck her straightaway that it was the same thing that her mother had. Joe, we didn't know then about the hereditary business. I don't know if the doctor mentioned it or not but we were probably too upset to take it in. We would have told Mary. She'd have had to find out in case she had any children. We didn't know that part of it until about a year ago. Or maybe we knew before but it didn't register.'

'That doesn't matter, Dad. It doesn't matter at all.'

'It tormented her. She was worse over that than she was over her own trouble. The thought that she passed it on to you and Mary, and that you might give it to other children. Her grandchildren.'

'We can find out now. There's a test.'

'I know.'

'Did Mam ever say . . . Did she ever mention me?'

'She couldn't bring herself to talk to you. She didn't hold anything against you this past while, but she couldn't bring herself to contact you first. And then lately her head was going. Terrible rages. Shouting.'

'I never meant to hurt her.'

'Paranoid. That's the name I was trying to think of. Seemingly a lot of them get paranoid.'

'It explains a lot.'

There was something lifeless about his eyes, something gone from them. I had not noticed it before. How long had it been missing?

'It makes them very hard to live with.'

'She read too much into it,' I said. 'That book was not about her. The woman in it, I made her up. I never thought Mam was mad. Not once. It's just that, the collecting, it was a beautiful metaphor.'

'You were nearer the mark than you knew, maybe.'

'Oh Christ. I never meant it.'

'Mary. I never thought she'd take it like this. The things she said. Nobody should say that to a father. Did you see her? The hate?'

'She'll get over it.'

He shook his head. 'Not in this family,' he said. 'It doesn't happen.'

In the silence that grew around that remark I began to see the thread that ran through our lives. I saw it as clearly as if I were analysing some formulaic tragedy, the ghost of Sophocles shambling through the plot. All of childhood was a false peace, each of us circling the one fatal falsehood, like people circling a firecracker just out of range, waiting for the fuse to burn down, waiting for the big bang. At the heart of the drama were three things: God, madness, love. Disguise was the mode of existence. Each of us believing ourselves alone in our own suffering. *Thou art a soul in bliss and I am bound upon a wheel of fire that my tears do scald like molten lead.* A variation on a theme. In the catastrophe the impossibility of true communication, true reconciliation is apparent. The good are punished equally with the wicked and order of a kind is re-established, founded on the same shabby ignorance, embraced with relief. I saw it all with an icy coldness that I knew was one step away from hate, irony about to tip over into self-disgust.

I knew that I should keep Suzie out of it. She would be here this morning, stepping into the scene unarmed. But I lacked allies. I was weak and lost. I needed her strength.

I took a deep breath.

'Dad, my girlfriend is coming today. I arranged it before all this happened.'

He looked suddenly terrified. 'Don't say a word.'

'No, no,' I lied. 'I won't say a thing.' At least she would know where the dangers lay. I could give her some small advantage.

'Suzie? Isn't that her name?'

'She won't be in the way.'

'She's welcome into this madhouse,' he said. 'She might bring a bit of sunshine with her.'

A still day. The leafless trees engraved on the sky. The fields were sorry-looking, ponds full, rivers bubbling; at one point a spring spilled across the road and the wheels splashed through a river on the tarmacadam. A grey-blue mist robbed the distance of detail. The car radio was on when I turned the key. I left it to play pop tunes, repetitive, monotonous rhythms like a computer program on an endless loop, punctuated by a breathlessly enthusiastic disc jockey. It occupied the spaces between my thoughts, demanding nothing.

The phone had rung as I was coming out. I picked it up and heard Matthew's voice for the first time in years. It was 6 a.m. in Seattle, he told me. I commiserated with him. I asked him what the weather was like and he said it was raining. Claire was fine, he said, and his job was going real well. He asked for Mary. I told him she was out. 'Gotta go to work,' he said. 'Tell her I called. Tell her I said the test results are in. They came out fine. She's in the clear.'

I remember thinking about the laws of probability, trying desperately to resurrect something from Honours Maths. Did the fact that Mary was clear affect my fifty-fifty chance? Between two children there was a fifty-fifty chance of having the gene; what if we know that one of those children does not have it? Does it or does it not change the probability for the second? What hope had I still of avoiding my inheritance? Each toss of a coin, I thought. Each one has the same probability. The fact that you have already tossed and come up heads doesn't mean it's more likely to be tails next time. Then I began to wonder whether God knew that, whether he allowed for the laws of probability, or whether he worked with a weighted coin, taking a twisted pleasure from the chagrin of the fall-guy.

Suzie was sitting on a bench outside the Elm Tree Bar and Lounge, face tilted back to catch the weak sun. Above her head a windmill that drove a toy man to saw a piece of wood; its motionless blades were a slanted cross. The elm itself had long since succumbed to Dutch elm disease. Its stump took the place of two cars in the customers' car park, rotten in the centre, cupping a standing pool mantled with petroleum waste. Behind Suzie was a frozen food van that said *Pierre's Fresh Ideas Served Fresh*. She hugged me hard, her cheek to mine. She said she was sorry over and over again. The door was open and there was a hint of stale beer in the air. I could hear the radio playing behind the bar and recognised the metallic guitar and nasal tones of Woody Guthrie. His certainties counterpointed the fake pain of the pop on my car radio.

We drove in silence for a time, back over the same roads, crossing the same river. At one point she tried to catch my hand in its flight from the gearshift to the wheel, fumbled it and settled for my sleeve.

'When is the removal?'

'Tonight.'

'I'll go home after that.'

A boy driving cattle held the road ahead of us. I slowed and stopped to await the enormous bodies, the noisy huffing and blowing, the clop-clop of hooves, the curious-incurious faces, the sour tang of hides filtering past. The boy waved his thanks, stopped, looked again and came over to the window. I rolled it down. I recognised his face but could not put a name to it.

'I'm sorry for your trouble, Mr Lyons. I heard this morning.' He nodded towards Suzie.

'Thank you. It was a happy release.'

'Still and all,' he said.

He was away again, holding out his hands like a scarecrow as a lively whitehead made a break for home.

'Pull over up here,' Suzie said. It was a wide gravelled space in front of the new school. I pulled in and we came to a rumbling halt close to the playground wall. She unclipped her seat belt and swivelled towards me. Behind her head a hungry-looking rat scuffled across the road and through the school gate.

'You're in a state of shock, Joe, and I want to get a few things straight,' she said. 'Firstly, this thing could be hereditary, right?'

'It is.'

'You're going to be tested for it?'

'I don't know.'

'You are. That's the first thing. The second thing is, I love you and I don't care what the test is. All I want to know is, do you love me?'

I thought of my mother's place in the bed, the impression of wire and plastic rather than anything human, the burnt-out look in her eyes. 'I love you, Suzie,' I said. I said it because love can push back the darkness, push out the light. Or at least because there was nothing else that I knew could do it. Which is not the same thing. But also because I had come to believe in the possibility of love, having watched my father, thought about what he had done and why; for the first time ever I had some inkling of the boundlessness of that bond. That perhaps there was no quid pro quo, the thing itself as mythically powerful as the dreamers said it was. How else to explain my father? My mother? This past isolation and certainty, the foreknowledge of ruin: how else could they have lived with it?

She kissed me. 'I'll mind you,' she said.

'Suzie, my father told me a while ago that I don't deserve you. I'm beginning to think he was right. Maybe he was right about more things than I gave him credit for.'

The boy's name came to me at that moment and for no reason. The way ideas came from the air. Barry. His father used to be a fishing buddy of my father's. No, it must be his grandfather. Pa Barry. Pa for Patrick.

A bell began to ring. Children's voices filled the car. We watched their flying bodies through the bars of the school gate, and as best I could, without any apologies or excuses, I told Suzie how my mother died, knowing as I did so that I was breaking their trust for the second time. She listened calmly, nodding her head occasionally, wincing when I repeated my father's words about the 7-Up.

She was silent for a while. I sensed her seriousness, her charged presence on my left, somehow, inexplicably, at the circumcentre of my life, an intangible line scribed in the air connecting us, dismaying in its frailty. What would her next word be? I desperately wanted her to understand. I felt like pleading for my father, for my mother – for myself too – a whole family of unlikely suits awaiting her judgement.

At last she took a deep breath and, still staring at the windshield, said: 'He did the right thing, Joe. Don't you think so?'

I nodded. There was too much in my throat to speak, a whole heartful heaved from below.

I saw that she was crying.

'He was very brave. Who'd want to go on like that? It was what she wanted too. He took her out of her agony. That's courage.'

'Yes,' I said. 'But more than courage too.' What more I could not say.

'So, what happens next?'

I shrugged. 'I'll have to keep an eye on him. Apart from that – I don't know.'

'What about Mary?'

'She's angry. Very, very angry. But I think it'll blow over. I think she'll wait for the funeral and then go back to the States. It's just about possible that she's angry enough to walk out now.' I thought about that for a minute. 'I think she'll want to put a good face on it. She won't want the neighbours to find out. Like all pious people she's more concerned with appearances than you might think.'

'And us?'

I took a deep breath. 'Suzie, I've been thinking a lot . . .'

'Oh no, Joe. I know what you're going to say. Don't say anything.'

'Suzie, I know what's going to happen. I saw it.'

'You only saw the end.'

'An inevitable end.'

She was leaning sideways against the door, staring at me. 'It's not all endings, Joe. There's more to it than that. Think about the beginning. Think about all the time between.'

I shook my head. 'I couldn't do it to you.'

'I'm frightened. But I'm not walking away.'

'It scares the living shit out of *me*.'

'I worked it out too. I knew you'd say this.'

'You have to think about it. You have to.'

'I will. I won't change my mind.'

The school bell rattled, a corduroy-coated teacher swinging the bright brass. It reminded me of a thurible, swinging in the air, little puffs of incense escaping, such a tiny cloud above the altar boy's head, but the sweet smoke filled a whole church and drifted out into the night, a blessing. The children were forming uneven giggling lines. And then another man came, clapping his hands rhythmically, a thunderous slow clap, and the lines began to move, vanishing into the shadows beyond the school doors.

I started the car. 'I don't think I have it,' I said. 'I've thought a lot about it the last two nights. I think if I had it, I'd know.'

'We'll talk about it again. After everything.'

I saw that my hands were shaking. A tiny tremor. An annoyance. Nerves, I thought. When I took Suzie's hand I felt that she was trembling too. It was consoling, love's seismology, the graph of the epicentre. We held onto each other between gear changes and the world reeled by, home on the line.

19

The sweet smell of bacon and cabbage. Helen O'Leary had called while I was out and put the meat in the pot, cleaned and chopped the cabbage. An irregular stream of neighbours intent on the curious ritual of handshaking and reminiscing had kept my father occupied. Now they were gone, taking their voices and their ancient consolations with them and leaving behind a faint suggestion of other people's clothes. My father greeted Suzie at the door and welcomed her in, leading her through the smell of my childhood into the warm kitchen.

She was saying that she was sorry for his trouble. 'It's terrible for you, Mr Lyons. Can I help at all? If there's anything I can do.'

'Sure I have great help. But I'm delighted you came down. Joe and Mary . . . and my neighbours – what would we do without neighbours?'

Briefly forgetful, holding beautiful Suzie by the arm, he was brighter-looking, not so worn. He had something of his old bantering charm.

'He's always talking about you, you know.'

She laughed. 'As long as he's not giving out . . .'

'I know. I know. He has a foul tongue in him. Did you read that book he wrote? The eff word on every page. Eff this, eff that.'

'I wonder where he got it?'

My father's mischievous smile. 'The effer didn't get it from me anyway.'

He conveyed her to a chair. 'Will you have a glass of wine?' Sherry had materialised in the house at some stage during the morning and every woman who called had been given a tall thistleful. Men drank whiskey or got nothing at all.

Now the glass of chestnut red appeared in front of her – Harvey's Bristol Cream from a weird blue bottle.

'You'll miss her,' she said, and he stared at her. She had the key: his heart was open to her. The soft words that realigned his despair. Which of us would have thought such a simple truth, Mary or me, trapped in our own troubles, forgetting that he had lived and loved one person for over forty years and now she was gone?

She touched his hand, a brief movement, as though brushing something from his skin, and then there were tears in his eyes.

I lifted the meat out onto a plate and strained the cabbage. Steam clouded the day beyond the window, daylight on a distant fog-bound sea. My father sliced the meat in neat rounds. 'She gets it at McCarthy's,' he said. 'Helen does. I never go in there, but they say he has good meat. We get all our meat in Quinn's.'

'McCarthy's father was on the wrong side in the Civil War,' I told Suzie. 'And he was a blueshirt in the thirties. My father is of the other colour.'

'Ah, it's only all nonsense now anyway,' he said. 'Who shot who in 1922. Nobody remembers. Maybe I will go into Tommy McCarthy one of these days. It might kill him with shock' – a sudden inspiration – 'That'd be as good as shooting him.'

'But you weren't in the Civil War, Mr Lyons? You're too young.'

I laughed. 'He inherited a hatred of blueshirts from his father.'

'Along with a bit of land,' my father quipped. 'Now, have a taste of that.'

He put a plateful of meat in front of Suzie. She held up her hands in mock-horror. 'I'll never eat all that.'

'Sullivan's arrived just after you left, Joe.'

'I'm sorry I wasn't here.'

'Don't cut the fat off, Suzie. The fat is the best part. Don't take any notice of this health food crowd. Chancers. It's fat today, it'll be something else tomorrow. Eggs or cheese.'

He brought my plate and his to the table and we sat down. 'Sure we didn't need you, Joe. Sullivan's are used to this kind of thing. They have it all down to a fine art. They give you a menu, imagine that? A funeral menu. You decide about flowers and a kind of a visitors' book and who plays the organ and about ten other things. You just tick them off.'

He reached forward suddenly and scooped a knife-load of butter and dabbed it into his potatoes. A peel of cling film lay along the edge of the dish and it occurred to me that Mary covered everything. That morning when I went to put milk on my tea there was an invisible barrier of plastic over the mouth of the jug. I stared stupidly at it, still half asleep, wondering why the milk would not flow – until I saw the wrinkled edge.

'It sounds very cold, Mr Lyons.'

'That's it now, Suzie. Cold is the word. Your mother would have liked a proper wake in the house, Joe, but I couldn't do it. If it was me went first your mother could have organised that. She was like that. But I couldn't do it.'

I remembered the time she came to the school to save me, how they must have talked it over and agreed that she was the one to go, of the sun in the tea-shop and the silver pencil with the concealed chamber.

'She was very organised?'

'She had the business mind.'

We lapsed into silence, filling our thoughts with food. When he spoke again his voice was wavering a little, as though he were barely mastering himself.

'Anyway, the removal to the church is tonight. Funeral tomorrow after eleven o'clock mass.'

'There'll be a big crowd, Dad.'

'A good send-off. A lot of people would be fond of her.'

The creak of the knife-blade on the plate.

'I don't know if Father O'Shea will do the funeral. There was that row.'

'He'll rise above that.'

'He will. You're right, Joe. He's a bigger man than that.'

Suzie was watching us. I knew she was thinking: here's Joe and his father, together in mourning. She was thinking of what my father had done, the enormity of his actions. Did she see the looming shadow between us? Character isolated by a deed, Yeats called it. The phrase had stuck in my mind a long time ago. My father was the hero of this particular tragedy, but the relationships were wrong, skewed by some perverse god; I should have been the slayer, my father the target of my sword. Instead, laughably, here sat the hero and his son, blood on their hands, eating bacon and cabbage. The wrong body lay on the bier. Not Oedipus but a blackface Othello, Iago the son he never had.

'So what's this thing I see you writing these days?' He winked at Suzie and then continued loading his fork with meat and potatoes.

I didn't think he had noticed. I tried to think when he might have seen me. Had he been in my bedroom when I was out? I imagined him wandering the house, hating the silence, drifting from room to room. This house was his, had been theirs and mine. Possession. A house is possessed by its occupants. Its spaces filled with their hopes. There is no vacancy in a family home – even the attic cluttered with lofty dreams and yesterday's prizes. And no real privacy.

'Just another book.' I hated to talk about it – superstition, like not mentioning cancer. God bless the mark. 'I'm not exactly writing at all. Now anyway. Not since I came down. I haven't been concentrating. It's about school. Among other things.'

He chuckled. 'They'll get a fright so. Going by your last one.'

I stared at him. Did he see it that way too?

He turned to Suzie, still chuckling. 'We all saw ourselves in the last one. That's the way people are. If they see a photograph of a hurling match they were at, they spend all day trying to pick out the place they were standing. If I was one of them priests I'd be quaking in my boots, going by the stories he used to bring home with him.'

I used to bring stories home; I had forgotten that. The first night home, Mary asking me to tell her everything. The Tales of Winker Walshe, Ratty Hanratty, the President and his pompous sermons, the icy cold of the showers, the bog of a pitch we played on, the friends, the fights and the beatings. The thousand and one nights. Behind his *Examiner*, the pages turning slowly, studying the notices of cattle-marts, auctions, certified seed for sale – all the time he had been listening to a boy's tales of school. Did he envy me? I used to think of him as remote, noble in his devotion to work and family, his poetry, his fishing – an impossible ideal. But he had been listening from beyond the barrier of the newspaper, containing his mirth.

'I might sell the house,' my father said. 'I don't want to be on my own out here.'

I looked at Suzie. 'I'll stay for a while,' I said.

She nodded to me.

'But in the end I'll be on my own.'

I looked steadily at him. 'We'll cross that bridge when we come to it. I'm in no rush to get back to my flat.' I was wondering how long my resolve would hold; more importantly, how long could I bear to live in the place of my own death.

'Don't make any rush decisions, Mr Lyons. This isn't the time. You might regret things later.'

'Dad, where's Mary?'

'She'll be back.' Curt. He could wait for her to turn.

'Anyway,' I said, 'Mike O'Leary is not too far away. He's a good neighbour.'

He nodded solemnly. 'The best.'

I noticed that the colour had drained from his face again. There was a hunted look in his eyes. 'Joe, did you . . . Does Suzie know?'

'I do, Mr Lyons.'

'About everything?'

'I know what might be in store.'

He shook his head. I saw that his eyes were moist. 'I have

a duty . . . Eily . . . I always thought it was insanity. I knew all about her mother. It often occurred to me that she could have it too. But I still married Eily. We were made for each other. That's what I always thought.'

'You were in love with her,' Suzie said, looking directly at me.

'That's it. I was. I was mad about her.'

'You understand so.'

He said nothing for a moment. I had noticed a habit he had developed of looking towards the ceiling. The first day I came down I saw it. Then I guessed he was thinking of my mother. He was looking up now when he came to speak. 'I was often lonesome. That's easy to believe. You see, she was a different person once this bastard of a disease got hold of her. Not at the start, but when it really got going. There was nights here when I thought I was going mad myself. Times when I thought I might as well kill the two of us. One night I loaded the shotgun, would you believe that?' He laughed. 'By Jesus, I unloaded it fast enough when I came to my senses. You never saw anyone unload a gun so quick. I haven't a cartridge left in the house now. I gave them all to Mike O'Leary. I'd say he had an inkling what I was doing.' He pushed his plate away, the food half eaten. 'Helen used to stand in for me from time to time. She understood the situation, being a nurse herself. I used to go fishing mostly. That's lonely enough too, on your own.'

Suzie reached a hand out and rested her small white fingers on his fist. 'Mr Lyons, I often think, when I'm singing, I often think that I'm only the instrument and a song that was made two or three hundred years ago is singing through me.' Without warning, almost without catching her breath, she began to sing *'An Droighneán*

Donn,' slowly and with delicate ornament. The verse wound its tortuous way to the final statement – *Agus tá mo ghrása mar bhláth na n-airní ar an droighneán donn.*

'It means: my love is the haw-flower on the top branches of the thorn. The last part.'

'Yes,' he said. He nodded slowly. 'It's not a word of a lie. The flower on the blackthorn. Don't sing any more, please. Your voice is beautiful. It upsets me.'

And I was watching her, my heart drumming in my chest. It could be simple, but it never would be. Love was no boys' story. Where would all the old songs be if the outcome could be predicted? What famous lovers would she sing about if their love wound its way to a comfortable end in a quiet house?

He held up his fingers and looked at the nails. Then he began to worry at the quick of his left index, pushing back the skin. There was something savage about the way he did it. Something hawkish.

'Joe, I said things before . . . I didn't mean them. The truth is, if I was going to tell you, I could have said it straight out. But I never did. It's no fault of yours that you couldn't read my mind. And I knew that the whole row came down to her disease. I often ask myself why didn't I break my promise and come straight out with it.'

'Dad, it's over and done with now. I gave up too soon. My pride got in the way.'

'Family failing?' We smiled at each other.

'Runs in the blood,' I said.

I heard the front door open. 'Mary's back.'

I heard my father draw a deep breath. Then she walked in. I think I knew, even then, what she was going to say.

*   *   *

Suzie was the first to react. She stood up and held her hand out. Mary looked at it as if she were going to leave it there untouched. 'I'm so sorry for your trouble,' Suzie said. The simple statement disarmed Mary and she took the hand and shook it. Her eyes were red as though she had been crying and they stood out like coloured saucers on a white damask. 'I'm Suzie, Joe's friend. You look very tired.'

'Yes, thank you. I am,' Mary said. She seemed to be off balance, uncertain. Then she let the hand go, straightened her shoulders and looked past Suzie at the window. Involuntarily we followed her gaze, my father and I, but it was just the window, the same grey sky beyond.

My father turned back. 'Have a bite of dinner, Mary,' he said. 'Helen O'Leary put on the bacon and cabbage this morning, God bless her.'

'Where's my mother?'

Suzie panicked. I could see that. I knew the signs. She looked around her and then sat down, leaning over her plate and making sudden cutting movements across a piece of meat. I could see also that my father had begun to tremble. I could see they were afraid. Mary seemed taller, more resolute, fiercer. I could not account for it.

'She's gone, Mary,' he said. 'Are you all right? Your mother's gone to God.'

Mary made a quick, short, chopping gesture. 'Do you think I don't know? Where is the body?'

'Sullivan's came this morning,' he said. 'The removal is at half past six this evening.'

'Funeral after eleven o'clock mass tomorrow.' I wanted to keep the banalities going, to postpone the coming catastrophe. Let Tiresias pass the time of day, chat about the weather, the dirt of the streets. Whatever happens don't let him come to the point.

'You had no right to take her out of the house,' Mary said.

'It was Sullivan's,' my father said lamely.

'Why not, Mary? This is the natural process. This is the way it always is. There'll be prayers. She'll lie in the church tonight. Mass tomorrow. It's good. It's the way it's done now.'

'I've been to funerals,' she spat. 'Normal funerals.'

'Sullivan's are used to these things. They have their own ways.' He picked up his knife and fork and bent his head to his food. It was a brave gesture, indicating a clear conscience, a no-nonsense approach to Mary's hysteria. But his knife rattled on the plate.

'It's illegal. Removing evidence from the scene of a crime.'

'What!'

I was on my feet, staring at her. Suzie was looking up at me, her mouth open, her eyes wide open. But my father was still trying to separate a piece of fat from a forkful of bacon. With absolute clarity I heard his knife grating on the hard glaze.

Mary said, 'I've made up my mind.'

'No,' my father said, shaking his head slowly. 'No. You'll bring a coroner's court into it. There'll be an inquest. I couldn't stick it.' He did not seem to grasp the full implications.

'Mary, it'll kill him,' I said.

'Justice,' she said.

'No.'

'Yes. He's not God.'

'It was love, Mary.'

She made the same small cutting movement with her hand. 'Thou shalt not kill. I am the Lord thy God, thou shalt not have strange gods before me.'

'What are you saying?' Suzie was lost. Mary's mind was *terra incognita* for her. But I knew what it meant, every word a hieroglyph and I had the parallel text. We had, after all, lived in contiguous worlds for most of our lives, twin universes, one ruled by a vindictive and autocratic god, the other a self-perpetuating pointless place.

'Mary, people have a right to choose their own way of going.'

'Thou shalt not kill.'

'No. You're hurt. We're all wounded. All hurt. We have to try to understand.'

'Do what you like.'

'Don't turn away now.'

My father sat back and looked at her face. He had given up on the food. His fork lay athwart the plate, a piece of bacon like a section of lip with a rime of fat skewered on the tines.

We all heard the hammering. My first thought was that she had already informed the police and they were battering at our front door, demanding access, arrest, waving a warrant. My father looked at the ceiling again. His lips seemed to have gone completely white. Suzie gasped.

'What's that?' Mary said. 'What's that knocking?'

'Don't do it, Mary,' I begged.

It came again, this time obviously outside the house.

'The gate,' my father said, relaxing suddenly. 'That's Mike O'Leary. He's straightening the gate.'

'I backed into it the other day,' I told Suzie, glad of a

distraction from other subjects. 'I broke a tail-light.' Her lips smiled up at me but her eyes were dark.

I looked at Mary and she returned my look without flinching. I knew what was driving her. 'This is revenge enough,' I said. 'Don't take it any further.'

'Before we talk about taking it further,' my father said, 'we'd better get it straight.'

'I can see straight enough. You killed my mother.' Her mouth was set in a thin line. Her eyes were dry. Her hands hung by her side so that she looked like a lost child, so thin and frail, a refugee from despair who has found that the refuge is gone. 'You were always like that.'

What did she mean now? Where was this leading?

But an extraordinary calm had settled on him. He straightened his knife and fork on the plate. He tilted the chair on its back legs.

'She read it all up a long time ago. Do you know what the biggest trouble is for someone who wants to do away with themselves? Someone in earnest, now?'

I shook my head. I could not take my eyes off him. I felt cold. I wanted, absurdly, to stretch my hands towards the range, a dull glow on the other side of the kitchen.

'I'll tell you what. They're always afraid they'll botch it. They'll wake up in some hospital bed with tubes coming out of every part of them. They'll know they're still alive. But they'll have done so much damage that they'll be ten thousand times worse off than before.'

'What are you getting at?' For the first time since she came in Mary moved away from the door. It was as if she believed we would try to prevent her leaving and had kept close to the escape route all along. But now she moved towards the sink, farther away from him, as though to resist the pull of his voice.

There was something hardening in him that I could not recall seeing before, a violence, and a cold contempt. Then I recalled his blind fury on Durrus Strand, battering a fish on a stone, the dull thudding, and I saw in a flash what Mary meant. *You were always like that.*

'The thing is,' he said, 'you can't be sure of the sleeping tablets. That's what I read. You can't just rely on them.'

The hammering was finished. I heard Mike O'Leary's whistling, the sound of tools being tossed onto the metal floor of his jeep.

'The more you take the less you're able to swallow. Like this law of diminishing returns they're always talking about.'

Nobody moved. Suzie was still looking at me. I thought she was holding her breath.

Then my father said, 'Better be sure what you're going to tell the guards.'

The carving knife was behind Mary. I actually worried that she might use it. 'What the doctor said. Helen said it too. The breathing went on her.' Desperation was apparent in her voice, fear struggling with anger. 'Death by asphyxiation, that's what they call it. From the pills.' He shook his head.

'Heart failure,' I said. I was defying him too. Or it was a ward to the coming blow?

He stared back. 'Seemingly there's some sign. When a person chokes.'

'The doctor said it was heart failure.'

He coughed and looked down at his fist curled into a ball on the table. With a visible effort he relaxed the hand, the fingers unrolling. There was nothing inside. 'I had a box of cling film ready,' he said. 'After she took the tablets, the 7-Up.' His face was blanched by the pain. I imagined him sitting by the bed, making estimates – would she live or die – knowing he had no head for numbers. His voice was cracking a little, small hesitations between phrases. 'Cling film would be the best. The way it would – it would cling to her face. It would be so light she'd hardly know it was there. I tried it myself.' His hand moved to place an imaginary film between his mouth and the air.

He turned to Suzie but I don't think he saw her. 'Eily never liked anything over her face,' he said. 'She never even liked a scarf. And her throat was delicate. But this stuff is so light you'd never know it was there.'

Mary was staring, her mouth slack.

'Otherwise she might wake up worse than she fell asleep.' His face was breaking. Twisting out of shape. I hardly recognised the lines of it.

'The whole world is gone mad,' he said. 'We're all lost.'

'Don't say any more,' I said. 'That's enough.'

I heard Mary's anguish but I did not look at her. 'You've done enough damage,' I said. 'For Christ's sake, she was our mother!'

'We worked it all out together,' he said. 'Except that.'

'Please,' I said. 'Don't tell us any more.'

How long did the paralysis last? We stared at each other across a barren tableland, strangers trying to recognise in each other something of the expected, hoping to identify the traits of the rescuer, the search party come to restore us to the comfortable lowlands. But what we saw was so different as to be unrecognisable, beyond communication. The nearer we came, the stranger was our world.

My father stood up abruptly, his chair tipping backwards and crashing into our silence. When he was upright the movement seemed to lose its force and he just stood there, one hand on the table, one on his upper abdomen. I saw a vein thickening at his left temple. I recall consciously deciding that a sudden catastrophic stroke would resolve everything.

Then Mary walked out.

I read somewhere that scallops can see. Who would have thought it? A whole row of eyes glitter like tiny ball-bearings among the tentacles fringing the gape of its shell. Imagine the tiny scallop spats jerking away from a marauding crab or diver, their shells opening and closing like thin-lipped mouths, not driving others away but using the watery speech to escape. Crabs smash the tiny scallop-shells. The anemone *Anthopleura balii* tears the scallop limb from limb. Oh give me my scallop-shell of quiet, Coleridge begged. Who would have thought it? Deep down in the imperturbable sand, safe in its shell! It is not too much to expect that some lives are tranquil.

When Mary came back we were waiting for her. She came down the stairs with her suitcase in her hand. A pair of flesh-coloured tights hung out at one corner like a dog's tongue on a warm day.

She stood at the end of the stairs for a time and shouted at us. She called my father 'a Kevorkian' and I tried to recollect where I had heard her use the term before. When she had exhausted her anger she wiped her eyes and her mouth with the sleeve of her coat. 'Why didn't you wait for God to take her?' she asked him. Plaintive. I thought there might be hope there. She was lost, like the rest of us, a child astray in the dark.

'I'm sorry to say,' my father snapped back, 'that God has his own way of doing things and I don't agree with it.'

'Blasphemy.'

'It's the truth. I had long enough to think about it.'

'It's an excuse.'

'Let him judge me when the time comes.'

'He will!'

'I'm not afraid!'

They were shouting again.

So we followed her out to the yard. The sky was clearing from the west and the afternoon sun hung like an underripe orange from the lowest bank of cloud. On the distant hills the cattle threw shadows as big as trees.

'Where are you off to?' I said.

She told us that if we thought blood was thicker than water we were wrong. She saw what he was doing. She put down the suitcase to count his transgressions: the doctor, bound by patient confidentiality; the priest and the secrets of the confessional; and the children, with ties of blood – her fingers folded down one by one. 'Well, not me,' she said. 'Honour thy father and thy mother, yes. But what if a Christian be placed under an obligation to commit an act which is contrary to God's Law? Conscience is a higher authority.' That was the child, word-perfect on her catechism. 'Murder is murder. You're going to pay for everything.'

We heard the sound of a car coming to a stop at the end of the boreen, turning onto the main road. Down among the ash trees we saw the indicator on Mike O'Leary's jeep blinking slowly, like a child with a lazy eye.

'Don't go,' Suzie said. She took two steps forward, hands held out, like a mother welcoming a child. 'Don't do anything while you feel like this. This is just shock.'

'Go home now while you have a chance,' Mary told her.

'No.' Suzie shook her head. 'I love him.'

'You fuck him, you mean!'

'Mary!' My father's reaction was automatic.

The jeep had stopped just a few yards along the road. Mike O'Leary rented two fields down there, one with the valuable resource of a stream. He had divided the field with an electric fence and I remembered him saying that he was having trouble with it, that sometimes the cattle just walked straight through as if there was nothing there.

'You don't know what the word means,' Mary was saying. 'A baby that never looks at you . . .'

'Please,' my father said. 'We have trouble enough.'

'You should have thought of that first!'

The jeep was moving again.

'She didn't want to live, child.'

'Who gave you the right!'

'As far as that goes,' I said, 'I don't think you have the right either.'

Mary picked up the suitcase and walked towards the gate. There was a shake of rust like faded blood under the bottom rung and I could see the coin-shaped indents where it had been hammered straight.

'Don't forget about Claire,' Suzie called.

Mary stopped. 'What about Claire?'

'Don't go,' I said. 'Stay and work it out. We're all in this together.'

'What about Claire?'

'Everything will come out in court,' Suzie said. 'You'll lose her, Mary. She'll go into care.'

'You told her!' she said to me. 'Who gave you the right to tell her?'

She began to cry and at the same time I heard barking. It was O'Leary's dog, the one that had followed her the day before, head low, racing through the slanting sun. For Mike? Or for Mary? I saw him come through a distant five-bar gate without pausing in his stride. In a few moments he would be here with us in the yard, jumping with excitement, yapping and whipping his tail around. At that moment I knew she would never report what had happened. She would walk through the gate and out onto the road where other worlds flashed by and in the intervals of silence she would realise that there was too much to lose.

I was thinking that after all Mary had walked into a trap, not now but years ago – when she had loved that other man, when she had miscarried – or further back, in the gracious keep that is the family. The simplest snare is magnificent in its complexity – the calculations of probability and improbability that bring the hare from its set to this precise point at the circumcentre of the shining copper coil; the smooth equilibrium of force and compression, friction, torsion. There was the complexity of the machine and of the animal, and even now when she tore free there would be something left behind in the wire.

20

He was wearing his best dark suit, the elbows and knees shiny from other people's funerals. 'An hour and a half's time. We'll have to be there early.' He looked from Suzie to me and back again and something in the way we looked provoked a change of mood. He threw back his head a little and in the voice he used for reciting poetry, learned at school but grown habitual over half a century, he said, 'That food that to him now is as luscious as locusts shall be to him shortly as bitter as coloquintida.' He gave us a weak, guilty half-smile. 'I think that's it anyway. Whatever coloquintida is.' He indicated the tea and toast he had left on the table. 'I thought I was hungry but I can't face it.' To Suzie: 'You're very good. I'm sorry.' He pushed his chair back and stood up.

Suzie shook her head. 'Don't worry about it, Mr Lyons.'

He looked desolate. He closed the door quietly.

Suzie looked at me.

'He likes to quote poetry,' I said. 'They used to learn huge chunks at school in his day. "The Deserted Village" is his favourite. He knows the whole thing still.'

'What does it mean?'

'Oh,' I said carefully, 'I just think he meant he can't eat.'

'What's it from?'

'Shakespeare. *Othello*, I think.'

'And what was the food?'

With a visceral tightening I told her that the food in the play was love. She did not reply and I did not say that coloquintida was a bitter drug. A purgative.

Time seemed to have stretched. I noticed that movements that once seemed instantaneous, to have no appreciable subdivisions, now appeared to be made up of numerous graceful increments, like a demonstration of one of Zeno's paradoxes. I had registered the slight swivel in my father's wrist as he pulled on the door handle, the swing of the door itself and the rotation of the hinge. Now I saw the turn of her head and it felt as slow as the winding of a planet on its axis.

Earlier he had stood beside me at the front door, smelling the air, and said, 'What'll be the end of me, Joe? What am I going to do next?' He was trembling – tiny violent flickerings that felt like sound. I put my hand on his arm to steady him and the contact transferred the energy to me. I felt it in the heart, the racing blood. This is murder, I thought then, matricide, we are all under interdict.

'We'll have to mind him,' Suzie said. 'He's keeping it all inside.'

'That's his way. He never talks much.'

'And he'll be worried until Mary goes back to the States.'

'So will I.'

'I still think she might turn on us.'

'No,' I said. 'In the end she won't do it. Blood *is* thicker than water. And she'll understand it eventually. That he had no choice. Anyway, she's not fanatical enough to risk going to gaol. To risk losing Claire.' But I was thinking of the evening when she told me about Claire's silence. *She's my responsibility*, she said. It had a wintry sound to it.

'I think he was brave. Incredibly brave. I couldn't do it.'

'That's the problem, isn't it, Suzie? None of us could.'

'Last night I had a terrible dream,' Suzie was saying. She came towards me and backed up to my stomach. I clasped my hands around her waist and pulled her back. 'The first thing I remember was seeing the words *El Niño*. They were printed on some kind of huge map. Like a weather map. Then I saw this piece of ocean. I knew it was the Pacific. It was a big circular piece, a different colour to everything around, and there were things floating in it. When I got up closer I could see that the things were dead fish. There was every kind of fish, mostly the coloured ones you see in nature programmes. Then I could see the water bubbling up, as if it was boiling, and then I could smell cooking.'

'That doesn't sound too bad. Bouillabaisse, the French call it. Chowder. Was there more to it?'

'No. You don't understand.'

'You're letting the doom-merchants get to you. The end of the world is nigh. Nostradamus strikes back.'

'It's not that. It's just that I woke with a terrible feeling. Like dread. Like something terrible was going to happen.'

'Well, it has,' I said quietly. 'But I think it's over.'

'We'll be late,' she wailed. She rummaged in the black knapsack that she kept her clothes in. A black leather jacket and black skirt were draped across the chair. 'I know I brought them,' she said. She was wearing only panties and I watched the way her breasts fell straight down, culminating in the blunt pencil-tip of her nipples. I was off balance, unused to the sight of a naked woman in my childhood bedroom. 'I wanted to impress you,' she said, straightening up and turning to face me. She looked childish, innocent almost. 'Coming down I wanted to be sure you'd fall for me. I didn't know your mother was gone then. To make you want me enough to marry me.' Her hands hung loosely by her side. 'I wanted to seduce you.'

'Again,' I said, smiling.

'And again and again.'

'So you brought these earrings you're looking for?'

'They're Egyptian. Magic. The woman at the stall explained it all to me. They stand for Isis and Osiris. The gods of love.' Earlier she had deftly twisted and removed the single earring from her left ear, holding it out for me, a broken silver circle on her lifeline.

'They were brother and sister.'

'Oh. I didn't know that. I don't think the woman knew either.'

'Mary was into all that stuff. She had this picture over her bed. She was always on the lookout for anything weird. She got phases. A vegetarian phase. A Legion of Mary phase. This was the Valley of the Kings phase. More religious mumbo-jumbo. It's no surprise to me she turned out half cracked. The thing is, Isis and Osiris, each pharaoh took his sister as wife.'

'No wonder they all died out.'

The last word was stopped short, choked off on a falling cadence. I could see the sudden resistance in her stance.

'Suzie, sometimes I wonder if things could have turned out some other way. Could I have changed anything?'

She looked severely at me. 'It's not a book or a story, Joe. You have no control over it.'

'The whole thing is so complicated. It should be all strung together, so you could tug at part of it and the way it was related to everything else would show, but it's not. It's all fragmented. It should be that if you thought hard enough about something you should be able to see how it has turned out.' The thought had been obsessing me: that I had not spent enough of my life trying to understand what was happening to me. An unexamined life.

'You said this before. You're beginning to repeat yourself, you know.'

'It's impossible to know what the right or the wrong was, even in hindsight. I don't think I inherited common sense anyway, whatever else came down to me.'

But what if my true inheritance was a destructive gene, a breaker of bonds? What if all my loves and friendships were marked? Long before I knew she was sick, from the time she sat at the mahogany table with her list of quotations, I was afraid of what she might have given me – the power to sever friendship, to walk away from home, to live without love, and the power to assemble words and images in dangerous relations. But I was misreading the code. It was all about the strength of loving bonds and the duty of sustaining them, the necessary piety towards familial and household deities. And so she must have bequeathed me the power to love too, the gift of loving Suzie, for she and my father had been the perfect pair.

Suzie leaned forward and kissed me quickly on the forehead. The dry touch of our skins, the smell of hair and make-up and the musty closed-up air of the room. I closed my eyes and heard the house of long ago full of noisy mysteries, but when I opened them she had moved away and I was looking at the one strip of wallpaper that was out of line, a sequence of embossed roses and twining stems that didn't quite connect to the patterns on each side.

'We'll be late,' she said. 'We'll talk later.' She moved away and pulled on a black camisole.

I caught her hand as she brushed past and lost it again in her rush.

'There it is!' Lying on the arm of the chair where the camisole had rested was the other earring. She tilted her head and fitted it into place, one hand stretching the lobe a little, one hand inserting the wire hook.

'Will we go back to Coinlín some day?' I asked her. Would there be way-leave from the insular gods? There might be a grace in the withering March wind – salt for the cure – blowing out of the sunrise.

'How will we go?' she said. 'As friends?'

Her face was serious; her eyes followed mine steadily, unblinking. Then, like a stone falling into water, the seriousness dissolved and she was grinning like a kid. 'Stop looking at me, you dirty old man!'

I caught her arm, managing this time to hold on. 'I'll get by, Suzie. I'll manage. Won't I? Nothing is as bad as it seems before it happens. I'll be able to face it when the time comes.'

'As long as we have each other,' she said. 'We'll get by.'

The old clichés. Every lover needs them, means them. They mend themselves in a billion instants of intimacy, the fingertip of the god of love charging the empty phrases, igniting the dry kindling of worn-out promises.

'I'm starving,' Suzie said. 'I can't go to the funeral without something.' She was fixing her skirt now – too short for a graveyard, she said, but all she had with her.

'There's cold meat in the fridge.'

A look of distaste. 'No thanks' – the chunk of meat with its frosting of plastic – 'I'll have a cut of bread.'

'Suzie,' I said, 'I'm thinking – I should stay with my father. I owe it to him, to try to make up for things a bit. I owe it to my mother. But . . .'

'Yes,' she said. 'I see that.' She was paused in mid-movement, about to pick up a shoe.

'But, there's more to it. There's you. What will we do?'

She had not moved. 'You'll have to marry me. Your father wouldn't have us in the house unless you made an honest woman of me.' She smiled weakly.

I could not hold her eye and looked away – upwards – conscious as I did so that it was possible to catch even reflexes from one's parents. For the first time since childhood I noticed the way the ceiling sloped down to one wall, following the pitch of the roof outside, the laths tongued and grooved and darkened by age; once again I saw that the knots in the planks of the ceiling formed strange shapes – solar systems, landscapes, contorted faces whose eyes glared or winked. For a terrible moment I felt that the gods were scowling down at me out of a jumbled firmament, sternly admonishing me to do no harm. I shook my head, trying to resolve some kind of clarity out of the crazy excess of design. 'I'm going to be very sick,' I said. 'I can see into the future as well as anybody.'

'There's a fifty-fifty chance . . .'

'No more.'

'Still . . .'

I remembered suddenly that I had not told Mary that she was in the clear. Good news waiting for her; perhaps it would have made a difference, changed her mind. She should be here, I thought, not running away. Her room too had the sloped ceiling, the scowling knots, the gods watching the roll of the dice that simplified or complicated things. She should have stayed and seen things through. That was a duty too. Not to remake oneself over and over in escape, but to face the inescapable reality of things as they are. How many years had it taken me to learn this simplest of virtues?

'I'm very frightened, Suzie. Petrified, in fact. I can hardly think with it. One minute I think it can't be happening to me, the next I think I can feel a shake starting. If my leg twitches I panic. Last night, every time I drifted to sleep my body jumped. It was terrifying.'

'That happens to everyone.' She spoke sharply, defensively.

'I know that. But what I want to say is, I don't want to go like that. That pointless way. I'd want to die with some sort of dignity.'

'That's where you're wrong. There's more than one kind of dignity. There's dignity in suffering too.'

'What Dad did for my mother, that's how I . . .'

'Don't! Don't say it, Joe.' Her face flared red with anger. She held a hand out, palm towards me, arm rigid, the universal stop sign. 'I don't want to think about it. Do you hear? I don't want to think about it.'

'It's what's in front of me.' Like a ship's course on a chart, all the variables calculated, due allowance made for set and drift, the vagaries of the helm: the ultimate port of call was there, not a safe haven but a breaker's yard, a shambles, a charnel.

'No!'

After a moment she got up and straightened her hair in the dressing-table mirror. 'I'm dreading this,' she said. 'I'm the odd one out.' I saw her watching my reflection in the glass.

Somehow, without uttering an unenciphered word, we had advanced the truth. We knew where we stood now – or so I thought. We looked at each other and there was a space opening between us even as we looked. I knew what had to be done and that it had to be at once, before the everyday complicity of neighbours and handshakes made the whole thing unbearably weighty, invested power in our pairing, the trust of introductions and explanations. Until then our connection had been a physical thing, and more, something in the heart, private, nameless, intrinsic, but in an hour it would be seized upon by a dozen people, spoken of, criticised, formalised, a public event. I said, 'I can't bring you into this, Suzie.'

She stared at me, started to speak and then stopped. I could not hold her gaze.

'I've thought a lot about it. What Dad went through, I wouldn't wish it on my worst enemy. I know' – I too held my hands out to stop her speaking – 'I know why he did it. I'm beginning to understand that too. How they managed. And why. Love – it's taken me a long time to see what it really means. And I know what you're going to say next, but it's too much.'

'Too much what? Too much for who?'

'I can't do it to you.'

'*You?* Do it to *me?*' She was suddenly defiant and angry,

but brittle also. I knew she would crumble in a moment if I let her. 'What gives you the right to say that?'

I could have said love, because I hoped that was what it was. More than anything I hoped it was not self-pity or selfishness or any kind of histrionics. The future could be a trap, a life-long waiting-room; waiting for the doctor to come out and say, 'Next'; waiting for the door to swing wide and the instruments to be exposed, the bedpans, the tubes, the pastel-coloured pharmacopoeia; waiting for the coin to stop spinning, heads or tails, one or zero; the first coded warning. And all the ifs and buts, I have it or I have it not. I knew I would never take the test, to be told that I would die in the throes of a demented dance in the company of ghosts and chimeras; and Suzie did not deserve to spend her life awaiting what was, after all, my inheritance.

'It would only ever be a half-life,' I said. 'Waiting. Guessing. Watching.'

'It'd be ours.'

'You deserve better.'

'But I'll never get it.'

'No. I don't believe that.'

'Does it occur to you' – coldly – 'that I might have thought about it too? Why don't you trust me, Joe? You worked all this out and you never said a word. Why?'

'Time to go.' My father's voice from the hall, and at the same moment the phone rang, a bell in the bedroom next door and an echoing metallic rattle in the hall downstairs. Abruptly Suzie began to cry. I put a hand to her shoulder but she swivelled out of its touch.

'Get away from me,' she groaned.

I said, 'We'll talk when it's over,' and she shook her head.

'Get away,' she said. 'You haven't changed, Joe, you haven't learned anything. You're the same as you always were – closed up and careful.'

I shook my head, but she wasn't looking.

'It would become pity,' I said. 'In time love would turn to pity.'

I heard my father shouting: 'It's for you, Joe.'

'And what's wrong with pity?' she said.

I stood at the door, my hand on the doorknob. I would walk through as I had done ten thousand times before but never truly understanding until now how each passage was irrevocable, that there was no going back. I would walk down the stairs and face my father. Together we would do the necessary thing. Suzie would always be here, in this room, hurt and alone. A troubling tenure.

I was aware of things outside the room: something clattered downstairs, the plastic flip-up phone book falling from the table – I knew the sound; a bird went by outside the window, a small and colourless thing in flight. I put my back to the door.

My father called again.

'Suzie,' I said, 'Suzie.' Something inert and unmanageable almost arrested the words.

She turned.

'Suzie, I don't know. What's wrong with pity?'

'Nothing,' she said. 'It's a kind of love.'

'But will it be enough?'

'It'll be what's needed when the time comes.'

When I came down the stairs he had his hand over the

mouthpiece. He watched me coming down with that rheumy blank look I had seen more than once in the past few days. One eyebrow lifted interrogatively, but I shook my head.

'I think it's her,' he hissed, 'but I didn't ask.' As if he didn't know her voice.

He passed the phone to me and walked away, something like relief in his step.

The line shuffled forward. Mike O'Leary was there. 'How are you managing, Mr Lyons?'

'Don't worry about me, Mike.' A sideways nod – 'Joe tells me he's coming home. What do you think of that?'

But Mike had already moved on and now Helen was standing there. 'Well,' she said. 'She got a great send-off. I don't know how many cars I counted. I lost track.' She held his hand. 'If you want anything . . .'

'Ah, sure Joe is moving back. He's fed up with the flat, he says. I have an idea himself and Suzie might be . . .' The line moved again and he was left gazing at a distant cousin. 'How are you?' – the name lost to him – how close? How far? One of Eily's crowd? A round-faced woman in a waxed coat, her head nodding continuous rapid-fire sympathy. Something horsy in her bearing.

'Poor Eily,' she said. She shook his hand and moved on and in the brief interval before the next face he saw the rim of the grave and a piece of ribbon worked loose from under the plastic film of a sheaf of flowers, like a wisp of escaped hair; he wanted to step forward and put it to rights. She was always careful about her appearance, always checking in the hall mirror before going out. How do I look? Grand, Eily. They hadn't filled the grave in yet, only covered it with a kind of fake grass. He felt panicked at the thought that night was coming and she hadn't been covered. He wanted to roll his sleeves up and shovel the earth over her. He thought of pulling the quilt up to her chin, tucking her in. Goodnight now, Eily. The gravediggers stood at a discreet distance, their shovels thrown aside. Behind them was the yellow bulk of a Hymac leaning on its claw.

Joe was holding his arm. 'Father O'Shea,' he said. He steered his father towards the priest. 'We want to say thanks, Father,' Joe said.

'Yes, Father. You're very good to do this.'

'God bless you,' the priest said and turned away abruptly, folding his chasuble as he did so and leaning slightly towards an elderly woman on his left. His face was red.

'That's the doctor over there,' Joe said, turning him again. 'And Suzie brought the car down. It's at the gate. We'll just say thanks to the doctor and we'll be gone.'

'Still no sign of Mary?' he said.

'She's just angry, Dad. She'll be on her way home by now. Flying on to Heathrow anyway. She doesn't mean half the things she says.'

'I don't know whether or which. I'm sorry she's not here to say goodbye to her mother.'

The doctor too shook his hand. Greeting, farewell and consolation – how many handshakes were there? No need for a secret signal, every conceivable gesture held its own burden of ritual, of unacknowledged intent. The free-masonry of death was universal; they had all lost to it in the past, would lose themselves in the future. But the doctor's hand was offered, taken and withdrawn. There was sympathy in it, but also disquiet. Its meaning hung in the air in the space vacated by the handclasp, the knotted fingers, interlocking palms, a topology of remorse.

'I'll call in tomorrow on my early rounds. See how you are.'

'I'm grand, doctor. Don't you worry about me.'

'Still . . .'

'Do you know what,' he said, shivering as he said it, 'graveyards are the coldest places in the world. I was never at a warm funeral.' The doctor smiled.

Where was Joe? One of the Sullivans was tidying things on the polished oak floor of the hearse. The brass rails looked fake. Joe was walking – striding – through the gate, out onto the road.

'Joe,' he called. He was surprised by how feeble his voice sounded. It occurred to him suddenly that unknown to himself he had become a very old man. His voice barely carried in the still air. His legs felt weak. Here was the doctor supporting his left elbow as they walked, piloting him between the headstones and unruly kerbs.

'Make that son of yours take the test,' the doctor said. 'You know they're making advances all the time. And forewarned is forearmed.'

'I will, doctor. I wanted to thank you for all your kindness. I don't know what we'd do without you.' Suddenly, bubbling up from deep down, the monstrous ferment of loneliness: there was no more *we*, no Eily, no care, no purpose, no common being. He almost spoke it. Instead he looked down at his hands, choking back the cry. Absurdly he remembered the man who had taught him in his last year in school, pacing in front of the boys and declaiming Shakespeare while brushing ineffectually at his palms: *Out, damned spot.* There had been a burst of giggling because one of the boys had a dog called Spot. Eily loved that story. She often got him to tell it to visitors, especially when the children were still at school. It was true, nothing would wash away the mark. His hands were untouchable. He should take care not to spread the contamination.

'There's no going back, doctor.'

The doctor didn't seem to hear. 'I didn't see Mary.' How many people had said it? *And poor Mary had to go back? Still she was here when it counted. Poor Mary.*

'Mary has her own share.'

'I don't want you to let this get in on you.'

'I did the right thing, doctor, didn't I?'

'You did. You never let her down.'

'That's the main thing, isn't it?' After today there would be no more talk. The doctor, the priest, Joe: they would never talk about it again. It would be over on the outside; it would become a secret, but it would never be over in his head. He wondered if things like that really ate away inside as they did in books. He imagined a trapped rat gnawing at him, a small knot of muscle and bone that was capable of eating concrete. And the bones of a rat were so fine, a tiny miracle of construction.

'Joe is moving in with me.'

'The very best thing that could happen now.' They smiled to each other and then the doctor turned away and began fishing in his pocket for his car keys, and for the second time he was left alone on the point of saying that Joe and Suzie had made their minds up. He looked around and there was no one else he could explain it to, that here was something hopeful after all, that maybe everything would turn out for the best, that someone was not afraid of the future. He found himself scanning the lingering clusters of mourners for Eily – Wait till I tell you, he could hear himself saying, Joe and Suzie are going to tie the knot – but his eye fell instead on Pa Barry Junior deep in conversation with Mike O'Leary. They were watching him too but they did not acknowledge his glance. Someone had told him a few weeks back that Mike O'Leary was standing for election next time round. He had the contacts anyway.

Car doors were slamming and engines racing. An indicator winked like a navigation light at the gate, luring him out past the last danger, into the open road where Joe and Suzie waited. Who were they talking to? Lately he had been finding it hard to distinguish things in the twilight. The eyes going. It could be Mary; her way of standing, even since childhood there had always been something defensive in it. There was time for that by and by.

Twilight was erasing the edges of things, blurring the contours. Sometimes when you knew a place like you knew your own hand, the slightest change was enough to make it look foreign. The shallow hills that faced him looked like unexplored country now. Across the road the slate roof of a cottage had fallen down in folds, the skeleton of a buddleia thrust up through, its arching arms still encumbered by the remains of last season's flowers. The garden on either side of the gate was overgrown with wizened fuchsia, and in the twilight the tiny sprinkling of late flowers glowed like fairy lights. There was something remote about the headland where a harrow stood against a gate, the tips of its teeth gleaming still high up in the evening sun while the valley where he stood was settling into night. The white scut of a rabbit bobbed like a false beacon on the slope. A hawk hung still and dangerous nearby. A pigeon dropped down on folded wings and, at the lowest point of its fall, clapped once, twice, and rose again, rapid wingbeats clawing the air. Even if you found a rabbit in a snare you'd break its neck, he thought. A dog with the chancre. A bird with a broken wing. Voices were calling goodbye or arranging to meet. Someone two graves away was saying the old platitude: *We only ever meet at funerals these days*. The ghost of the words forming in gusts of fog. The notion came to him that the worst was over, that perhaps they could all make a fresh start. He heard the pigeon's single handclap again and knew that somewhere above him the bird was applauding a calm evening. And, he thought, that must mean something.

POSTSCRIPT

'I'll tell you a true story,' Suzie says in that serious way she has of beginning a joke. 'A man's son is going to America in the days when no one ever came back. The man is broken-hearted about it. If only I had more cattle and a bigger house, he says to himself, Martin would never have to leave. He walks him to the crest of a faraway mountain, the farthest he can go in a day's walk, so that he can watch him for as long as possible. At last when the boy is out of sight he turns to go home. What does he see but a very small, very old man sitting on a stone in the ditch. I can give you three wishes, the old man says, or I can give you luck. Which do you want? The father says he'll take the three wishes. Very good, the old man says. The father wishes for three times as many cattle, twice as big a house and his son returned to him for ever. Go home, the old man says, and it will all come true. The father goes home. As he comes into his own country he notices that there are three times as many cattle in the fields but he has the same amount of land and already they have eaten all the grass. When he gets to his own house he sees that it is twice as big but there's only himself in it. When my third wish comes true, he says, I'll have Martin back again and he'll know what to do with all this. But that night while he's sitting by his fire a knock comes to the door. All his neighbours are outside in the dark and the women are crying. The men are carrying

a box on their shoulders. Then the father knows that all
his wishes have come true.'

'He should have asked for luck?'

'The trouble is nobody really believes in luck.'

Suzie smiles.

Acknowledgements

I found the title in Marina Warner's book *From the Beast to the Blonde*, in the passage quoted in the epigraph, and I am grateful to her for permission to use it. I am indebted to her work, here and elsewhere.

Some of the observations about the Gaelic *sean-nós* style of singing were formed after hearing an interview (broadcast on Radio Telefís Éireann) with the great Munster singer Iarla O Lionáird.

I would like to acknowledge my gratitude to Dr John Whelan for his advice, but more particularly for his patience in listening to what must have seemed a rather abstract exploration of a rare and tragic disease coupled with an outcome that offends his commitment to palliative care. Any inaccuracies that may have found their way into the medical information are entirely my own.

I am especially grateful to my agent Gill Coleridge and to my editor Carole Welch for their painstaking reading and rereading, constructive criticism and invaluable advice.

Website
The website cited in Chapter Five exists and I am grateful to the webmaster and Johns Hopkins University for permission to quote from the definition used there. The URL is:

http:/ /www.ncbi.nlm.nih.gov/omim/

(Online Mendelian Inheritance in Man, OMIM (TM). McKusick-Nathans Institute for Genetic Medicine, Johns Hopkins University (Baltimore, MD) and National Center for Biotechnology Information, National Library of Medicine (Bethesda, MD), 2000.)

WILLIAM WALL

Alice Falling

Alice Lynch appears to have everything – brains, beauty and wealth – yet she harbours a barely concealed hatred of her husband. What the student she dallies with doesn't understand is why she doesn't leave him. Alice, haunted by the ghosts of her rural Irish childhood, knows it's not that simple, but that she has to find a way out. In this powerful and hypnotic tale, William Wall traces the corrosive effect of a dark secret on a group of friends and lovers, and illuminates a shocking aspect of life in Ireland's recent past.

'Vivid and disturbing . . . an excellent debut' *Irish News*

'Instantly gripping . . . a brutal, brilliantly written, deeply unsettling novel' *Sunday Business Post*

'While this book is certainly disturbing, it never seems bleak or oppressive. This is largely due to Wall's poetic handling of words, which suffuses the book with a lyrical rhythm, while at the same time he manages not to slip into lush romanticism' *Time Out*

'An intelligent and well-crafted book . . . the haunting eloquence of Wall's prose makes it an evocative and compelling read' *Irish News*

'Dark, visceral and unflinching . . . Wall's uncluttered sentences are delicate and detailed, and his night-time landscapes are softly evocative of small-town Ireland' *The Times*

'The sort of book that renews your faith in Irish fiction . . . a deeply affecting novel' *Books Ireland*

SCEPTRE

WILLIAM WALL

Minding Children

Josephine Strane has never known a real family when as a teenager she goes to work for Dr and Mrs Casey, caring for Baby Jean. Soon she has made herself so indispensable that when things go wrong she is able to move on with a glowing reference. Then comes an American couple with their small son Robin, who charms everyone with his laughing blue eyes and cheeky ways – the perfect family. What they do not realise is that Josephine is anything but the perfect child-minder.

'I enjoyed it enormously. He is such a writer – lyrical and cruel and bold and with metaphors to die for.'
Kate Atkinson

'A beautifully written novel, with layers and layers of fine writing like snowdrifts . . . The story – so softly that you feel the menace before you ever understand it – thrusts at the heart of motherhood . . . Wall brilliantly, relentlessly, reveals how our natural senses of superiority ensure that we can be completely taken in by the simple, good face worn by genuine evil.' *Independent*

'A beautifully choreographed "danse macabre" of Catholic guilt and implosive rage' *Daily Express*

'Wall perfectly matches form to content: his measured prose, calm and deliberate, like his main character Josephine, contains within it a quiet, brooding menace . . . an intimate tale, well told, that draws the reader into a world both familiar and frightening.' *Irish Times*

'*Minding Children* is, among other things, a masterful horror story . . . But Wall is interested in far more than just the horrific, and his compelling study of the fractured childhood of Josephine Strane, and the tragedy it begets, is a more deeply troubling thing indeed . . . it is precisely Wall's refusal to paint her as a mere sadist that lifts this story above a thriller.' *Sunday Tribune*

'A haunting, compelling novel . . . Wall has succeeded in producing a rare thing: a page-turning work of literary fiction.' *Books Ireland*

S

SCEPTRE